Seeking HYDE

MAX GRIFFIN

Dreamspinner Press

Published by
Dreamspinner Press
5032 Capital Circle SW
Ste 2, PMB# 279
Tallahassee, FL 32305-7886
USA
http://www.dreamspinnerpress.com/

Seeking Hyde
Copyright © 2012 by Max Griffin

Cover Art by Reese Dante
http://www.reesedante.com

ISBN: 978-1-62380-038-3

Printed in the United States of America
First Edition
October 2012

eBook edition available
eBook ISBN: 978-1-62380-039-0

"Ariadne's Thread"

Against
Chaos and dread,
Hope, truth, and steadfast love
Stitch profane to sacred between
Lost souls.

The Missing Cinquains
—Arpad Laszlo

Chapter ONE

BRENT squinted against the late afternoon sun and wondered again why his mother had insisted he come home this weekend. When he pulled his aging Chevy pickup off Highway 52 and headed west, his knapsack slid across the seat and thudded to the floorboards. He glanced down to make sure none of his homework had fallen out before he returned his attention to driving.

This was supposed to be the "Great River Road," but instead of a vista of the Mississippi, endless rows of corn stretched to infinity in all directions. In less than a mile, though, the tedious farmland gave way to limestone bluffs. Brent gripped the steering wheel as the road climbed up the rocky hillside in steep curves, coiling like a rattler with a broken back. Thick underbrush and low-hanging trees scraped against the sides of his truck as he twisted along the narrow gravel lane. He slowed further, while his stomach growled. He was in no hurry. In just a couple more turns he'd be at the top, where he could stop at Ruby's Filling Station, Bar, and Museum and get a snack.

As he headed toward the final bend, a black SUV careened around the corner in front of him and fishtailed in his direction. A yellow cloud of dust billowed behind the vehicle as it fought for traction on the loose gravel of the switchback.

A frigid chasm opened in Brent's gut while he hit the brakes. "Damn." He gripped the steering wheel and swung to the right. Little needles of adrenalin prickled out at his fingers. At the last minute, the SUV straightened and blasted past, horn blaring. A spray of rocks rattled against his truck. He coughed and blinked gritty dust from his eyes. The horn still sounded, Doppler-shifting to lower pitches and then fading to silence.

"What a friggin' idiot." He heaved a deep breath and edged forward. Ruby's awaited.

A sheet metal shack hunkered on the crown of the bluff, surrounded by a rutted parking lot. Two ancient, rusty gas pumps stood in front, and a neon sign announced "Ruby's" over the door. Brent's pickup creaked to a stop next to a battered van with a side panel that read "Middleton Shopper."

He clambered out, stretched, and combed dust from his short-cropped hair with his fingers. On the other side of a limestone fence, the bluff dropped back down to the valley. He never tired of the view from this height. Below him, the river was a silvery sword that cut through the verdant land. A barge crawled along its surface like a caterpillar inching toward sanctuary. He shook out his arms, still weak from the adrenalin shock of his near-accident, and inhaled the sweet scent of sumac and oak. An undercurrent of worry about his mother's cryptic e-mail to come home still gnawed, but the peaceful view reassured him. Nothing ever happened here. Maybe Dad had won a few dollars in the lottery. He'd know soon enough.

He twitched when a mild tenor voice interrupted his reverie. "That's quite a view. I never expected to see anything like that when I moved to Iowa." The man's precise diction made him sound like a TV news anchor.

Brent turned to face the speaker. "It's beautiful, all right." The newcomer was at least six feet, nearly as tall as Brent, but he was skinny as a floor lamp. The gentle breeze toyed with his shaggy chestnut-colored hair, and he looked like he hadn't shaved in a week. His spindly arms stuck out from a T-shirt that flapped in the breeze against his narrow chest. Brent couldn't help himself and flexed his pectorals.

The other guy's gaze raked over him, and a sardonic grin played across his features. "My name's Jason." He stuck out his hand.

His solid grip was a pleasant surprise. "Brent here. Nice to meet you." At least he didn't shake hands like a pansy. "You're not from around here."

"Nah. I'm from New Jersey originally. I moved out here to go to Collier's journalism school four years ago."

Brent nodded. That still didn't explain what this outsider was doing here. "Collier, huh? That's way over in Middleton, about fifty miles west of here."

"Right. I'm a reporter for a paper there. I'm working a story." He looked down and shuffled his sneakers against the dusty surface of the parking lot.

"Huh." *An outsider and a reporter.* A little swirl of self-reproach made him stop. *God, I sound just like my parents.* Brent tossed a grin at the fellow. "I'm a student at Collier too. Pre-med."

"Yeah? That's supposed to be tough—a world-class program. Say, do they still run that children's hospital out at the Grange Station?"

"I believe that's closed now. I think maybe the Stillwell-Holmes Institute has some labs out there, though." He paused, and then added with some pride, "I lucked into a work-study job at the Institute. I'm learning a lot."

Jason's head snapped up at his words. "You *work* there?" He pulled an iPhone from his hip pocket. "Maybe you can help me with my story? It's all about the Institute, and the Gerion Group that's behind it. I'd like to interview you."

Brent frowned. "I'm not sure Dr. Athair would like that. They're pretty strict about security."

Jason's head wagged back and forth, and he snatched a stray curl from his eyes. "I don't want to know anything current, except maybe some general background. You know Dr. Athair? How about Dr. Holmes? What're they like?"

"Sorry, I'm really not comfortable talking about them."

"So you're saying they won't let you talk to the press?" He held his phone closer. "Just speak up. It'll record your answer."

"What I *said* was that I wasn't comfortable talking about my job." Brent let an edge creep into his voice. "Please get that thing out of my face."

"So your answer is 'no comment'." Jason shrugged and pocketed his phone. "Whatever. I'm really more interested in things from twenty years ago. I'm here to track down a local who used to work there back then. Mary Hyde. You know her?"

Brent laughed on hearing his mother's name. "She doesn't know anything about what goes on at the Institute. Trust me."

"Maybe not now, but she used to work there. I want to ask her some questions about Grange Station."

Brent snorted. "You must have her confused with someone else. She doesn't know about the Institute or research in epigenetics. The only biology she knows is which side of a cow to milk. She's never worked any place but the family farm."

"That's not what my sources say. In any case, I'd still like to talk to her. Can you maybe tell me where she lives? All I know is it's someplace on 'FM 15H'." He pointed. "That's this road, right?"

"You bet. But Mary Hyde won't have anything to tell you, and I know she won't want to speak with you. She doesn't like talking to strangers."

"How can you be so sure?"

"She's my mother." He thought about adding "you twit," but decided to be polite. "Tell you what. Give me your phone number. I'll tell her we spoke, and she'll call if she's willing to see you." *Like that's going to happen.*

"That's all I ask." He stuck bony fingers into his blue jeans and pulled out a tattered business card. "My cell number's on here. I'm staying up in Bellevue tonight, so feel free to call me."

Brent glanced at the card and suppressed a snort at the name of the newspaper, a weekly tabloid stuffed with want ads. "You're a reporter for the *Middleton Shopper*?"

Jason's face turned red. "There's nothing wrong with that. A job's a job."

Brent blinked, and a twinge of guilt nibbled at him. "Can't argue with that, especially these days." He glanced at the sun. "Hey, I gotta run."

"Sure. Don't forget to call." Jason tossed his head to clear that unruly lock of hair from his forehead. "I'd still like to talk to you about the Institute. I'm really interested in the Grange."

"I don't know anything about that. I work on campus, and Grange Station is way out in the country."

Jason nodded. "I heard that there's proprietary research going on there, maybe even military work."

Brent squelched his irritation at the guy's persistence; he was just doing his job, after all. "Like I said, I wouldn't know. I work on campus, in Dr. Athair's lab." He looked the reporter up and down. He *was* kind of cute. *Maybe I should cut him some slack.* "I do have to go. Tell you what. Call me next week, back on campus. I'm in the online student directory. I just can't give you anything specific, okay?"

Jason looked like a puppy having its tummy tickled. "More than okay." He stuck out his hand. "Thanks again. And tell your mother I don't bite. I just want to chat with her."

"Will do." Brent shook hands, turned, and entered Ruby's without looking back.

Inside, the acrid scent of onion rings, cigarette smoke, and motor oil twanged in his nostrils. "Hey, Ruby. How's tricks?"

Her wrinkled face erupted in a leathery grin. "Brent, you little scamp. I saw you a-flirtin' with that fella out there. He gonna be your new squeeze?" Her voice rasped from decades of cigarettes, and her iron-gray hair frizzed about her head like a Brillo pad, but her blue eyes sparkled with affection.

Brent laughed. "Good to see you too, Ruby. And no, I'm done with boyfriends after what happened with the last one."

Her mouth turned down. "I remember. I met that *Gary* last time you passed through."

He shook his head. "You did, but he's not my boyfriend. He's just a buddy. You never met Matt. Gary helped me put things back together after we broke up. Anyway, I'm too busy with school for dating."

She glanced outside at where Jason's van was still parked. "Too bad. The reporter guy was kinda cute." She frowned. "Snoopy, though. And he talked like he was from New York City." Her tone suggested that was the furthest depths of hell. She spat in a can next to the cash register. "What can I get for ya, honey?"

"How about some chips and a coke? Something to hold me over until dinner."

"Don't you spoil your meal, now. I bet your Momma's been cookin' all day."

"I'm sure she has. You doin' okay, Ruby?"

"Sure, sure. Thing's is kinda slow these days, but I'm kinda slow myself." She rang up his purchase. "Send my greetin's to your folks, y'hear?"

"I'll do that. Good to see you."

The Middleton Shopper van had left by the time he returned to the parking lot. He fingered Jason's card in his shirt pocket, slipped back into his pickup, and opened his coke and chips.

The road wound through steep hills and occasional rock-strewn fields. In most places, the slopes were too steep for a tractor, and the ancient scrub forest had returned. Oak and maple trees swayed in the evening breezes, but the ground hid beneath a bramble of briars and impassable underbrush.

Fifteen minutes after leaving Ruby's, he arrived at the Hyde's little farmstead, nestled between two hills. The red barn needed paint, and the front porch sagged against a white frame house. A tiny pasture held three cows that chewed on cuds and stared with placid brown eyes as Brent got out of his pickup. He inhaled the familiar barnyard scents of oats and manure and grinned. His father's old Ford pickup was in the circle drive by the well, and his mother's rusty Buick stood in the driveway. A scrawny tomcat stretched in the sunlight and stared at him, as if wondering what he'd taste like.

It was good to be home.

He bounded up the front steps, avoiding the broken second tread. The front door was ajar, and a momentary frown creased his forehead. They never locked the front door, but they never left it unlatched either. "Mom! Dad! I'm home." He pushed inside.

No answer.

The scents of dinner wafted from the kitchen. Sure enough, an apple pie, still warm, sat on the counter by the stove, and a pork roast was in the oven. The table was set for three. The TV was on too, playing an episode of *Green Acres*. Brent cringed and shut it off.

"Hey. Where is everybody?"

Still no answer.

He roamed the little house: living room, dining room, his bedroom, his parents' bedroom. All neat and ordered, and all empty. He pursed his lips. Maybe they were outside.

Three cows lined up next to the barn and stared at him. "You need to be milked, girls?" Maybe that was it. For sure, Dad would take care of the animals before anything else. But the barn was empty too. It was clean, washed down from the morning chores and the milk tank was ready for tomorrow morning's pickup by the local dairy. The feed troughs were loaded and ready, but no one was there except the animals. One of them nuzzled the gate into the barn and gave a sorrowful low.

Brent frowned and headed back to the empty house. Both cars were here. Dinner was in the oven and the table was set. But his parents were missing.

Worry chewed at him. This wasn't like his stolid parents at all. He pulled out his phone and called his dad's cell. Ringing shrilled from the kitchen. He followed the sound and found his father's phone in a jacket hanging by the back door. Brent's phone announced in his father's gruff voice, "You've reached Chuck Hyde's cell phone. I can't take your call right now. Please leave a message." It beeped, and he hung up.

What was going on? Where were they?

He flipped open the phone book and looked up old man Zimmerman's number. The old coot lived alone in the only nearby farmstead, just around the bend, and never went anywhere. Maybe he'd seen something. When his phone rang with no answer, Brent frowned and hung up. His fingers tapped on the phone book, and then he looked up the sheriff's emergency line. Panic bubbled in his throat as he punched the number into his phone.

Chapter TWO

KIMBALL VERLOC chose a booth in a dark corner of Floyd's Pig Shack, where he could see without being seen. The stench of cooking grease and barbecue fouled his nostrils while country-western music twanged against his eardrums. The owners had wedged the menu between the Formica tabletop and a scratched sheet of clear plastic that protected the surface. He scanned the offerings. Barbecue, of course. Pulled pork. Corn on the cob. His stomach roiled, and he silently cursed his job for bringing him to Bumfuck, Iowa, or whatever this place was. He resolved that tomorrow, back in Chicago, he'd treat himself to a proper meal, maybe at Café des Architectes in Water Tower Place.

A waitress slouched to his table and slopped a glass of ice water in front of him. She had squeezed her orca-like body into a uniform two sizes too small. Kimball imagined that if she were to smile her eyes would disappear in folds of blubber. But she didn't smile. She pulled a grimy rag from her apron and swiped crumbs and discarded Sweet'n Low packets onto the floor and into his lap. A name tag on her dress announced that she was Mandy and that she wanted to help. He glowered.

She pulled out a pad and asked, "You ready to order, sir?" Her voice grated, as though Ozzy Osbourne had come down with laryngitis and taken a job waiting tables.

Bile crawled up his throat. Her orange-colored wig was askew, and strands of iron-gray hair leaked from the edges and curled in front of her ears. Runnels of dried sweat snaked through layers of makeup on her face and highlighted a rat's nest of wrinkles. Worst of all, she jiggled when she breathed.

Kimball swallowed and looked back at the menu.

"If you're not ready, I can come back." She started to walk away.

"No, wait." All he wanted was to finish his business and get out of here. He cast another forlorn glance at the menu. "What does the chef recommend this evening?"

Her eyebrows crawled up her forehead, exposing further fissures in her coats of Max Factor. "What?"

He grunted. "I'll have coffee and, uh, a piece of apple pie." They couldn't screw that up.

She made a note. "You want they should heat up your pie?"

He shrugged. "Sure. Why not?"

Moments later he regretted that decision. The cook plopped his pie onto the fry grill, next to a sizzling hamburger and an unidentifiable slag of gray meat. It sizzled and popped as the grease foamed about it. The bile returned, and Kimball sucked at his water to cleanse his palate.

His eyes narrowed when a wizened, gray-haired man entered Floyd's. The newcomer pulled leather gloves off his hands and adjusted his impeccable black suit. His steely eyes scanned the patrons like a hawk looking for a rat. His sharp, protruding nose gave him a cross-eyed look, but Kimball knew those bleak eyes missed nothing. A hint of a smile bent the man's thin lips, and then he headed to Kimball's table. He slipped into the opposite seat, his face cold and impassive. "Good to see you." His voice flowed like fine cognac, but Kimball knew the mellifluous tones cloaked a ruthless will.

Kimball nodded. "You too." The newcomer's clothes reeked with the sickly sweet scent of his cologne. Kimball's stomach gurgled, and he pulled an antacid from his pocket and swallowed it dry. "Did we have to meet here?"

"This was convenient. Your objective is in this community." The man slipped an envelope from his jacket and pushed it across the table.

Kimball fingered it, wondering at the thinness. "This has the specifications?"

"What you need to know, yes." He paused while Mandy returned with another glass of ice water.

"What can I get you, sir?" Her voice was flat as week-old beer. Sweat soaked her armpits, and her ample bosom threatened to ooze free from her spotted uniform.

"Just coffee for me, dear." The newcomer smiled, and Kimball wondered if his face would crack. His dark gaze followed her as she trudged away.

Kimball's mouth turned down, and he decided to risk a joke. "Thinking of asking her out for a date, Montel?"

The other's eyes snapped back to face Kimball and turned to liquid nitrogen. "No names, please. You know our protocols." He leaned forward. "Unless you want this to be your last contract."

Kimball snorted. "Last contract" could only mean one thing coming from Montel's lips. "Thanks, but I'd rather keep breathing, if it's all the same to you."

Montel's expression didn't change, and his gaze didn't waver. He just sat there, rigid and staring. Kimball's heartbeat accelerated, and his breath whispered in his throat. It was just possible he'd gone too far.

Mandy returned with two coffees and his now grease-soaked pie. She slapped the check on the table and mumbled, "Anything else?"

Montel broke his frozen pose. He smiled at her again, and his eyes seemed to glow with warmth. "That's all we require. Thank you, my dear."

A weary smile passed across her lips. "You need anything, just whistle." She plodded away.

Kimball frowned. *What the fuck is Montel doing flirting with this fat old hag?* "Your message said there was some urgency with this job?" It was unusual to get two jobs in one day. Unheard of. Not for the first time, Kimball wondered who hired his usual employers, Kingfisher Associates, for this afternoon's snatch job. Probably not Montel; his work almost always involved a hit.

Eyes dead as Caligula's gazed at him and sent icicles down Kimball's spine. Montel stirred sugar into his coffee before he answered. "Yes, there is some urgency. There's a reporter snooping around, and our… patrons are cleaning up loose ends before he gets too close. You must be both swift and discreet."

The same instructions he'd gotten earlier today. "No problem."

"See to it." He took a sip of his coffee, grimaced, and spit the liquid back into the cup. "Our employers insist there be no connection back to them."

Kimball kept his face impassive, but he raged at the suggestion that he'd be so careless as to leave clues. He was a professional. That's why they hired him. Then he wondered if he was the only specialist at work this week. His contact at Kingfisher Associates had called to offer him another job tonight, but he'd already committed to Montel. There must be a lot of loose ends that needed cleaning up. "I'll do it tonight or tomorrow. Need to study the situation some first."

Montel's attention returned to Mandy. "Of course. Best you review the folder soon."

Kimball nodded. "Any special complications?"

"No. This is simple. There's only one package, and you just need to dispose of it." Montel pulled a C-note from a silver money clip and left it under the check. "Tell her to keep the change. This is her lucky day." He stood and left without another word.

Kimball watched him depart before opening the envelope. It had the usual information: location, instructions on the disposition of the package, and a mobile phone number to which he would send a proof-of-completion photo. He scanned the attached photograph, and then glanced at Mandy.

She returned to the table, and her eyes widened at the sight of the bill under the check. "Is everything all right, sir? Can I get you anything?"

He shook his head. "I'm fine." He forced himself to choke down a bite of pie and a swallow of carbonized coffee. "Everything's fine. Really. I guess I wasn't as hungry as I thought." He tapped the check. "My companion said you should keep the change."

Her eyes glowed, and she beamed at him. "Thank you, sir."

"Thank him." He stood and left before she could respond.

He drove his black SUV to the outskirts of the little town and stopped in a church parking lot. From here he could keep an eye on the dented mobile home across the street. It sat on concrete blocks, and a porcelain garden gnome leered at him from the ragged front lawn. Someone had turned an old toilet into a planter for bedraggled pansies.

This was going to be easier than the job this afternoon. He switched his satellite radio to the opera station and settled back to the strains of *Die Walküre*.

Midway through Act I, the package arrived at the mobile home. Her ancient Chevy spewed a foul trail of smoke and coughed to a stop on the street. By the time Sieglinde expressed her undying love for her twin brother, the lights in the mobile home went out. Crickets chirped, and a dog in the next block barked, but sleep gripped the townspeople. Some things were easier in rural settings. Kimball waited for the end of Act II, just to be safe, before he pulled on latex gloves and stretched plastic booties over his sneakers. He patted the ankle holster that held his Taurus Millennium 9mm pistol before he slipped from his car. A clear plastic raincoat completed his ensemble. He crept through moonlight and shadow toward the trailer.

The metal treads on the entrance steps creaked under his weight. He hesitated and decided to try the door before using his burglar tools. Sure enough, it was unlocked. *Gotta love small towns.* He pulled out his pistol and screwed a silencer onto the barrel.

Moonlight marched in rows of shadow and light through the blinds in the living room. The stale odor of cigarettes and ancient dust filled his nose. He suppressed a snort at the velvet painting of a panther that hung above the sofa. A mangy cat coalesced from the shadows, yawned, and stretched. He let a small smile twist his lips, knelt and extended his hand. The animal approached, sniffed at his fingers, and then stropped against his legs. He whispered, "That's a good kitty," before straightening and scanning the rest of the room.

His ears caught muffled snores emanating from a hallway behind the kitchen. He advanced on cautious feet, sensitive to every creak of the floor. The bedroom door stood ajar, and the package lay sprawled in her bed, asleep. A frilly nightie clung to her corpulent body like a discouraged spider web. The snores ceased for a moment, and then she snorted and rolled to her back, her flesh quivering in the moonlight. The soft susurrations of her breathing whispered sweet nothings to the darkness.

Kimball's heart thudded in anticipation. He shuffled forward, savoring the knowledge that he would see her take her last breath. With the gentleness of a mother caressing her baby, he held his pistol to her forehead. She breathed in, then out, and then in again. The pistol gave a satisfying little *chuff*, and her body lurched. A sudden dark stain flooded across the bedding, and the scent of blood, feces, and urine filled the room. His eyes closed, his back arched, and an exultant breath shuddered from his open lips.

But then it was over. The gun dragged at his now languid muscles, and his soul slithered to a stop, torpid as a crocodile that's just fed. As always, the transcendent ecstasy evaporated and left behind a hollow shell of depression. Pleasure never lasted long enough to satisfy his hunger. He pulled out his cell phone and took two photos of the body.

He glanced around the bedroom. An old snapshot on the dresser caught his eye. It showed a younger and thinner version of the dead woman posing next to a woman who looked remarkably like the package he'd snatched this afternoon. They stood in front of an ornate metal gate. The sign overhead read, "Grange Station." It would make an excellent trophy. He turned to leave, but then his gaze landed on her purse. He dug inside and removed her wallet. He opened it and fingered the hundred dollar bill that Montel had left for her earlier this evening. A grin twisted his features as he returned to the silent mound of flesh on the bed. He dragged the tip of the silencer across her cheek while he murmured, "Well, Mandy, I guess this turned out to be my lucky day."

He slipped into the darkness and disappeared into the lonesome gloom that was at once his refuge and his torment.

Chapter
THREE

THE crushed rock in the driveway crunched under Brent's work boots as he trudged through the shadows toward the house. His muscles ached from unaccustomed labors, but at least the chores were done. A grim smile tugged at his exhausted features. His father would be pleased he'd taken care of the animals. Then he remembered his father was missing, and a ball of ice chilled his insides. He emitted a shuddering sigh, and he slumped on the back steps of the house. His feet ached, and his sweat-soaked work shirt clung to his body. He thought about his mother's clean floors and wiped the manure from his boots onto the grass.

For what seemed like the tenth time, he pulled his cell phone from his pocket and stared at the screen. No messages, no missed calls. It had been almost two hours since he'd talked to the sheriff's dispatcher at the county seat, and still no one had followed up. The continued silence from his parents worried him even more.

His gaze jittered across the farmyard. This was so like a normal night, back before he moved away to college. He cast a nervous eye over the homestead as he sought comfort in familiarity. Overhead, feathery clouds drifted over the Big Dipper. Lightning bugs flickered above the pasture. The light in the eave of the barn cast an amber glow across the ruts of the driveway and shimmered off the windshield of his pickup.

Yes, this was just like any night at home. Except tonight his parents were missing.

He pressed "talk" on his cell phone. It dialed the sheriff's emergency number, just as it had the last six times he'd called.

The woman's voice at the other end managed to be chipper and bored at the same time. "Jackson County Sheriff's Office. What's your emergency?"

"This is Brent Hyde. I called earlier about my parents. You said a deputy was going to stop by later tonight. Just 'anytime now' was what you told me."

"Yes, sir, I see your calls on the log. I dispatched Deputy Purcell to your location ten minutes ago. He should be there in an hour or so."

"Another hour. Dammit, it's been at least two hours since I called." He gritted his teeth and fought against the anger that throbbed inside.

"I realize that, sir. This is a big county, and we've only got four deputies on duty tonight. We've had two accidents and a drug bust to handle. He'll be there as soon as he can."

"Meantime, what about my parents? They could be injured or who knows what."

Icicles seemed to sharpen her words and stab at him. "All I can tell you is that the deputy will be there soon, sir. He'll take your information."

"Right." Brent regretted snarling at her. "Look, I'm sorry. I know you're following protocol. I'm just so worried about them."

"I understand." Her voice softened. "I've taken lots of these kinds of calls, sir. It'll probably turn out to be a simple misunderstanding. It usually does." She hesitated. "Maybe they're visiting relatives, or neighbors."

"We don't have any relatives. It's just us. The only neighbor who's anything like close isn't answering his phone." Despair sucked at him, and he leaned against the wall, but then headlights flashed over the hill and headed toward the farm. "I think I see him coming now. Thanks for your help." He broke the connection and stood, waiting.

Instead of a patrol car, though, he recognized Gary's blue sports coupe pulling into the drive. At least he wasn't alone anymore.

At the sight of his friend's lithe frame and lank ebony hair, relief flooded through Brent. Gary hopped out of the car and sprinted the dozen or so paces to his waiting arms. Brent melted into his muscular embrace and inhaled his fresh, masculine scent. "God, it's good to see you. Thanks for coming." His chin trembled, and he was grateful that his buddy couldn't see the sudden tears that pooled in his eyes.

"Where else would I be, babe?" Gary's voice, husky and reassuring, caressed Brent's ears. He pulled away and stroked Brent's cheek. "I'm sorry I couldn't come as soon as you called. The important thing is, I'm here now. We'll figure this out together. That's what friends do."

"I'm so *worried.* I called the hospitals in Maquoketa and Bellevue. Thank God they're not there. But where could they *be?*" He choked back a sob.

"Hey, if they're not in a hospital, that's good news, right? I called Middleton, and Dr. Athair Googled the ones in Dubuque, Iowa City, and the Quad Cities. No reports there."

"Thanks for checking. I'll have to thank Dr. Athair too."

"She said she'd cover for you at the lab if you need to spend some time here. We *care* about you, man." A drifting cloud exposed the moon, and for a moment his eyes shone with a crystalline gleam. "Maybe they just went shopping, or on a quick vacation."

Brent shook his head. "But dinner was in the oven. And no one did the chores. Dad would never have left the animals unattended." Fatigue pulled at him, and he collapsed onto the steps.

Gary nodded. "Well, there is that. We'll figure it out, though. Count on it." His nose wrinkled, and a grin toyed with his lips. "What's that smell?" He leaned forward and sniffed. "Have you been rolling in pig shit?"

Despite himself, Brent smiled. "We don't have hogs. Someone had to do the chores. Dad would have had a fit." He looked down at his grimy, sweat-soaked T-shirt and blue jeans. "I guess I don't smell so good."

"That's an understatement. Have you had dinner?"

"No. The animals came first. I took Mom's roast out of the oven, changed clothes, and did the chores."

Gary leaned over as if to kiss his forehead before pulling away. "I don't want to get foot-and-mouth disease, or whatever that vile smell is." He fell into a corny mock-cowboy twang. "Why don't you shower and get cleaned up, pardner, while I whomp up some vittles for you?"

A laugh bubbled up in Brent's throat. He fought it back, lest it turn to hysteria. "Purcell, the sheriff's deputy, is supposed to be here. 'Soon', the dispatcher said. I should be here to meet him."

"I'll meet him and hold him off while you scrape the manure off your body." He held out his hand. "Give me your cell phone, in case your parents call, or this guy Purcell."

Brent reached into his pocket and handed it over. "Thanks. Come get me if it's my folks."

"Will do. Now git! A shower will do your body good, and my nose too. That'll give me time to fix us both some chow."

Brent let Gary pull him to his feet, and he stumbled inside. "You remember where Mom keeps stuff in the kitchen?"

"Yeah. She even let me help with the dishes last time we were here, just like I was family. Go on, now. Get yourself all prettied up for the deputy, and I'll fix you a sandwich."

THE steamy shower turned the aches in Brent's muscles to an enervated languor. He toweled dry, and sudden hunger seized his body. He slipped into clean blue jeans without bothering with underwear, socks, or a T-shirt and headed to the kitchen. Gary stood at the counter, building a huge sandwich with Mom's homemade bread, lettuce, tomatoes from the garden, and fresh cheese from the dairy in Bellevue.

Brent snatched up a stray slice of pork roast. "Mmm. This is wonderful." He peered at the sandwiches. "Those about ready?"

Gary finished off two towering stacks with a flourish, sliced each diagonally, and put them on plates on the table. "All done. You want beer or coffee?"

The chair creaked when Brent collapsed into it. "I better have coffee, at least until after I talk to Deputy Purcell. No sign of him yet?"

"Not yet. You know this guy Purcell?"

"Don't think so. I wonder where he's at. Maybe I should call the sheriff again." Worry gnawed its way back into his consciousness, and he returned his sandwich to the plate.

"Have dinner first. Take care of yourself, or you won't be any good to anyone else." Gary set a steaming cup of coffee in front of him and doused it with cream. "This is the best stuff I've ever had. You can't get this in stores."

Brent nodded and spoke through a mouthful of Dagwood. "Fresh from our cows."

Gary cocked an eyebrow at him. "Really. So is one teat for cream and another for skim? Is there one for chocolate milk too?"

"Don't be silly. You watched me separate the milk when you were here last summer. It's just fresh, and we keep the best for here on the farm."

Headlights flashed through the open window, followed by the crump of tires in the driveway.

Brent looked up. "Well, that's got to be the deputy. About time." He glanced at the cuckoo clock that hung over the table. "It took him over three hours to get here. I called it in before seven." A heavy hand rapped on the front door. Brent looked down at his naked torso. "Shit. Would you get it? I need to put a shirt on."

"I'll get it, but stay where you're at and finish your dinner. I'm sure he's seen a guy without a shirt before." He left to answer the front door.

Purcell swaggered into the kitchen, all six feet four and three hundred pounds of him. He sat in Brent's dad's chair and thumped his notebook on the table. Handcuffs and a .45 dangled from the belt at his waist. Well, from below where his waist would be, if he had one. Sweat sheened on his bald head when he removed his Smokey the Bear hat and put it on the table.

Gary served him coffee without asking, and then settled into the guest chair.

Purcell heaved a sigh and opened his notebook. "Which one of you's Hyde?" The pungent aromas of cigars and Old Spice cologne hovered about him.

Brent spoke. "That's me, officer." He pushed a snapshot across the table. "Here's a recent photo of my parents."

Purcell's eyes narrowed, and Brent thought of Officer Wiggum on *The Simpsons*. "Deputy. I'm a deputy." He pulled a form from his notebook and slipped the photo underneath it. "So your parents is missin'?"

"Yes, sir. I was supposed to come home for dinner tonight, from college, but when I got here no one was home."

"Uh huh." He made another note. "So how you know they didn't jest forget?"

"Dinner was in the oven, the table was set. And no one had done the evening chores. Dad would never have left without arranging for the animals to be taken care of."

"Uh huh." More notes. "Anything missin'? Cars, money, jewelry?"

"Both their cars are here. They don't keep money in the house, and Mom doesn't own any jewelry."

"Any sign of foul play?" His eyes roamed over the kitchen, lingered for a moment on Gary, then a moment longer on Brent.

Brent wished he'd put on a shirt after all. He felt like a bug exposed under a microscope. "What do you mean, 'foul play'?"

The cop gave him a disgusted look. "Doors smashed in. Broken windows. Furniture fucked up. Don't you watch TV?"

Brent shook his head. "No, nothing." He thought for a moment. "The front door was ajar. That was kind of unusual."

"Nothin' else? Maybe neighbors saw strange cars or somethin'?"

"The nearest neighbor is over a mile away." Brent thought for a moment. "An SUV almost ran me off the road on the way here, over by Ruby's."

Purcell rolled his eyes. "You want me to investigate traffic violations too? I ain't got all night. Let's keep this to just the facts about your parents."

Brent flushed. "Sorry."

Purcell glared at him for a beat before continuing. "All right then. Your parents got any enemies? Use drugs? There was that bunch over by Monticello what was raisin' marijuana. Maybe gambling debts? Any reason why anyone would want to hurt 'em?"

Gary scowled and fidgeted in his chair. He seemed about to speak, but Brent beat him to it. "No. They're just plain folk. Dad works for a software firm in Dubuque. The farm is just kind of a hobby for him and Mom."

"Uh huh." His gaze raked over Gary. "Who are you, bud?"

Gary's eyes seemed to throw daggers, and his voice dripped with venom. "I'm a friend of Brent's, from college. He called me when his parents turned up missing, and I came to support him."

Purcell snorted. "That your car out there with that *rainbow* sticker on it?"

Gary turned white. "Yes. What of it?"

Purcell's mouth squirmed like he wanted to spit. He glared at Gary for a beat before looking back at his clipboard. "Just askin'," he muttered. He made another note and turned back to Brent. "You and your folks get along okay? No conflicts over your... friends?"

Gary shoved his chair back and leaned forward. His jaw muscles jerked like they were spring-loaded. "What the fuck's that supposed to mean?"

Brent's face heated, but he held up a hand. "This is a loving family, Deputy. Gary's only visited a couple of times, but my parents went out of their way to make him feel welcome."

"Huh." Purcell closed his notebook. "Look, son, they've not even been gone four hours. I'll have Beulah call the hospitals, but there ain't nothin' we can do tonight. It's not illegal for folks to disappear."

Frustration boiled in Brent's chest, and his throat tightened. "But they're missing. What if they're kidnapped?"

"Now why would anyone want to do that? You jest told me they don't have no enemies." He stood. "I've been on dozens of these calls. In every case, the so-called missing person jest turned out to be out visiting, or on joy ride, or some other misunderstandin'. They'll turn up, probably later tonight or tomorrow."

Brent scowled and snapped, "This isn't a misunderstanding."

The deputy pulled a card from his pocket. "Tell you what, son. If they don't show up in a couple of days, you call me back and we'll talk. Right now, I got real crimes to investigate." His boots clumped against the linoleum and left black heel marks on Brent's mom's immaculate floor as he left.

Brent slouched at the table, his mouth agape. "What the hell was that?" He felt as though his last hope departed when the deputy's car pulled out onto the gravel road and sped away.

Gary stroked his hand. "Babe, I more or less expected this. Let's get a good night's sleep, and tomorrow we'll figure out what to do.

Some of my trainers at Grace Development have contacts with law enforcement. Maybe they'll have some ideas." A tight grin played across his features. "And who knows? Maybe it'll turn out that asshole's right, and your parents will show up."

"I don't think so. I'm telling you, there's something about this that doesn't add up."

They both jumped when someone rapped at the front door. Brent frowned. "Who's that? It can't be Purcell. Did you hear a car drive up?"

Gary shook his head. "I thought I heard thunder. I suppose it could have been a car. Maybe the deputy forgot something. Stay put. I'll check." He pulled a cleaver from the rack on the counter and winked. "Just in case." Then he headed to the front door.

Chapter FOUR

ASTON MINOCK poked at his campfire and dreamed of better times.

The plastic sheets of his shelter rustled in the night breeze, and an owl sang a distant dirge. The moon and stars hid behind low, scudding clouds. A trickle of grease dribbled from the rabbit roasting on a spit over his fire, and sparks flickered into the darkness. The stench of his unwashed body and his grimy clothes seemed almost homey against the pungent aromas of burned meat and rotting vegetation that wafted across the darkness. A chill shivered through his bones, and he clutched at his tattered jacket.

He contemplated the shattered windows and boarded-up doors of Building Three. The firelight flickered through fifty feet of dense woods to cast a ruddy glow on the walls. He could just make out the words "Grange Station" in faded crimson lettering over the entrance of the ramshackle structure. Memories of when he had reigned there as a guard, controlling the lives of patients and workers alike, brought a tight smile to his lips. But then the fire crackled and returned him to the present. Now his kingdom consisted only of the abandoned facility and the surrounding bramble. Now he held dominion only over rabbits and squirrels and the other creatures of the wild.

A chill breeze swept through the weald, and a whisper of dried leaves rustled against the tangled thicket surrounding him. From afar, laughter danced with the night, and inchoate voices skittered into the silence. Adrenalin sent a chill tingling down Aston's spine, and he stroked the empty shotgun that rested by his side. Memories burned at him, and cold fear sucked strength from his limbs.

Last spring, a laughing gaggle of teenagers had invaded his kingdom. They terrorized him and his friends, a bedraggled group of homeless people who had squatted here in the old Grange Station. He'd tried to scare the bullies off with his empty shotgun, but they just taunted him. They snatched away his gun and tossed him from one set of youthful arms to another. He rubbed his knuckles, and a hoarse chuckle bubbled in this throat. He remembered the satisfying crunch his fist had made when it smashed into one of the smirking faces. But then his chuckle turned to a cough, and old pain gripped his ribs. They had pushed him to the ground and kicked him. When they grew bored, they had left him bleeding and broken, to be tended by his homeless friends. Later, the police came, and he'd hidden in the tunnels under Building Three. The cops had handcuffed the other squatters and taken them away in cattle trucks. He sighed. Now he was alone in his Grange. Just as well. People were trouble.

The rabbit sizzled over the flame, and his stomach growled. But then the laughter sounded again, louder now. The murmur of indistinct voices broke the peace of the night, and the fear he'd felt that earlier day returned.

He stood and reached for a cracked plastic container that read "Meadow Gold Ice Cream." It held only brackish rainwater tonight, and he used that to douse his fire. Steam sputtered, and the fire smoked as he extinguished it. He crouched low next to the glowing embers and tipped his head to listen.

Footfalls crunched through the woods. A male voice, full of bravado, called out. "I can see the buildings. That's where the boogeyman is supposed to hang out." He made mocking "ooOOoo" sounds and broke into giggles.

A female voice responded. "Stop it, Clark. That's not funny." Her contralto shook with a faint tremor. "So now we've seen it. Let's go."

"Don't be such a fraidy-cat. I want to see what's inside."

Another male voice broke in. "Hey, if Cindy wants to go, we should go. We agreed that we'd leave when she said."

Clark's tenor took a mocking tone. "What's the matter, Jimmy? You scared, like a girl?"

"Stop it, Clark." Cindy's voice snapped now and was sharper, shriller. Thunder rolled across the sky, and a chill wind swirled through the branches of the trees. "It's going to rain. We're leaving. You can do what you want."

"Go ahead. I didn't come this far just to run away like some faggot."

Aston gripped his shotgun and wished he had ammunition.

"Come on, Jimmy. Let's go," Cindy commanded. The tremor in her voice had vanished.

"Chickens." Clark clucked like a drunken hen. "Go ahead. Wait for me at the cars. Scaredy-cats."

Cindy snorted. "Whatever. I'll give you fifteen minutes, and then I'm going with Jimmy. If I'm not home by midnight, my parents will freak."

"Let 'em freak." The croak of a frog and the chitter of crickets filled a moment of silence before Clark spoke again. "Don't get lost in the woods, little girls."

Footsteps crunched, this time retreating away from where Aston cowered by his shelter. The black plastic fluttered in a sudden gust of wind, and he silenced it with a hasty fist. Overhead, dark clouds raced across the sky. Thunder grumbled in the distance.

Clark muttered, "Fucking pansies."

His voice rang louder. He must be closer now. Aston pointed his empty shotgun in the direction of the footfalls. His hands shook.

A shadow drifted between him and the entrance to Building Three. He narrowed his eyes and the form coalesced into a human shape. It must be Clark. The figure stopped, and, when he looked back, the moonlight gleamed in his eyes. He turned again and hesitated before he edged forward. The stairs leading to the entrance creaked under his weight, and then the door rattled against the chains and padlock holding it closed. Clark turned again, and Aston cowered deeper in the shadows. Clark muttered, "Fifteen fucking minutes. What losers. Faggots, that's what they are." The chains clanked as he tested the door one more time. "Fuck this." He kicked the entrance and then turned and retreated.

He stopped and turned full circle. "Shit. Where's the trail?"

Aston held his breath. The empty shotgun hung heavy in his hands. He sucked at his lower lip.

Clark took a step forward, directly toward Aston. He stopped and knelt to touch the soil. Aston knew he'd find the broken shards of a sidewalk that would lead directly here, to his hiding place. Clammy sweat chilled his torso, and his fingers tightened on the stock of the rifle.

Clark stood and pulled out his cell phone. His rugged features and spiked hair glowed in the light of the screen while he dialed. A jeweled stud glimmered in his left earlobe.

Aston waited. Lightning flickered, closer now. His legs ached from crouching, and he shifted his weight. A twig snapped.

Clark's head jerked up, but then he spoke into his phone. "Hey, are you faggots at the car yet?" His words held an edge of worry now, perhaps even fear. He paused, listening. "Nah, it was locked." He waited a beat longer. "Look, I got turned around, and I'm not sure which one of these fuckin' trails leads back to the car. Can you start Google Latitude on your phone? I'll use your location to figure out which way to go." Another moment of silence. "Ha ha. Very funny. I'll see you in a few."

The screen lit his face again, and he held his phone in front of him like a compass while he rotated about. His motion seemed jerky as lightning flashed in the clouds and illuminated the scene like strobe lights. In a moment, he faced back toward Aston and started walking along the crumbled remains of the walkway.

Aston's breath clogged his throat, and he scuttled back, deeper in the shadows. He wanted to scream as a sudden cramp gripped his calf. He tried to shift his weight, but the leg gave way and he crashed to the ground. His arm disturbed a log sticking out from the remains of his fire, and sparks flew skyward.

Clark's voice held an edge of panic now. "Who's there? What the fuck's that?" He stopped and his head tipped forward. "Cindy? Jimmy? You guys better not be fuckin' with me." He held his phone like a flashlight and panned it across the underbrush. He inched forward, and his breath husked into the night. "Who's there?"

He was less than ten feet away when Aston's shelter flapped in a sudden gust of wind. Clark whirled, and his gaze fell first on the plastic whipping in the wind, then on the ruddy glow of the coals from the fire, and finally on Aston. "What the fuck," he whispered. "You're that old hermit." He stepped forward, and his voice rose. "You hit me in the nose, you asshole." He towered over Aston now and kicked him in the shin. "You fucker," he screamed. "You think you're funny, scarin' me like that? I'll teach you to fuck with me." His voice shrieked, octaves higher than before.

Aston rolled backward. His shotgun thudded to the ground, and his fingers crawled across the sandy loam seeking something, anything for defense. They found one of the heavy logs protruding from his fire. He tugged it free and used it to lever himself to his feet.

Clark crouched with his arms in a double arc. He circled like a champion wrestler, confident and certain of victory, looking for weakness in his opponent. A beam of moonlight lit his features. A grin slashed across his face. He bared his teeth, and they glowed as though lit by neon.

Aston gripped the log with both hands. The rough bark bit into his fingers, and the acrid scent of smoke burned his nostrils. He swung it like a lumberjack chopping wood. The heavy weight dragged against his muscles, and his tendons screamed as torque stretched his torso.

Time slowed. Clark's eyes widened until they seemed to be nothing but whites. He dodged, but he was too late. The log smashed into his skull with a satisfying crack, and he collapsed as though his bones had turned to water.

Aston's heart pummeled his chest, and his breath tore his throat. He swung the log once more, and something warm and wet splattered on his face. He licked his lips and savored the salty taste of Clark's brains. He swung the club again, and yet again. It had been too long since he'd killed, since he'd exulted in death. His arms pounded like a flywheel, and his chest heaved like a piston. Again and again the club thudded. He beat Clark into the earth, turning muscle to pulp and bone to splinters. At last, he stopped and dropped his weapon. He knelt and ran his fingers through the gore of the smashed body. An ecstatic croon passed his lips while organs slithered through his grip.

Heavy drops of rain splatted onto his head and dribbled down his cheeks like tears. The wind whipped at his shelter, and it tumbled into a tangle of briars and ragged sumac. Lightning sparkled from cloud to cloud, and thunder crashed. He tugged at his jacket and decided to head back into the tunnels.

First, though, he'd have to hide the remains. He knew just the place. There were already dozens of decaying remains there. One more body wouldn't make any difference.

Chapter
FIVE

CONCERN pulled Brent's lips into a grim line as Gary left the kitchen, cleaver in hand.

A fist pounded again on the front door, and a muffled voice cried out, "I need to talk to you."

"That voice. I'm sure I've heard it before," Brent murmured. He stood and peered out the kitchen window. Lightning shimmered in the distance, and dark clouds raced across the face of the moon. The yard light cast an amber glow over the vehicles in the little circle drive: his pickup, Gary's sports car, his dad's truck, and a van with writing on the side. The deputy hadn't returned, then. The sight of the van jiggled at his memory, but his fatigued mind couldn't quite make the connection.

Gary's snarl reached him from the front door. "Who the fuck are you?"

"Jason Killeen. Who are *you?*"

Brent rolled his eyes. *Of course. The reporter from this afternoon. What an asshole.* He headed toward the front door.

The cleaver gleamed in Gary's fist, and he towered over the little would-be reporter. The latter looked like a lamb headed to slaughter. A skinny lamb. A thick manila folder bulged in his left hand, and his keys dangled from his right.

Gary sneered. "I'll ask the questions here. What do you want?"

The wind whipped at Jason's hair, and his eyes widened when Brent approached from the kitchen. His voice shook as he asked, "Are you all right? I think you might be in danger."

After everything else, having a reporter show up was the last straw. Pent-up anger and fear spewed from Brent's mouth. "I'm just great. My parents are missing, the fucking sheriff won't do anything, and now I've got an asshole reporter beating on my door. "

Gary gripped Brent's hand when he reached the door, but his eyes didn't leave Jason. "He's a fucking *reporter?* What, that dumbass deputy blabbed to you, and now you're looking for a cheap story about Brent's parents being missing? Don't you fucking vultures have any decency? Can't you just leave him alone?"

A puzzled look flooded across Jason's features. "What do you mean, your parents are missing?"

Brent hesitated, not sure if a news story would help him find his parents or not. Maybe he should talk to this loser, after all.

Apparently, Gary had no doubts. "There's no fucking story here for you. Go away." He held up the cleaver. "Git!"

Jason raised his right hand, palm forward, and the keys jangled. The wind slapped at the papers bulging from the manila folder in his other hand. "You don't understand. I'm not here for a story. I got a call from one of my sources. He told me that Brent was in danger, and I should warn him. I tried calling his cell, but he didn't answer, so I came here."

Gary stepped in front of Brent and pushed Jason's chest, making the little reporter stumble backward. "I said git! Didn't you hear me?"

Brent put a hand on his friend's shoulder. "Just a minute. I'd like to hear more." He stepped onto the front stoop and looked over Gary's shoulder at Jason. "What source? What's his name? What did he tell you?"

"I don't know his name. I don't even know he's a he. Whoever it is, he contacts me from a throw-away cell phone. But everything he's told me has been right so far."

Brent rolled his eyes and tried not to shout. "Can't you come to the point about anything? *What did he fucking tell you?*"

Jason opened his mouth and closed it, and then he spoke. "He said that the Gerion Group is cleaning up loose ends, and that you're one of them. They know you're here, he said, and they were going to send an assassin after you tonight."

Gary snorted. "An assassin. Like Lee Harvey Oswald." He glanced over his shoulder at Brent. "He's a wacko conspiracy theorist. Why are we wasting our time listening to this bullshit?"

Jason shook his head. The wind lashed his dark curls into a Medusa's crown of snarls. "Not like Oswald. More like a mob hit man,

I think." He held up his folder. "You wouldn't believe the stuff I've got on them." Lightning crackled, and scattered raindrops splatted onto the trio. "Right now, though, you've got to get out of here. He was really clear."

Gary advanced and showed him the cleaver again. Jason retreated once more and missed the top step on the porch. His arms spiraled, and he tumbled onto his butt on the walk. Gary leaned forward and pointed to Jason's van. "The only one who needs to leave here is you, asshole. Now."

A buzz, like a bumble bee, whizzed past Brent's ear, and the glass in the storm door exploded inward. An instant later a sound like a firecracker snapped from the cow pasture. He swiveled to look, and his foot caught on the broken step. His arms pinwheeled for balance, but to no avail, and he landed facedown on his mother's pansies. The firecracker sound snapped again, and this time he saw a red flash behind the fence. He knew what that was. Muzzle fire. "Get down! Someone's shooting at us!" He rolled for cover behind the front porch.

Gary dropped the cleaver and dashed back into the house. Jason clawed at the mud and crawled on his belly to hide next to Brent. His voice shook when he whispered, "Are you all right? Did you get hit?"

Brent's shoulder ached from the fall, and he'd scuffed the heels of his hands. "He missed me. I'm okay." The rain turned to a steady drizzle, and he wished he'd stopped to put on a shirt. He risked peeking around the porch. "I can't see a fucking thing."

"Do you believe me now?" Jason's hoarse whisper rasped against his ears.

Brent snorted. "Where did Gary go? He didn't get hit, did he?"

"Your boyfriend dropped that fucking butcher knife and took off inside. He looked okay to me. Maybe he'll call the cops."

"Maybe." He reached into his pocket, but it was empty. "Shit. Gary's still got my cell phone, or I'd call 'em."

Jason patted his shirt, and then pointed to where a mobile phone lay near the stairs. "I guess mine went flying when I tripped and fell. I can't call either."

Lightning lit the barnyard, and Brent hunkered closer to Jason. "We can't stay here. Whoever shot at us could circle behind us. We'd be sitting ducks." He thought for a moment. "The entrance to the cellar is on the side of the house. If we go down there, we can get back upstairs and get to my .22. My dad's got a shotgun too."

"That's better than nothing, I guess." Jason shivered. "Which way?"

Before they could move, a shotgun roared from one of the front windows, and Gary's voice shouted, "I've called the sheriff. They've got a deputy less than two minutes away." A siren wailed through the storm sounds. His voice turned softer. "Brent! Talk to me. Are you all right?"

"I'm fine. So is Jason. We're hiding."

"Stay put. I've got your .22 along with your dad's shotgun. If he fires again, I'll nail him. They said Purcell would be right back."

An engine purred to life from behind the barn. A black BMW fishtailed into the drive in a spray of mud and gravel. The yard light revealed two figures in the front seat before it turned and raced down the road, toward Ruby's and the river. "I think they just made a getaway," Brent called out. "It looked like there were two of them."

Jason piped up. "There was at least one more in the backseat."

Brent started to clamber to his feet.

Gary snapped at him, "Stay put. There could still be snipers out there. Wait until Purcell gets here."

Brent rubbed his shoulder and shivered.

Jason turned a mud-smeared face in his direction. "I tried to warn you, man. My source says these guys are fucking nasty."

"What could they possibly want with me? I'm just a student." His hands trembled as the adrenaline took its toll. "What have they done to my parents?"

"I don't know, man." Jason rolled a bit to one side and tapped the manila envelope that lay underneath him, protected from the rain. "I know just enough to scare the shit out of me."

The deputy's patrol car screamed over the hill and lurched into the circle drive. The siren wailed and the light bar on the roof flashed a maniacal red. The driver door slammed open, and Purcell's copious form crouched behind it. Brent jumped when the deputy's voice roared from loudspeakers. "Throw down your weapons and show yourselves."

Jason shuddered and squirmed closer to Brent. His bony body rubbed against the bare skin of Brent's chest and left a trail of mud.

Brent reflected that being shot at must be erotic, in some sick kind of way, since Jason's touch aroused other sensations as well. It sure as fuck couldn't be the obnoxious reporter that did that to him.

The loudspeakers thundered again. "You there, behind the porch. Come out now."

Brent levered to his knees and lifted his hands over his head. "It's just us, Deputy. The shots came from over by the barn." He squinted and held an arm to his eyes against the glare of a searchlight from the cruiser.

"That other guy there with you? What's his name? Gary?"

"Gary's inside. This is a reporter who showed up after you left."

"Let me see him."

Jason followed Brent's example and rose to his knees, with trembling hands over his head. He squinted against the light and muttered, "I hope the bad guy's not still here."

Gary emerged from the front door, his hands raised. "I'm here, Deputy. I'm pretty sure the shots came from the pasture, down by the barn."

The searchlight focused on him for a moment before it panned across the farmyard: Brent's truck, his parents' vehicles, Gary's sports car. It lingered on Jason's van and the lettering on the side before it moved on to the pasture.

Breath huffed from Brent's throat when the spotlight shone on his father's cows. "What the fuck?"

Jason followed his gaze. "I didn't know cows slept lying down."

"Yeah, they do. But not like that." He stared at the two cows in the pasture and shuddered. Their bodies sprawled into grotesque, motionless heaps, their heads twisted backward at impossible angles, and their mouths gaped in silent screams.

Chapter SIX

THE DEA Jeep bounced over the rutted road, and rain drizzled against the windows. Special Agent Rachel Morrison's Kevlar vest pinched at her right armpit. She winced and loosened a strap. A lightning flash broke the darkness and illuminated the swampy forest on either side of the gravel road.

Jake Sibley, the DEA agent sitting crowded next to her in the backseat, asked, "Everything all right, Agent Morrison?" His voice held a mocking tone.

"I'm fine. These damned vests weren't designed for a woman's anatomy." She twisted it into a more comfortable position.

Sibley's hand brushed against her knee. "We wouldn't want our FBI Liaison to be injured on our little operation," he purred. "Maybe you should go back and wait in the rear, with the ambulances."

Her skin crawled at his touch. "The meth lab's on US government property. I'm going in. That's why I'm here." The Jeep lurched again, and muddy rainwater splattered against the window at her side.

Sibley raised his fingers to the receiver wedged in his ear. "Good." A tight smile bent his lips. "Our Coast Guard friends have the gang's dock in sight."

She sighed. Calling in the Coast Guard to do the assault from an Iowa river seemed overkill to her, but she didn't argue. Sibley was in charge of the Joint Task Force, and he'd set up the rules of engagement to assure the only job she had was to observe. What a waste of training.

The Jeep sloshed to a stop at a picnic area beside the road. Three more vehicles, with only parking lights on so as to not alert anyone in the cabin, maneuvered alongside. She rolled her eyes. Sibley's Special Ops team included DEA agents, sheriff's deputies, Iowa Highway Patrol officers, and Coast Guard ratings. He'd commandeered an ambulance from the hospital in Savanna, three miles away across the Mississippi River in Illinois, and it hid in an abandoned barn a quarter mile back from here. He'd used every excuse to expand his command, as if that somehow expanded him. Rachel hid a sneer as she thought that the only thing he expanded was his fat head.

She still resented the orders of her boss, Montel Strorm. He'd told her to "be a good girl" and "just observe." Since this friggin' swamp was federal land, owned by the Corps of Engineers, she was to be the eyes and ears for the Bureau. God knows why they would care what happened here.

Sibley's radio buzzed again. Each contingent of the JTF sang out their position and readiness. Sibley acted like he was commanding the D-Day landing instead of raiding a meth lab run by a couple of hick farm boys. What an ass. Sure, it was always a good idea to use overwhelming force against these kinds of creeps, but this was ridiculous.

He turned to her, and his slimy fingers squeezed her knee again. "When we go in, you stay in the staging area, Agent Morrison. Let the Special Ops team do what they're trained to do."

Lightning flashed again and, and for an instant, filled the dark woods with light.

His voice rasped into his microphone. "On my mark, at 10 p.m. sharp, just like we planned, men." Rain clattered against the roof of the Jeep. He consulted his watch, and his lips moved while he counted down the seconds. "Go!"

Rachel stepped out of the Jeep, and her feet sank ankle-deep into muck. The DEA Special Ops team exploded out of their van and rushed ahead, their black, hooded outfits vanishing in the night. She joined Sibley, the sheriffs' deputies, and the highway patrol officers, who took up positions behind their vehicles. The officers and Sibley drew their weapons, but Rachel didn't bother.

The rain muffled the sound of the DEA team pounding on the door of the meth lab. She couldn't make out their shouted words, but she knew that they were announcing their warrant and demanding entry. She had to admit Sibley was smart. There was no probable cause to support exigent circumstances, so his team used correct "knock-and-announce" procedure to preserve the search from court challenges later. She counted off the seconds, and when she reached fifteen, the sounds of the team smashing down the door thudded through the woods. A flare arced through the rain and soared above the dock at the river, announcing that the Coast Guard team had begun their phase of the operation.

Less than two minutes later, a grin split Sibley's features. "All clear. The lab and the dock are secure. Let's go, men." He waved the officers forward.

Rachel's lip curled at the reference to "men," but she held her peace and trotted after them. Ahead, yellow light spilled out of the open door of the cabin. Rain beat down, and she swiped at her eyes with the back of her hand to clear her vision. The officers streamed into the pathetic shack, leaving trails of mud on the floor. The roof sagged in the middle, and plywood covered the windows.

She sauntered into the chaos of the building. Inside, three scruffy-looking youths lay sprawled facedown on the floor, barefoot, their hands bound behind their backs with plastic handcuffs. One of the DEA Special Ops team was already stuffing their shoes and socks into a plastic bag. One of the perps turned his head and stared at her as she approached. His eyes, their pupils narrowed to pinpoints, rolled in his head. Her nose wrinkled at the stench of cooking meth. It still smelled like rotten eggs and cat urine.

One of the DEA agents knelt on the back of a fourth man, in a far corner of the room. Another crouched next to them and shackled the man's ankles. The commander of the Special Ops team stripped off his black hood and showed her a .45. "That asshole pulled a gun on us."

She nodded. That was aggravated assault of a federal agent and resisting arrest. The US Attorney would pile the charges on. She was glad.

Sibley swaggered up to her. "Looks like we've got this under control." He raised his voice. "Good job, men." His radio squawked and his eyes narrowed. "Shit."

Rachel kept her voice smooth, professional. "Is there a problem, Agent Sibley?"

He glared at her. "Nothing we can't handle." He turned to face the officer who had been shackling the suspect. "This one been Mirandized?"

"Yeah. We did all of 'em."

Sibley nodded and squatted next to the suspect, who still squirmed under the agent's knee. "What's your name, bud?"

The guy twisted his gaunt features to face the DEA agent. One of his eyes was swollen shut, and he looked like he hadn't shaved in a week. "Get this asshole off of me," he sneered. "I'm filing police brutality charges." Sores ran down his boney arms, and his veins were blue ropes underneath pallid skin. A user, then, besides a manufacturer.

"You pulled a gun on my agent. You're lucky he didn't blow your brains out." Sibley leaned closer. "I asked you your name, creep."

"Fuck you. Ask my lawyer. You ain't gettin' nuthin' from me." The man's eyes rolled and looked too big for their sockets, like bloodshot billiard balls.

"The boat down at the dock is registered to Fred Merrick. That you, bud?" He nodded to the officer on the perp's back, who pulled away so Sibley could get at the man's wallet. "Driver's license here says Fred Merrick. The picture matches your ugly mug too. I guess that's you, bud."

"What of it?" The man twisted his head, and a greasy string of black hair fell across his wasted features.

"You use the nets on that boat to fish? That's illegal, you know."

Rachel frowned. This had to be going someplace, but where?

A laugh bubbled up from Merrick's throat. "So sue me."

"We'll do more than that, asshole. There's a body in those nets."

Rachel's forehead wrinkled before she remembered to stay cool.

Merrick snorted. "I don't know nothin' about no body."

"Yeah, well until we find someone else, I think you'll do." Sibley stood. "Let's go, men. Time to start processin' this friggin' scene." He glanced again at Rachel. "I guess you've got something to do after all, honey. Murder on federal property falls under the FBI, right?"

Rachel clenched her jaw and nodded.

"Right. Just remember, I'm still the special agent in charge of this joint task force. You answer to me."

"Got it, Agent Sibley." She turned on her heel.

"Hey!" Sibley shouted. "Where you going?"

"To inspect the body, of course." She stepped into the rain and headed toward the dock. She wished for coffee, lots of it. This promised to be a long night.

Chapter SEVEN

RAIN drizzled on Brent's bare torso. Mud squeezed between his toes as he set off toward the animals that lay contorted and still in the deputy's spotlight.

Purcell's voice roared from his loudspeaker. "Hey, where you goin'? Stay put until backup gets here."

Brent paid him no need. "Look at the cows, Deputy. I need to check on them."

"God damn it, I said stay put."

Jason's footfalls sloshed beside him. A grin slashed across his features, and he panted, "What's he gonna do? Shoot at us?"

Brent detoured to tread on the sandy loam of the yard rather than the graveled drive. He quickened his pace.

A siren howled in the distance, while thunder rumbled and lightning flickered. Brent reached the gate to the pasture and raced inside. He knelt by the nearest cow, a black-and-white mottled Holstein his father had acquired three years ago. His stomach churned, and he swore under his breath. "What the fuck did they do to her?"

Jason skidded to a stop next to him, and the flash on his iPhone camera lit the scene with a bizarre white glare. "Its mouth is all screwed up." The camera flashed again.

Brent ran his fingers across the wounds. "They've cut away her lips." He pried the mouth open. "Her tongue's gone too. This is sick."

"There been any other cattle mutilations around here?" He circled around and took a photo of the cow's rear. "Look at this."

"What?" Brent crawled over to inspect what Jason was pointing at. "Fuck. It's like they cored the poor thing."

"Yep. The udders are gone too." More flashes from his phone. "Notice anything else? No blood."

Sirens screamed into the farmyard, and two more patrol cars joined Purcell's. His voice roared again. "You two get back up here. Do it now, or we'll fuckin' cuff you and drag you."

Sour bile rose in Brent's throat. He pushed to his feet and turned away. "I don't want to see any more of this." He trudged back toward the farmhouse, where he rubbed mud from the pasture off his feet onto the wet grass.

Purcell grabbed his arm before he got to the front porch. "When I give you an order, boy, you better follow it." He jerked him toward the house.

Jason's camera flashed again, and his voice sang out, "Jason Killeen here, officer. I'm a reporter. Would you care to answer a few questions?"

Purcell's head jerked around, and his eyes narrowed. "Right now, you're a fucking witness. Put that damned camera away."

Jason held his phone higher. "Could you speak up, officer? I want to be sure I record your exact words."

Purcell released Brent, snarled, and took a step toward Jason. A uniformed arm grabbed his shoulder. "Take it easy, Fred. Why don't you go inside and see if Joleen needs any help?"

Purcell's jaws jumped like he'd been struck by lightning. "We can't let these punks push us around, Sheriff."

Jason smiled. His voice was smooth as freshly drawn cream. "As nearly as I can tell, it was Purcell doing the shoving. Want to see the photos, Sheriff?"

"Thank you, that won't be necessary Mr. Killeen."

A soprano voice sang out from the door to the house. "Sheriff. The guy in here got hit. I need the tactical first aid kit from your cruiser."

Brent's heart stopped. "Gary got shot?" He ran toward the house and pushed by the female deputy in the doorway. His friend sat on the living room sofa with a bloody handkerchief tied about his arm. "Oh my God, Gary! You said you were all right. What happened?"

A wry grin played with his lips as he spoke. "Seems I got wounded. I didn't even notice it until Deputy Sherman over there told me. She's been good enough to give me first aid."

A gentle hand touched Brent's shoulder, and Joleen spoke in soft, certain tones. "It's not bad, sir. A through-and-through. He's lucky. It looks like it missed the bone and any major blood vessels. We've called an ambulance, but I can fix him up for now. I used to be an EMT." She opened a plastic chest the size of a woman's purse and pulled out latex gloves. She nodded to a pair of scissors in the kit. "Maybe you can cut his shirt off so I can get at the wound?"

"Yeah, sure." Brent's hands shook, but he managed to snip through the fabric below the makeshift bandage. "Jesus, Gary. You could have been killed."

The sheriff, Purcell, and Jason thumped into the room, tracking mud all over Brent's mother's spotless carpet. "How's he doing, Joleen?"

She tore a bandage pack open with her teeth. "I can fix him up for now with this kit. Not much blood, don't see any major tissue damage. He'll need transport to the hospital, though. What's the ETA for the EMTs?"

"Dispatch called them same time as us." He glanced at his watch. "Should be no more than fifteen minutes."

She nodded. "He'll be fine. This won't take long."

The sheriff turned to Purcell. "I want you to investigate the crime scene. The shots came from the barn?"

Gary nodded. "The pasture, actually." He winced. "Careful. That hurt."

The sheriff nodded to Purcell. "Get to it." He leveled his gaze at Brent. "If you don't mind, son, I'd like to take your statement. Maybe we can go someplace else, while Joleen takes care of your friend?"

"Yeah, sure." Brent stumbled toward the kitchen.

Jason tried to follow, but the sheriff stopped him with a hand to his shoulder. "I'd like to talk to Mr. Hyde alone, if that's all right. Why don't you stay with Joleen, in case she needs help?"

Jason nodded, and his eyes narrowed. "You'll give me an interview after you complete your investigation tonight, Sheriff?"

"I'll give you a statement, yes. But we'll need to talk to you too."

"Sure, no problem." Jason pocketed his phone and trailed mud back into the living room.

Brent slumped into a chair at the kitchen table. The lights seemed too bright, and the murmur of conversation from the other room fluttered at the edge of audibility, as if in a dream.

The sheriff pulled a notebook from inside his jacket and sat opposite him. His silver hair shimmered in the fluorescent kitchen light, and his face wrinkled with a sympathetic smile. "Okay, son, can you tell me what happened here tonight?" His gentle but firm voice somehow carried comfort and authority at the same time.

Brent raised weary eyes and stared at the man's kindly face. He reminded Brent of his high school wrestling coach. Despite his age, he still carried himself with the confidence of an athlete, and the furrows that lined his features echoed more smiles than frowns. Brent shook his head. "I don't know where to start."

"The beginning is always a good choice."

"Yeah. Well, I guess that would be when I got home this evening and my parents were missing. But you know about that."

"You're parents are missing? No, I don't think so."

"I called it in. Purcell even stopped by earlier. Took him forever to get here too."

The sheriff scowled and made a note. "So you called in a missing person's report to my office? What time was that?"

"I don't know. Maybe six? Won't your dispatch have a record?"

The sheriff lifted his eyes for a moment and nodded. "Of course. So they were missing. Do you live here?"

"No, I'm a student at Collier. I was just coming home for the weekend."

"And your two friends were with you?"

"My two friends? Oh, you mean Gary and what's-his-name. The reporter. No, they came later."

The sheriff sighed. "Tell you what. Tell me everything that happened, in order, from the time you arrived home."

By the time the ambulance arrived, Brent had finished recounting events. The sheriff closed his notebook and stood. "Son, you can't stay here tonight. Do you have someplace to go? A friend or relative, maybe?"

"Not really. We don't have any relatives, and my friends are all away at college."

Jason stepped in from the other room. "I've got a motel room up in Bellevue. He could stay there, with me."

The sheriff glared at him.

Jason blinked. "Hey, the EMTs chased me out of the living room. I had to go someplace."

That earned him a grunt. The sheriff turned back to Brent. "That works, Mr. Hyde. I just don't want you staying here, alone. I'm sure Mr., uh—" He hesitated and consulted his notes. "—Mr. Dixon will be spending the night in the hospital."

Brent stared at Jason and remembered the touch of his body earlier tonight, behind the steps. His face heated, and he looked away. "I guess I could rent a room at the motel. I do want to be close to Gary."

The sheriff nodded. "Tell you what. We can transport you all to the hospital. Mr. Killeen, I still need your statement. I'll take it once we're there. You may ride with Deputy Purcell, if you wish."

Jason snorted. "I'll drive myself. I can look up the location from my van. I'll meet you there. I still want to interview you too, Sheriff."

He nodded. "I haven't forgotten. After I take your statement and Mr. Dixon's, the two of you can figure out sleeping arrangements."

Brent frowned. "What about my pickup? How will I get back here to get it?"

Jason's answer was a little too eager. "I can bring you back. No problem."

Brent was about to argue, but the sheriff's phone rang. He flipped it open and growled. "Watkins here."

His eyes widened, and his gaze turned to Brent. "Where was that again?" He got out his notebook and scribbled. "What's your number? Uh-huh." He glanced at his watch. "I can be there by midnight. I've got a case here I need to turn over to my deputies. What's the condition of the body?" Silence. "So we'll need dental records or DNA for a positive ID?" He glanced at Brent and walked to the living room, where his side of the conversation was no longer audible.

Purcell stomped into the house and followed Joleen into the kitchen. "I'm tellin' ya, I never seen nothin' like this before. It's like an episode of *Ghost Hunters*."

She rolled her eyes. "You watch that crap?"

"Yeah, what of it?" He eyed Brent. "How many cows you got, boy?"

"Three."

"Yeah, well, they're all dead. Some sicko mutilated the poor bastards. Cut out their mouths, their teats, and cored their asses, like an apple."

Brent's shoulders sagged. "I don't get it. Who would do a thing like that?"

Jason touched his hand. "I'm so sorry. On top of everything else, that must be hard."

Purcell glowered at them and grunted. He pulled a pocketknife from his pants and scraped mud from his boots onto the floor.

Brent stared at the little clods of manure and mud that plunked onto the linoleum, and his face burned with anger. "Will you *stop* that? This is my *home*. Where were you raised? A barn?"

Purcell scowled at him, but before he could answer the sheriff returned, cleared his throat, and sat opposite Brent. "Mr. Hyde, I'm afraid we may have bad news. That call was from Special Agent Rachel Morrison of the FBI. During a drug raid near Green Island tonight, the DEA discovered a body in Bear River. I'm sorry to have to tell you this, but there was an ID found with the corpse, and, well, it was your father's driver's license."

The last vestiges of strength fluttered out Brent's chest. Without thinking, he gripped at Jason's fingers. "What are you saying? My father's dead?"

"Don't jump to conclusions, son. The ID was in a brown suede jacket. Someone might have stolen your father's wallet."

The sheriff's voice seemed to have come from miles away. Brent blinked. "Dad had a brown suede jacket. But he always carried his wallet in his pants pocket."

The sheriff nodded. "Like I said, we won't know for sure until we get a positive ID."

"What about my mother?"

"They only found one body." He hesitated and glanced at Purcell. "I'll get my deputies on her case right away, looking for her. We'll do our best for you."

Brent stood on liquid legs. "I want to see him."

"Son, I don't think that's a good idea. Like I said, we don't know it's your father. All we know right now is that whoever it was had his ID. The current dragged the body for a while, and it might have got caught in a propeller. You wouldn't be able to recognize what's left." He hesitated. "We'll need dental records for a positive ID. Do you know who your father used?"

Brent stared and muttered, "Old Doc Jacoby in Maquoketa." The room floated about him, dreamlike and unreal. He mused, "Green Island is less than twenty miles from here. But you said the body had been in the river for a while? Maybe it's not him. Besides, how would he get there from here? We're a good ten miles from Bear River here."

The sheriff shook his head and clasped a hand over Brent's shoulder. "Those are all good questions, son. We just don't know anything right now. Why don't you go on to the hospital and sit with your friend for a bit? They can give you something to help you sleep. Tomorrow, I'll know more. I'll brief you first thing in the morning, as soon as I know anything. I promise." He glared at Purcell. "Deputies, if you'll join me in the living room for a moment, we'll let Mr. Hyde compose himself before we leave."

Tears welled in Brent's eyes. "I don't get it. Why's all this happening?"

Jason leaned forward and whispered, "I've got some ideas."

Chapter EIGHT

RACHEL sagged into the sofa in the hospital lobby and heaved a sigh. Her phone buzzed, and she blinked gritty fatigue from her eyes as she read the text message. *Why the fuck is that spook Montel sticking his nose in this, anyway?* The message demanded that she wait for his arrival before inspecting the body. *Why should he care about a body found at a drug bust? I thought he was a hotshot working industrial espionage cases.* She pursed her lips. There could be a bright side. Maybe the presence of a honcho from DC would keep that pig Sibley off her back.

She stared at the hospital entrance and longed for sleep. When Sheriff Watkins trudged through the front doors, she rose to greet him. "Good morning, sir. I hope you managed to get more rest than I did."

A weary grin flashed for an instant on the older man's haggard features. "I managed a catnap, thanks. I imagine you've been busy since we met last night too." He shook her hand and then looked around. "Is the medical examiner here yet?"

"They'll page me when he arrives. The Bureau is sending in a specialist, too, and an assistant director from the Chicago office is going to join us this morning."

His eyebrows crawled up his brow. "An assistant director? Is that normal?"

She shrugged. "We found this body during a DEA raid. When you connected it with a possible kidnapping, well, it seemed to pique his interest. He was in Middleton last night, so he should be here soon. He just sent me a text telling me to hold up looking at the body until he gets here."

He snorted. "I guess bosses are the same everywhere, huh?"

"Right." If only. She rubbed her eyes and then pointed to the cafeteria next to the lobby. "I could really use some caffeine. Care to join me?"

"Sure."

After she paid for both of them, she loaded hers up with three sugars and extra cream. She led the way back to the lobby and picked a pair of chairs from which she could watch the entrance. "So, Sheriff, what can you tell me about the late Mr. Hyde?"

"I didn't know him well. Salt of the earth, as near as I can tell. He had a steady job at a software company up in Dubuque, and his wife stayed at home. She went missing yesterday too."

She blew on her coffee before taking a sip. "No sign of her?"

"None. We're checking with neighbors."

"Good. Maybe she'll turn up alive." At least that was still possible, for now. "I thought Hyde was a farmer?"

"They had a small spread, yeah, but it was more of a hobby than a working operation. Just a few animals and some subsistence crops. The land in that part of the county is too hilly for heavy farm equipment, and most of it's gone back to forest."

"So it's isolated, then."

"Right. Their son came back from college, found dinner cooking in the oven and his parents missing. The house was in order: no evidence of a fight or anything. It was like they'd just gotten in a car and driven off."

"Except that both their cars were there." The coffee singed her tongue when she sipped at it, and she winced. "What do you make of the later assault?"

He leaned back and frowned. "Now that's weird. Almost like an episode of one of those crazy TV shows. You know, the ones that find ghosts and flying saucers everywhere. Someone took potshots at the son, Brent, and a couple of his friends. Hit one of 'em too. But then they drove off, like the shots were just to cover their escape. But the strangest thing was what they did to the cattle."

"Mutilations, you said. You ever seen that kind of thing before around here?"

"Never. When the deputies first told me about it, I figured it had to be some kind of wild animal attack, maybe dogs or something."

"But now you don't think so."

"No. Some sick sadist killed those poor beasts, and then cut them up just for the pleasure of it." He scowled. "I've got a local vet checking out the carcasses, and he says he's never seen animals do anything like that."

She nodded. "Except the two-legged variety. They seem to be capable of almost anything."

His expression soured. "I know what you mean. We don't get much of that in these parts." His Adam's apple jiggled as he swallowed coffee. "Whoever did it, I'm sure it wasn't space aliens or ghosts. But I'm not sure the cattle mutilations are connected with the missing parents, or with Mr. Hyde's death."

"You think it's a coincidence that they happened the same day?" Her fingers jittered around her plastic cup of coffee as the caffeine did its work.

"It don't make sense that they'd be connected. If the Hydes were snatched, why would the kidnappers come back? And why on God's green earth would they mutilate the family cows? What else could it be but coincidence?"

She mused, "I don't believe in coincidence, Sheriff, although I admit nothing in this case makes sense." She paused. "Maybe their son had something to do with it. Or his friends. *Something's* going to tie these things together."

"It's more than my department can handle, that's for sure. I'm glad to have your help."

She let a grim smile bend her lips. "We'll figure it out. We always do." An older, gray-haired man entered the lobby, and she stood and waved. "The assistant director's here."

She wondered how Strorm could look so perfect this early in the morning. The creases of his blue suit hung in geometric planes from his rail-thin body, and the part in his steel-gray hair was razor-sharp. His weathered features twisted into what passed for a grin as his gaze turned to her. "Special Agent Morrison. So good to see you."

When they shook, his fingers scraped against her palm like leather-coated splinters. "Assistant Director Strorm, this is Sheriff Watkins. He's been most helpful."

"Call me Montel, Sheriff," he purred while scanning the man's face. "We've got ourselves quite a mystery, here."

A chime sounded, and the soft voice of a hospital operator replaced the drone of the Muzak that filled the lobby. "Rachel Morrison, please pick up a white paging telephone. Ms. Morrison, please pick up a white telephone."

She nodded. "That'll be the ME. Just a second."

She found one of the phones back near the coffee shop. When she picked up the handset, it rang twice before a female voice answered. "How may I assist you?"

"This is Special Agent Rachel Morrison. You paged me."

A moment later, the woman replied, "Yes, Ms. Morrison. Dr. Gilliland asked that you join him in the morgue. Do you need directions?"

"I'm sure that won't be necessary, thank you." She hung up and returned to where Montel and Watkins stood talking about football standings. She avoided rolling her eyes, while wondering how men could be so vapid. "Sheriff, I'm sure you know where the morgue is located. I wonder if you'd be so good as to lead the way? Dr. Gilliland is ready for us."

She followed the sheriff and Montel down a corridor, past Radiology and to a set of stairs that led to the basement. Hospital smells of Pine-Sol and antiseptic seemed to have settled in the gloomy subterranean corridors. The soles of their shoes clattered against the polished tiles of the floor. Watkins stopped and pressed a red button next to a door marked "Morgue, Do Not Enter."

The speaker under the button emitted a thready voice. "Yes?"

"It's Sheriff Watkins and the FBI, Frank." The door buzzed, and he held it open for them.

The hospital odors disappeared inside the morgue. Rachel shivered at the chill air. It carried a stale, cold scent, like the inside of a freezer that hadn't been cleaned in years. A double row of square steel doors, with latches like those on an old-style refrigerator, lined one wall. The naked body of a middle-aged man lay exposed on an examining table. Someone had attached a white tag to his left big toe. A balding man clutching a clipboard nodded when they entered. His lab coat looked like it was made from a wrinkled mattress cover, and it didn't conceal his stained chinos or wrinkled Oxford-cloth shirt.

The sheriff's voice bounced off the hard surfaces of the room. "Dr. Gilliland. This is Assistant Director Montel Strorm and Special Agent Rachel Morrison of the FBI. They're here to assist us in our investigation."

Gilliland's head bobbed like a ping-pong ball. "Nice to meet you." He nodded to a cluttered office that adjoined the morgue. "There are gowns, masks, and gloves in there if you need them."

Rachel circled the table. "I'll pass, thank you. Is this Mr. Hyde?"

Gilliland's head bobbled again. "I won't have positive ID until I get the dental records, but that's the body you found last night. I've held off my autopsy as you requested, Sheriff."

She leaned down and examined the corpse's left hand. Three of the fingers were reduced to stubs, with splintered bones protruding from pinkish tissue. Similar wounds marred the other hand and the man's face. "The points are abraded. The current in the river must have dragged him for a while. These look postmortem."

The doctor nodded. "Agreed. There's certainly no gross evidence of healing. We'll have to confirm with tissue samples, of course."

She continued her circle around the table, peering at the wrinkled skin. "Any guess how long he was in the water?"

Gilliland shrugged. "It depends on where he entered the river and how fast the current was. If it was fast enough, and the bottom was rocky, it wouldn't take too long for those kinds of wounds to form."

Her survey turned to the man's face, or what was left of it. "He's got foam in his mouth. He could have died from drowning."

Gilliland looked smug. "I don't think so." He pointed at the man's forehead. "Look here. That's an entrance wound for a bullet. It's easy to miss, what with the third degree abrasions from being dragged on the river bottom. But it's there."

Her eyes narrowed as she inspected where he was pointing. "Looks like a nine millimeter entrance wound." She lifted her gaze to the doctor's face. "Any exit wound?"

"I didn't see any, but I've not done the autopsy yet."

The sheriff spoke from over her shoulder. "Maybe it wasn't fatal. Foam in the mouth indicates he drowned, right?"

"Maybe," she muttered, "but it's not conclusive. Head wounds can cause that too. No exit wound suggests it might have been a hollow point."

Strorm touched her shoulder, and she almost cringed. "So it could have fragmented on impact. Good work, Agent Morrison. I think we can take as our working hypothesis that this is a murder. It could even be a professional hit." He turned to the physician. "Dr. Gilliland, thank you for your help. A specialist from the Bureau's forensic lab in Virginia will be here before noon to assist you with the autopsy and tissue samples."

Gilliland nodded. "Good. The avulsion injuries have masked any gross evidence, like gunshot residue. It'll take electron microscopy of the collagen fibers to find traces of GSR. I'm glad we'll have access to a full service forensics lab for this one."

That got him a tight smile from Montel. "We're here to help." He squeezed Rachel's shoulder. "Agent Morrison, I wonder if I might have a word with you? In private."

Gilliland grunted. "We done here?"

"Yes, we're done for now, at least until the special agent from Quantico gets here. I wonder, could we use your office for a moment, Doctor?"

"Sure." He shoved the body back toward the wall of square metal doors. "Sheriff, you want to join me for breakfast in the cafeteria?" He tugged open one of the slots, and the metal rack holding the remains clanked inside.

"I guess I could use more coffee." The sheriff turned toward Montel and Rachel. "Perhaps you'll join us? We should discuss procedures."

"Certainly, Sheriff. I agree. We'll be along in a moment, as soon as Agent Morrison and I consult."

Montel pressed Rachel toward Gilliland's office and closed the door. He sat in the chair behind the desk. Papers and charts were piled in the only other chair in the office. Rachel stood and waited.

He tented his fingers and stared at her. "Agent Morrison, there are aspects of this case that trouble me. I think there is more to it than a murder or kidnapping. Much more."

"Yes, sir. What makes you think that, sir?"

His features relaxed. "Just a feeling." The chair squeaked when he leaned forward. "I'm reassigning you full time to this case. Until further notice, you report directly to me. I want you to find out what happened here. Understand?"

"Yes, sir." She hesitated. "This is a little unusual, sir." What was he doing, anyway, bypassing the command structure to task her directly?

"This case is unusual. Trust me. There are considerations that I can't share with you. At least not yet."

She kept her face impassive and her tone respectful. "Sir, if you know something that will help the investigation, shouldn't you tell me?"

His tone sharpened. "For now, all we know is that we found this body on federal land. That's enough for the Bureau to take jurisdiction. I want regular reports from you. Daily. If you find this is any more than a routine murder, then I'll decide what you need to know. Is that clear?"

"Yes, sir. Perfectly." She didn't think it was clear at all.

He leaned back and mused, "Based on your preliminary report, I think you'd do well to focus your efforts on the younger Hyde and his friends. That reporter's part in all this is especially suspicious, if you ask me." He stared at her for a beat, as if measuring her for one of the cold storage cells next door. "All right, then. It's in your hands." He pushed back from the desk. "Now let's go make nice with our bucolic colleagues."

She followed him back to the lobby while wondering what she'd gotten into.

Chapter NINE

BRENT sat on the edge of Gary's hospital bed and tried to focus. A dull ache had taken up residence in his brain, somewhere just behind his eyes. He blinked when he realized that Gary had spoken. "I'm sorry. What did you say? Whatever the doctor gave me last night to sleep has turned the world to fuzz."

Gary frowned, and his voice grated with impatience. "I said, I wonder where the damned nurse is at. I'd like to blow this place." The late morning sun streamed through the windows of the room, and his brown eyes gleamed and turned to liquid gold as he raised the bed to a sitting position.

"I'm sure he'll be here soon." He stroked the sling on Gary's arm.

Gary flinched away. "Ouch! Dammit, be careful." His features relaxed after a moment. "Sorry, I didn't mean to snap at you. I hate fucking hospitals."

"I'm sorry. You've been through a lot. Does it hurt much?"

"You know, at first I didn't feel a thing. Then, when the cop showed me I'd been shot, it hurt like hell." His teeth flashed in a merry grin. "But then we got to the emergency room, and the docs there gave me some dreamy drugs. You should try it."

"Don't joke. You could have been killed." Brent hated the girlish whine in his voice.

"I don't think so. It should have been a turkey shoot for anyone who knew their way around guns. It's less than thirty yards from the pasture to the house. I don't think they meant to kill us at all. I think they were warning shots. Barney Fife couldn't have missed us."

Despite all that had happened, a grin tugged at Brent's lips at the mention of his parents' favorite TV rerun. "Yeah, but Andy didn't let him have any bullets." Worry and fatigue dragged at his features again.

"I'm just glad you're all right." He ran a finger down his buddy's cheek. "You need a shave."

"I don't know. I kind of like the scruffy look."

"Well, truth be told, it is kind of sexy. All the guys back at school will chase after you." He glanced out the door where a nurse bustled by. "How soon before they'll let you go?"

"Well, the doctor said any time, but then the nurse told me he's got some insurance forms for me to fill out. Stick around. The nurse is really cute."

"I can hardly wait." He turned at the sound of knuckles rapping against the door.

"Hey, guys. May I come in?" Jason was even more disheveled than earlier this morning, when he'd dropped Brent off at the hospital.

Gary scowled and pulled his hand away. "What are *you* doing here, creep?"

Brent hopped off the bed and waved Jason into the room. "Gary, please. He drove all the way to the farm to warn me about being in danger when he knew it wasn't safe. Be nice to him, okay?"

"He's a snoop. All he wants is to use you for a story." His fist kneaded the sheets, and he sat up on the edge of the bed.

"Of course he wants a story. That's his job. But he's got information that can help figure out what happened too. Give him a chance. I think you'll like him."

Jason's gaze shifted from one to the other. "Hey, I don't want to make problems between the two of you. I'm just trying to help." He turned to Brent. "I went back to our motel room after I dropped you off and got our stuff. Your knapsack is down in the van."

Gary's face flushed crimson, and his eyes flared. "Did you say *our* motel room?"

A tinge of dismay chilled Brent's stomach. "The sheriff suggested I stay in a motel last night."

Gary started to speak, but a nurse with curly red hair and a sunny smile burst into the room. He clutched a clipboard in one hand and wore bright pink scrubs. "Mr. Dixon. How's my miracle patient this morning?" He stopped to check the chart hanging at the foot of the bed. "I've never seen a patient respond so quickly to treatment."

Gary's jaws jumped, and he glared at Jason before turning his attention to the nurse. "So, when can I get out of here?"

The man *tsked*. "Now, now, don't be impatient. Most patients would have had to stay at least one more day with a wound like yours. Your recuperative powers are really remarkable." He seemed to notice the two visitors and beamed at Jason. "I'm Rick, Gary's day nurse. You must be his friend, Brent? He was right. You *are* cute." His enthusiasm foamed into the room like an effervescing bottle of soda.

"Uh, he's Brent." Jason blushed and pointed.

"Oh." Rick's blue eyes scanned Brent from sneakers to blond crew cut, and his face fell. "Well, muscle boys can be cute too." It didn't sound like "muscle boys" were his type. He plopped on the bed next to Gary and gushed, "Now, let's run through these insurance forms. It'll take about fifteen minutes. After that, you can sign the release and be on your way."

Brent's phone buzzed, and he stepped out into the hall. "Hello."

He recognized the sheriff's weary voice. "Hello, Brent. This is Sheriff Watkins. I've got some good news for you. Your father's dental records don't match the X-rays the coroner took of the deceased."

His knees turned to rubber as relief flooded through him. He braced himself against the wall and closed his eyes, while he murmured, "Thank God. There's still hope, then." He heaved a deep, cleansing breath, but then realized the sheriff's voice was still coming from his phone. "What was that, Sheriff? I kind of zoned out for a moment, there."

"You got every right, son. I said, I'd like to speak to you, if I may. Where are you at?"

"I'm at the hospital. Gary's being discharged."

"Excellent. I'm downstairs in the cafeteria right now. Perhaps you could join me?"

"Sure. Give me five." When he turned back toward the room, he bumped into Jason. "Hey, I'm sorry about Gary giving you a hard time. He's really a nice guy."

"S'all right. I might be testy too, if I'd been shot." He looked at the phone that Brent still gripped in his hand. "Was that the sheriff?"

"Yeah. The body wasn't my dad!"

"Hey, that's great news. So, do they have any leads on what did happen to your parents?"

"I dunno. He wants to see me in the cafeteria. I'll let you know what he says."

Jason squeezed his hand. "Do you want someone to go with you? For support?"

He heaved a sigh. "No. I'll be fine." Rick's laughter brayed through the open door. "I'm not up to facing that ditzy nurse, though. Would you tell Gary I'll come back up when I'm done with the sheriff?"

"Sure. I'm still planning to drive the two of you to the farm, too, to get your vehicles."

"Thanks. I really appreciate it. You've been great." Brent took a shuddering breath, trotted to the elevator, and headed downstairs.

Only a few scattered customers sat in the cafeteria at midmorning. Brent spotted the sheriff sitting in the back with a petite, dark-haired woman. Her hair was clipped in a short, no-nonsense bob, and the little smile lines at the corners of her mouth folded downward this morning. When he got to their table, they both stood.

"Gary, this is Special Agent Rachel Morrison. She's going to be helping local law enforcement with the investigation."

She shook his hand with a strong, solid grip that inspired confidence. Her solid body and lean features made him think of a champion gymnast or a martial arts expert. He'd seen this type before, in the weight room at school. She must have spent hours in training. "Special agent. Like in the FBI?"

"Yes, sir. We're taking jurisdiction over all aspects of this investigation." Her face softened. "I know you must be worried about your parents. We've got them listed in the FBI missing persons' database. We'll find them, one way or another."

One way or another. That brought it all home, as if she'd slapped him with what had happened, with what might still happen. He gripped the table while the room spun about him.

The sheriff's hand on his shoulder steadied him. "You all right, son? Have a seat." He pulled out a chair.

"Yeah. Just give me a minute." He took a deep breath and collapsed into the seat.

Concern pooled in the special agent's eyes. "Put your head down, between your knees, and take deep breaths."

He complied. Breathe in and out. Just like Dad used to tell him before a big wrestling match. His breath shuddered in his chest, and he hated himself for being weak.

Her fingers caressed his hair. "It's all right. Let it out."

He swallowed, sat up, and wiped his eyes. "I'm sorry. I'm not usually like this." His voice quivered, and he swallowed.

The corners of her eyes crinkled in concern. "You have every right. Would you like some ice water?"

He squeezed his eyes closed. Two more deep breaths. "No, I'll be all right. Really." He looked at the sheriff. "You have positive ID then, on the body?"

"All we know for sure is that he's not your father. We're checking missing person reports right now. But the medical examiner was certain it's not Charles Hyde."

"So why did he have Dad's ID on him? I don't get it."

The sheriff shrugged. "No telling, son. But that makes us think he might be connected in some way to your parents' disappearance. It's a clue."

"A clue. I guess that's a good thing." Brent lowered his gaze and nodded. He couldn't look at them. It took all his concentration just to remember to breathe. In and out. He bit his lip. "Do you have any other leads?" he whispered.

The FBI agent shook her head. "Not yet, sir." Her voice was firm, comforting. "When we ID this body, we'll know more."

Brent tried to remember her name. Rachel something. She had kept her voice calm and distant, professional. He held onto that. "But there's still hope."

"Yes, sir." She gripped his hand. "I promise you that the full resources of the Bureau are on this case. If anyone can figure out what happened, we can."

He heaved another sigh. "So what's next?"

She patted his hand and then straightened in her chair. "We have a team processing your parents' farm right now."

"My parents' farm? There's nothing there."

She shook her head. "They'll find things you and I would miss. Fibers, tire tracks, footprints, shell casings from last night. We'll have to go through your parents' papers, computers, and financial statements too. Trust me, we will be most thorough."

He sighed. "My truck's at the farm. Gary's car is there too. We'll need to get those."

"We have to make casts of their tread marks, first. The team at the farm will do that. But I don't want you going back to the farm right now. It'll take us at least a day, probably more, to finish up, and then it'll be secured as a crime scene. Sheriff, is there an impound lot where they can pick up their vehicles?'

"I'll have a deputy deliver them." He paused. "It rained pretty hard last night. I'm not sure tire tracks will do you any good."

"You never know, Sheriff. Better safe than sorry. This way, we'll have a comparator set, for elimination."

He nodded. "In that case, you'll need to do the same thing on three of my patrol cars and the EMTs' ambulance. There's that reporter's van too."

"Mr. Killeen. I already made a note to contact him."

Brent's head swayed from one to the other. Things were happening too fast. "You mean Jason? He's upstairs. His van is out in the parking lot. He'd offered to take us to the farm to get our cars."

She shook her head. "No. No one goes to the farm, at least until we're done processing." A frown creased her pretty features. "Perhaps he can drive you someplace nearby?"

"There's Ruby's. It's about fifteen minutes due east, on the county road."

"That'll do. I can have a couple of agents drive your vehicles there, and they can make casts of Mr. Killeen's tire tracks at the same time. Sheriff, perhaps you can collect their keys and have one of your deputies deliver them to our agents at the crime scene?"

"No problem, ma'am."

She turned back to Brent. "I know this is difficult for you. Is there someplace you can stay? Maybe with relatives or friends?"

"No relatives. I was homeschooled until I was sixteen, so I don't really have many close friends around here, and all of those are away at school." He thought for a moment. "I can't go home?"

"If you mean your parents' farm, no. I'm afraid that's going to be secured as a crime scene for quite a while."

"Then I want to go back to my place in Middleton. It's only an hour away."

The sheriff nodded. "I agree, Special Agent Morrison. The sheriff over there's a good woman. I thought Brent should probably go back to school, where he's got a support structure, so I called her this morning. She's happy to cooperate in any way you need." He frowned. "Strangest thing. She's working her own missing person's case."

The agent quirked an eyebrow at him. "Really? Any chance it's connected to our DB?"

"First thing I asked. Hers is way too young to be our guy. She says it's just some wild kid joyriding last night who didn't come home. He's probably sleeping it off someplace."

"Hmph. Can you keep me briefed, Sheriff? You never know what turns out to be important." She shook her head. "You just never know."

Chapter
TEN

JASON stirred his coffee and tried to ignore the macabre array of taxidermy in Ruby's back room museum. The diorama in front of him, with cute little stuffed chipmunks and squirrels frolicking together, wasn't so bad. That is, until you noticed the fox that leered at them from behind dusty foam-rubber shrubs. The fire-hose-size rattlesnake in the display behind him was even creepier. He'd almost tossed his breakfast, though, at the sight of the bizarre two-headed calf that dominated the center of the room.

He glanced at the little dining alcove in the front room where Brent sat speaking in low tones to Gary. Jason wondered, not for the first time, what Brent saw in the guy. Brent was so nice, and handsome too. If he didn't already have a boyfriend… but then, a hunky guy like Brent would never go for a geek like Jason.

Gary rolled his eyes and held up his injured arm, now in a sling. "That's all you can think about when I've been shot?"

Jason frowned and edged closer. This guy was a real piece of work.

Brent's shoulders slumped, and he reached across the table, but Gary scowled and pulled back. Brent held his face in his hands, while Gary scanned the room like a snake looking for a mouse. He caught Jason staring at them, and his eyes narrowed. He leaned forward and stroked Brent's hand, but his eyes, cold as ice, never left Jason. For the barest instant, a Cheshire grin flashed across his lips, and he winked. Then he focused his attention to Brent, and concern seemed to flood his features.

Jason flushed and turned back to the displays in the museum. *Not my business.* He pretended to read the cards propped in front of a clutter of pottery shards and broken arrowheads and thought about the Gerion Group and conspiracies.

The floor creaked, and Brent's soft voice broke his reverie. "I'm afraid this isn't much of a museum."

Jason gave a little start and slopped some coffee on his hand. "Well, it's interesting, I guess." He tilted an eyebrow toward the stuffed owl that hovered over his head. "It's sort of taxidermy hell. I keep expecting Norman Bates to show up."

A smile tried to flicker across Brent's features and then faded. "I used to feel like that when I was a kid coming here. Ruby's husband was way into this stuff." He rubbed fingers across red-rimmed eyes. "She lost him about five years ago."

Jason wanted to touch him, to comfort him. "I wish I could do something, man. I feel so bad about all this."

Brent heaved a shuddering breath. "Thanks. I don't know what I'm going to do. It's like I'm all alone, now."

"Well, you've got Gary, right?" *Like that putz would be any help.*

"Yeah. I don't know what I'd do without him, even though sometimes he can be a little...." His voice trailed off.

"Self-centered?" Jason prompted, and then regretted it. "Sorry, I shouldn't have said that."

"No, it's all right. He's a good guy, really. He's just a bit obsessive and goal oriented. Kind of like me." That forlorn smile tried to emerge again. "He's in training for a job in industrial security, and getting shot like this throws off his schedule." Brent glanced out the front display window. "He's outside right now, watching the CSI techs take casts of the tires of your car. Said he wanted to watch real-world investigators."

"Never a missed opportunity, I guess." Jason sipped at cold coffee. "What's next?"

Brent stared at the stuffed chipmunks. "I dunno. I can't go back to the farm. Even the animals are gone. The sheriff said the vet came and got them for a necropsy."

"A what?"

"Necropsy. It's like an animal autopsy. At least I won't have to take care of the poor things' carcasses. The sheriff took care of all that for me."

"Sheriff Watkins seems like a good guy. The FBI agent seemed professional too. Let me know if there's anything I can do, okay? You've got enough on your plate."

"Thanks, but right now it's all with the FBI." Brent squeezed his eyes shut and took a shuddering breath. "I appreciate the offer, though."

"You got family you can turn to?"

He shook his head. "No. It was always just us." A lone tear seeped from his left eye. "I want to get back at school. Maybe work and studying will help me think about something else."

Jason's heart ached. "They're going to find them. I'm sure of it."

"You think they're all right?" His voice shook and then turned sharp. "Why would anyone *do* this?"

"I don't know, man. But I'm going to do my best to find out."

Brent gave him a hollow stare. "I feel so helpless."

"Look, I know this isn't the time, but when you're up to it I want to talk to you. I think this might all be connected somehow to the story I was working on."

"Really? I don't see how. I'm sure my mother never worked at the Grange. And whatever you've got, that was all twenty years ago, right?"

"Maybe." Jason frowned. "Look, you're tired. You need to get back to Middleton and get some rest. How about I call you tonight, maybe take you to dinner? Then I'll tell you what I know."

Brent shrugged. "You're right. I just want to get home, crawl into bed, and pull the sheets over my head. Maybe tonight. You've got my number." He stared at the two-headed calf. "Right now, I don't want to think about anything."

Jason nodded. "Yeah." He followed Brent's stare. "You want to go back out front to sit? This two-headed calf freaks me out."

Brent's eyebrows crawled up his forehead. "It's not really a two-headed calf. It's got just one head, with two faces. It's called cranial-facial duplication, or diprosopus. That was the topic of my science fair project in high school."

"Don't know much about science, here."

"But it's connected to what we do at the lab." Brent's voice showed some enthusiasm, like a child with a new toy.

Jason decided the distraction might be good for him. "So, isn't a two-headed calf from, like, Siamese twins or something? I thought the lab did genetics?"

"Incomplete conjoined twins might result in two heads, but this is from the calf being overdosed with a certain protein in utero. It's called SHH, for sonic hedgehog homolog."

"You're kidding? The calf has hedgehog genes?"

"No, that's just the name for the protein. The name's kind of a joke. Anyway, it's like a teratogenic agent. It changes the way an existing gene is expressed without affecting the underlying DNA. Too much, you get two faces. Two little, you get narrow or even suppressed facial features. Just right, and you get normal facial development. I raised chicken embryos with two beaks for my science fair project." For reasons Jason couldn't fathom, pride glowed in his features.

"I get it. Too much, too little, and just right. It's like the Goldilocks protein for faces?"

"Sort of. The Grange has been studying this kind of thing for ages. The original goal was to learn more about birth defects, but now they've expanded to cancer therapy, and even gene therapy. The idea is that proteins and other biochemical agents change the way a gene is expressed. That's what epigenetics is about: studying heritable changes in gene expression caused by mechanisms other than changes in the underlying DNA."

"Heritable? You mean they could genetically engineer people?"

"Well, no. Here, heritable means generations of cells within the organism exposed to the teratogenic agent, not transgenerationally. Although there's some secondary evidence for that too."

Jason waved a hand over his head. "Whish. You lost me."

"It's easy." Brent's eyes flashed with enthusiasm. "DNA tells a cell what kinds of proteins to make, but not when or how much. That's usually controlled by other mechanisms. If you understand those, you can change the organism, sometimes in significant ways."

Jason looked at the calf. "Like making it a two-faced monster."

"Right. But the changes can be positive. For example, at the Grange, we've found a strain of *Mycobacterium vaccae* that makes rats run mazes faster. It's the same principle."

Jason shook his head. "Myc-oh-what? You lost me again."

"It's a common bacterium, first cultured from cow dung. Never mind. Dr. Athair said the rat data was an anomaly, anyway."

Jason frowned. "None of this could have military applications, could it?"

Brent snorted. "You're kidding, right? You mean like germ warfare or something? That's so far from what we're doing that it's laughable. This research is all about making people better."

"I don't know what I mean. But I've got a pretty good idea that the military has been funding the Grange ever since it started."

Brent's face fell. "You mean, back when you think my mother worked there. That doesn't make any sense. Besides, all of our funding comes from the Gerion Group and NIH."

Jason wanted to kick himself for reminding Brent of his worries. Before he could speak, though, a rough voice interrupted them. "There you are. You been hidin' out from me or what?"

Brent turned pale and rubbed the side of his face. "Deputy Purcell. What can I do for you?"

The deputy peered at them from piggish eyes. "The FBI is watchin' you, boy. You best be careful." His glance flicked toward Jason. "That goes double for *you*, boy."

Jason's upper lip curled as he pulled out his iPhone and held it up before Purcell. "Would you care to make a statement for the record? What role are you playing in this investigation, Deputy?"

Purcell scowled and shoved the phone aside. "You shut that blasted thing off, hear me? Unless you want me to run you in."

"And what would be the charges, Deputy? Failure to grovel?" He held the phone up again.

Purcell tapped the riot baton that hung from his belt. "I *said*, shut that damned thing off. I wouldn't want you to slip and fall. You might hurt yourself."

Brent touched his arm. "It's all right. Let's see what he wants so we can get out of here."

Jason glared at the fat deputy but swallowed his anger. "Whatever." He stuffed his phone back in his shirt pocket.

Purcell smirked. "That's a good boy. I knew you was smart." He turned back to Brent. "I heard you was leavin' the area."

"That's right. Sheriff Watkins knows. He suggested it, in fact."

"Yeah. Well, the FBI don't like it. Not one bit."

"Agent Morrison knows too, Deputy."

He guffawed and repeated in a singsong voice. "Agent Morrison knows too." He stepped forward until his gut pushed against Brent. "She ain't the only FBI agent around here. Her boss talked to me, and he don't trust her or the sheriff. I'm deputized special, just to keep an eye on you. So see to it you don't go no place without what you tell me first."

Brent's face turned ashen. "Well, now you know where I'm going, Deputy. I guess I should be extra safe now, with you watching me. Is there anything else?"

"Just you be careful, boy. I'll be all over you like a fly on shit."

Gary's voice rang out from the entry to the museum. "What's going on here?" He cracked the knuckles on his good hand.

"Nothin' you need to worry about, boy. The FBI ain't interested in you." Purcell swaggered away, but turned back at the doorway. "Just you remember what I told ya."

Gary's eyes threw daggers at the deputy as he left. When he turned back to face Brent and Jason, his face was hard and cold. "They've finished with the cars. We can go now."

Brent heaved a heavy sigh. "Good."

Jason took in his weary features and the tremor in his fingers. "Are you up to driving? You could stretch out in the back of my van, and I could drive you."

Gary strode forward and slipped an arm about Brent's shoulder. "He'll be fine. I'll follow him back to Middleton." He led Brent from the room, and Ruby's plate glass exit door slammed shut.

Jason walked to the front and stared after them as their vehicles pulled away in a cloud of dust, followed by Purcell's patrol car.

Ruby watched from behind the counter and muttered. "I'm worried about that poor boy."

"He's been through a lot."

"That he has, lad. But I was thinking of what that buddy of his is up to. That one's the devil, that's what he is." She shook her head and then exploded in a spasm of hacking and coughing.

He frowned. "Well, I don't like him much either. You all right?"

"Yeah. Damn cigarettes." She pulled one out and lit it. Smoke oozed from her lips, her head tipped back, and her eyes closed. "Ahhh." She tapped the ash into the can by the register, glanced at Jason, and offered him the pack.

"Uh, no, thanks. I quit." He hesitated. "Do you know something about Gary I don't?"

Her eyes narrowed to slits, and her mouth pinched into a little oh-shape that dribbled smoke like a discouraged chimney. "When you've lived as long as I have, you can't help but know stuff. Stuff you sometimes wish you could forget. Memory's the curse of old age." Another spasm of coughing interrupted her. When it passed, she took a deep drag on her cigarette. "Yes, sir, it's starting at last, after all these years, just like I knew it would." Smoke leaked from her nostrils and hovered about her face.

Jason turned to confront her. "What's starting?"

A laugh churned deep in her chest and then morphed to a wheezing, phlegm-filled cough. She tossed her cigarette into the tin can and watched with watery eyes while a trail of acrid smoke rose and curled about her features. "You'll see. The Lord says, *the beast that ascendeth out of the bottomless pit shall make war against them, and shall overcome them, and kill them.*" She hacked and spat into her can. "You'll see."

Chapter ELEVEN

WHEN the wizened man with the penetrating gray eyes entered the soup kitchen, Kimball dropped his ladle. He stooped to recover the utensil from where it clattered on the floor.

The woman standing next to him stopped serving green beans, put a hand on his shoulder, and cooed, "Don't worry, dear. I'll run back to the kitchen and get you a clean one." She turned a cherubic smile on the weary face of the homeless woman waiting for her portion of stew. "Just you wait right there, hon, and we'll take care of you. I'll be right back." She tucked a stray strand of gray hair back into her bun and toddled away.

The haggard woman's shoulders slumped, and she murmured, "God bless, Miss Amanda."

Kimball tried to steady his hands and took a cleansing breath. The scents of vegetable stew, strong coffee, and unwashed bodies filled his nostrils, and he wrinkled his nose. A cheesy recording of a choir singing "Down in My Heart" hung over the murmured conversations of the homeless diners and the clatter of pots and pans from the kitchen. Weary faces waiting in the now halted serving line peered over shoulders to find the source of the delay. The homeless woman scowled at him, so he tried giving her a tentative smile. "I'm sorry. I guess I'm just a klutz."

She narrowed her eyes and glared at his nervous fingers. "You usin', bud? Miss Amanda won't like it if you're usin'."

Kimball glanced at the end of the line, where the man with the wolf-eyes picked up a tray and clutched a black overcoat about his lean body. No question it was him. Kimball stooped to scratch at his ankle, reassured by the weight of the gun holstered there.

He flinched when the homeless woman gripped his hand. Grease and grime fouled her cracked fingernails. "Your hands is shakin'." She scowled. "What you on? Your eyes don't look like you're usin' meth or coke."

He jerked his hands back. "I'm not on anything. I'm just clumsy." He resisted the urge to slap her and kept his voice calm and caring.

Amanda returned and handed him a fresh ladle. "Here you go, Kimball, dear." She scooped a huge helping of green beans onto the homeless woman's plate. "Praise the Lord for the goodness He provides."

The homeless woman continued to peer at Kimball, but then lost interest when he scooped the thick stew into her bowl. "Praise *you,* Miss Amanda. The Lord ain't got nothin' to do with it." She stumbled on, and another battered soul replaced her in the line.

Amanda continued to serve green beans and potatoes, with a merry smile and a word of thanksgiving for each new patron. But when she stole a glance at Kimball, concern pooled in her eyes. "Are you all right, dear? You seem nervous."

"I'm fine." He nodded at the bedraggled people trudging through the line. "There but for the grace of God."

"Ain't that the truth, brother?" She stopped long enough to grip his arm. "We're all so grateful for your good works, Mr. Verloc. The Lord will reward those who help the helpless."

"I do what little I can." His soul soaked up her praise like a desert absorbs a drizzle of rain. His heart warmed, and life was worthwhile, at least at this moment.

Amanda beamed at him. "You do more than just a little." Another huge scoop of vegetables plopped onto a tray. "Your generosity last month paid for almost two thirds of our budget. Hundreds of people remember you in their prayers every night, praise Jesus."

Her words brought a smile to Kimball's lips, but then his breath caught in his throat.

Montel had advanced in the line and now stood before the two servers, a sly grin playing across his features. He held out his tray, and Amanda slopped beans onto his plate. His Cheshire smile broadened to reveal his teeth, and Kimball's heart chilled. When he spoke, his voice grated with the echo of hundreds of cigarettes. "Bless you, good lady."

"God bless you too, sir." Her words sang with the peace that passed all understanding, or at least passed Kimball's understanding.

He scraped the kettle. "The stew's almost all gone. If you'll wait, I'll get a new pot from the kitchen, friend."

Montel put his tray down. "I'll help."

Amanda put her hands on her ample hips and beamed at them. "You uplift yourself when you help others, friend. Thank you."

Kimball grabbed the kettle with two hot pads and headed to the kitchen. Inside, volunteers sweated over the ovens and ranges, preparing the hearty meals that the shelter provided. He dropped the empty pot off with the dishwasher, but before he could step to the stove to retrieve a new batch of stew, Montel's boney fingers dug into his bicep.

A predatory smile twisted the man's narrow features, and his eyes stayed cold and hard. "I've got another job for you. We need to talk. Now."

Kimball scowled and whispered, "I'm working. We'll have to do it later." He tried to pull away, but Montel's grip was too strong.

"I said now. Tell them you need to leave. Make something up." Command gleamed from his eyes.

Kimball contemplated his options for a few seconds and then shouted, "Hey, Larry. Can you fill in for me? I'm feeling kind of under the weather."

The man washing the dishes picked up a towel and wiped his hands. "Sure thing, Kim. No problem." He peered into Kimball's eyes. "You look a bit pale, brother. Everything all right?"

"Yeah, I'll be fine. I just need to sit for a while. Oh, we're out of stew on the line. You'll need to take a new kettle out."

"You got it." The man paused. "You need a lift someplace?" He frowned at Montel's fist, which still gripped Kimball's arm.

Montel turned to face him. He smiled with his lips, but his eyes glinted. Larry paled and took a step back, but Montel said, "That would be so kind of you, Larry, is it? But I can give him a lift in my car." He reached for his wallet. "Perhaps I can make a little donation to dear Amanda's shelter."

Larry's eyes roved over Montel's ragged clothes, and he snorted. "Yeah, you do that, brother." He glanced at Kimball. "You sure you're okay?"

Kimball sighed. "I'm fine. Look, I really appreciate you filling in for me. I'll owe you big time. Give my regrets to Sister Amanda, if you would. Tell her I was looking forward to the prayer service."

"Yeah, sure. God bless." He glanced at Montel. "You, too. Nice meetin' ya. Any friend of Kimball's is a friend of mine." He grabbed a fresh pot of stew and headed to the serving line.

Montel tugged at Kimball's arm and headed toward the back exit. "My car is parked in the alley."

The stale smells of piss and garbage filled the alley behind the State Street Holiness Project. The Red Line subway rumbled underneath their feet, and the skyline of the Loop towered into the night just a few blocks to the north. Kimball caught sight of Trump Tower and longed to return to his luxury condo. Montel pushed him toward a black Mercedes, where an impassive, muscular man stood waiting. Kimball noted the telltale bulge of a shoulder holster underneath the man's cheap suit coat. At a nod from Montel, the thug opened the rear door of the sedan and motioned for Kimball to enter.

Kimball glared at Montel and controlled homicidal impulses. He slid onto the plush leather, and the door slammed. Montel entered the rear from the other side, while the muscle slid into the driver's seat and started the engine. The car purred into the traffic, and Montel stretched and yawned.

Instead of speaking, Montel opened the little bar built into the front seat and poured two bourbons, on the rocks. He handed one to Kimball and then turned to stare out the window. Kimball tossed his off and waited while silence grew between them. He stared at Montel, clenched and unclenched his fists while a vein throbbed in his temple. His breath grew ragged, but still no one spoke. The flowery aroma of the agent's cheap cologne mixed with the scent of the leather seats. Kimball wanted to kill someone, anyone.

The car stopped at a red light, and Montel turned an indifferent eye in his direction. "Control yourself, Mr. Verloc. I'd hate for you to have a stroke. It would be a nuisance for Jeffrey to have to dispose of your body."

"What the *fuck* are you doing, Montel? Business is business, but you ain't got no call to be fuckin' with my life."

"Oh?" He tilted an eyebrow, and a cold smile played across his features. "You mean those sweet people at your little mission? Does it make you feel good, *saved*, maybe, to work there? Holy?"

"What I do when I'm off the clock is none of your fuckin' business."

"Yes, of course. None of my business." He looked out the window again. "We've got another job for you. One that requires finesse. Do you think you have finesse, Mr. Verloc?"

"I'm a professional." *Not like you, you fuckin' asshole.* He took a cleansing breath. "I'll do whatever the job requires. You know that."

"Whatever the job requires." He nodded. "You *have* been reliable, I'll give you that." He pushed a manila envelope across the seat. "Open it."

Inside, Kimball found several sheets of paper and some photographs. The one on top was of two young men standing in what looked like a convenience store. One was skinny, with a ruff of shaggy brown hair, and the other was lithe, blond, and muscular. "These guys my targets?"

"In a way. We need you to keep track of their location. For now, we've got other plans to neutralize them, but if those don't work out, you need to be in position to button them. But—" He stopped to tap the photos. "—we don't want them to know you're watching them. It can't be traced back to us."

Kimball snorted. "Easy enough."

"To be sure. Look at the next photo."

Kimball shuffled papers. "Who's this fat slug? Looks like Smokey the Bear, except fatter and dumber."

"He's a sheriff's deputy. Your assessment of his skills is accurate. He thinks he's keeping an eye on these two for the FBI, but he's just a decoy. He's there so they can give him the slip and then think they're clear. But you'll still be following them."

"I don't need no help. I can do this without some Barney Fife schmuck fuckin' things up."

"No doubt, but our patrons require extra certainty. Besides, if the time comes for you to act, he's the fall guy, the Lee Harvey Oswald."

Despite himself, a smile tugged Kimball's lips upward. "While the real shooter vanishes. I guess I don't mind the extra cover. There gonna be a grassy knoll?"

Montel rolled his eyes. "Hardly, Mr. Verloc. For now, it calls less attention to us if these two are loose. They don't really know anything right now, and one of them may have an intrinsic value to our patrons. But if they get too close to certain secrets, you'll get a text message. Minotaur. That will be your cue."

Kimball nodded. "Got it. Any preference on method?"

Montel's fingers fluttered in dismissal. "Your usual practice should be fine. Just hold off until you get the signal."

Kimball scanned the papers. "Shit. I've got to go back to fuckin' Iowa? That's the most borin' place on the planet. Nothin' happens there. "

"Our goal, Mr. Verloc, is to keep it that way." The Mercedes pulled into the passenger drop-off in front of Trump Towers. "We'll expect you on the job first thing in the morning."

"You can count on me." Kimball departed the car and pushed through the lobby to the elevators. He'd have to call Sister Amanda and let her know he'd miss his volunteer schedule for a while. He glanced at his watch. If he hurried, he'd have time for dinner at Cyrano's before he departed for the culinary hell of deep-fat-fried pork and catfish.

The elevator opened, and, when he entered, the Muzak version of John Denver's "Country Roads" oozed from the speakers. He grinned and hummed along to the lyrics. *Almost heaven. That's so perfect.* Delicious daydreams swirled in his head: the savor of a gourmet meal tonight, followed by a piquant dessert of torture and death in the days to come.

He could hardly wait.

Chapter TWELVE

JASON followed Ruby back through the museum and into the cubbyhole office that nestled between the restrooms. He perched on one of the two straight-back chairs that sat side by side in front of her desk while she dug into a dented filing cabinet. Old photographs, arranged with geometric precision, peppered the walls. Overhead, a stuffed owl hovered in midflight, suspended from the ceiling. Jason took a deep breath and inhaled the odor of stale cigarette smoke mixed with a delicate undertone of Ruby's lilac perfume. The radio crackled with an old version of John Fogarty singing "Bad Moon Rising."

A coil of steely hair dangled over her face while she searched. "It's right here. Mary and I was lookin' at it just last week."

"Mary? You mean Brent's mother, Mary Hyde?"

She pulled a battered scrapbook from the drawer and tucked the stray strand of hair behind her ear. "What other Mary would I mean?" She sat on the other chair, laid the book on her lap, and lit a cigarette. "We've been friends for years, you know. All the way back to when Fred, rest his soul, was stationed at Middleton and she was a student."

"Fred was your husband?" Jason pulled out his phone and turned on the voice recorder.

Sadness dragged at her features, looming behind a curling haze of smoke. "Yeah. We were so young." She opened the scrapbook and stroked a photograph of a smiling young couple. The man wore an army uniform with master sergeant stripes and a black beret. The woman's face glowed with a mischievous grin, and she clung to his arm.

Jason recognized a younger, happier version of the old woman who sat next to him. "You're beautiful, Ruby, and the two of you look so in love."

"That we were, lad. That we were." Silence stretched between them.

When she didn't speak, Jason asked, "You said he was stationed at Middleton? With the ROTC unit, maybe? I didn't think there was a military base there."

"No. He was an MP, assigned to security at Grange Station. It was good duty, and close to here, where we both grew up." Her voice mellowed now, as though memory softened the damage from years of cigarettes.

"So what can you tell me about those times? You said you've been waiting for something. What did you learn back then?"

She rubbed her eyes, and the cigarette in her fingers trembled. "They swore us to secrecy, they did. Threatened Fred with prison if he broke security." She lowered her hand, and her fingers toyed with the photo. "I reckon they can't hurt him, now that he's in heaven." She gazed into the distance and murmured, "It had snowed the night before, but that day the sun shone so bright it hurt your eyes." She bit her lip and used the coal of her cigarette to light another. The soft strains of "Scarborough Fair" hissed from the old radio. Her story came out through the fog of smoke, memory, and music, as though it all happened yesterday.

IT WAS so cold that morning that the snow squeaked when you walked on it. The winter air burned my throat like fire and numbed my cheeks. The sun shone in God's blue sky, but there weren't no heat to it. It was one of those January days that were as bright as the fourth of July, but as cold as the devil's kiss.

A frozen blanket of white covered everything, like sheets over a dead body. Hundreds of booted feet had pounded the walkway into a mini glacier of packed ice. Dirty little holes pocked the surface from where someone had scattered sand and salt on it this morning, but it was still slicker than snot. As cold as it was, I took baby steps to the guard house.

The door banged behind me, and I praised the Lord for the blast of heat from the kerosene stove in the corner. Fred already sat at his desk, fiddling with some kind of paperwork. His shift started at 7:00

a.m., an hour before mine. I peeled off my scarf, shook the snow from my boots, and ran up to give him a kiss.

He pulled away and whispered, "Watch it." He tilted his head toward where that asshole lieutenant of his sat, giving us the evil eye. I hated that bastard, always lording over us about how we needed to be more patriotic. We were as patriotic as anybody, what with Fred a twenty-year man and all! I forget that asshole's name. Storm. Something like that.

Anyway, I showed Fred my ID, like the regulations required, and he logged it in and had me sign the book. I leaned over and asked, "Pork chops okay for dinner tonight? Don't forget the Hydes are coming over for pinochle."

His eyes gave me that little twinkle that made my heart go flutter, and he nodded. "Sounds like fun." He glanced at the lieutenant, then added, "Everything's in order, Mrs. Skrivseth." Then he winked and whispered, "I'll be home by six. I'll get a couple of six-packs on the way."

I grinned back. "Love you." I pulled my coat tighter and rewrapped my scarf. It was a good hundred feet from the outer fence where the guard station was to Building Three. I mopped the floors and cleaned the toilets during the day and took care of Fred at night. It was an okay job, and let me at least be close to my beloved during the day.

Things was pretty normal in Building Three that day, at least as normal as they ever got. The place was always full of snooty scientist and doctor types in white coats who wouldn't even say hello to common folk like you or me. 'Ceptin' Mary. She was different. She'd take time to ask after Fred, and how was my gall bladder. She really cared about people. Her husband Chuck was the same way. We really took to them, and it was them who was comin' over for pinochle that night.

I took care of the first floor, where them scientists had their labs. Mary worked in them labs too. The patients, they was on the second floor, and I never saw them much. I heard about 'em, though. They was poor little things, children with horrible deformities, God bless their souls. The doctors, they kept 'em pretty much drugged up and asleep.

I was just gettin' my gear out to start on the bathrooms when the security guard for the building, Aston, came sashayin' up to me. He leaned on the door to my cleaning closet and gave me the once-over, like he was gonna hit on me. Good thing Fred couldn't see, even though we all knew he carried a torch for Mary. "How goes it, Ruby?" he asked, as sweet as can be.

"It's another glorious day in God's creation," I told him.

He snorted. Snorted! Then he said, "It's more like the devil's work today, it's so cold."

I didn't see no need to answer that, so I just pushed my cleaning cart down the hall. But he followed me. "Mary told me there's something big goin' on in the labs downstairs today." He always liked to act like he was a big shot, knowin' more than anyone else.

I just shrugged. "None of us can go down there, so don't make no matter to me." I propped the door to the women's room open and put up my "Room being cleaned" sign.

Aston followed me inside, just like he belonged there. "I saw three generals come in here this morning, and I heard that Mr. Stillwell himself flew in from New York. He runs the Gerion Corporation." I rolled my eyes at that. Everyone who worked there knew who Stillwell was. His name was on a plaque outside the main gate. Aston continued to babble at me. "There's a big confab downstairs about something, I tell you." He stopped while I flushed a commode. "I wondered if Fred heard anything about it."

Now it was my turn to snort. "Like that lieutenant of his would tell him anything. He's just an enlisted guy. Anyway, he's only got a month left and then he retires." I smiled. "He's so short, he could sit on a dime and his legs would dangle. They ain't gonna tell him nothin'."

It was just about then that somethin' went *bang*, the lights went out, and sirens started screamin'. We found out later that the steam heat lines had frozen over, and then backed up into the boiler in the subbasement. Damned thing went *blooie*, just like that. Shook the whole building like we was in California durin' an earthquake.

When I went back out into the halls, they was full of people in white coats, all wild-eyed and runnin' around like chickens with their heads cut off. I heard 'em shoutin' about biohazards and massive containment failures, but that didn't mean nothin' to me. The only calm one was Mary. She came up, held my shoulder, and said, "Ruby, there are people trapped in the basement. Can you help me get them out?" Her face was all calm-like, but her voice was tight, and her eyes told me it was serious.

It didn't sound none too safe, but if people are in need, God tells us to help. Besides, 'bout then Fred came runnin' through the front door, lookin' like he'd seen a ghost. He tore through that crowd like a pig through corncobs and ran right up to me. "Ruby, are you all right?" God love him, his voice shook like a babe lookin' for his momma, and my heart went right out to him.

I squeezed his shoulder and shouted over the din, "I'm good, hon. But Mary here needs some help. There's some folks trapped downstairs."

Fred, bless his heart, was always ready to help those in need. He turned to Mary. "It'll be locked. You got a key?"

She nodded and shouted, "I got keys." Her hands shook while she pulled a bulky chain from her pocket. "I know the code too. Hurry. There might still be time, if the seals haven't broken."

We pushed through that crowd of idiot scientists and down the corridor to the double steel doors that led to the basement. She used the key to unlock them, and we entered another room, with metal walls. Mary closed the outer doors again and turned a little crank on the inside. The air went *whoosh,* kinda like at a meat locker when the door seals. Then she entered some numbers in a keypad next to an inner door. This one slid open, and concrete stairs led down to the basement. It was like a theater, what with red emergency lights on the steps and on down into the hall.

It was as still as a coffin, and the air smelled like a hospital, full of Lysol and Lord knows what. I held Fred's hand, and we followed Mary down into the depths. I swear, I felt like we were going right into Satan's lair, and if I'd known what we was going to find, I'm not sure I would have been brave enough to go there.

The corridor was maybe fifty feet long, and thick greenish glass windows lined each side. They opened up into little hospital rooms, but they was mostly empty. Until we got to the end. A long crack snaked up this last one, like a serpent sent by the devil. And inside the room, a little critter stared out at us. It wore a hospital gown and was maybe four feet tall, skinny like a scarecrow, and with gray skin. It leaned against the wall, and I could tell it was sick. Its little chest heaved up and down, and its mouth pumped like a fish out of water. But its eyes! Those were enormous gray things that just stared right into your soul.

Fred reached for his service revolver. "What in the Lord's name is that thing?"

Mary grabbed his hand and restrained him. "He can't hurt you. He's just a child, a child these monsters created for their evil purposes." She pointed at the little beast while he staggered forward. "Look, he's sick, the poor thing." She peered into the room. "What did they do to you, honey?" She placed a palm on the glass, and the critter put his palm on the other side, right opposite where hers was. He wavered back and forth, like he was gonna pass out.

JASON'S sweat-soaked T-shirt stuck to the back of his chair, and he squirmed in his seat to free it. The radio's scratchy speakers murmured Johnny Cash's version of "Ghost Riders in the Sky" while Ruby leaned back, closed her scrapbook, and stared into the distance. When she didn't speak, he asked, "Then what happened?"

She lit another cigarette and stared at Jason with vacant eyes. "'Bout then, a bunch of military brass stomped into the room, along with MPs and men in suits. They pushed us back upstairs and out into the cold. Kept us there for over an hour, freezin' our butts off, until they was good and ready. Then they took us back inside, and made us sign papers where we swore never to tell anyone what we saw. National security, they said. And that we'd all go to prison or worse if we told."

Jason frowned, not sure what to make of her story. "So you saw space aliens?" She'd been so intense, he didn't want to make fun of her. But really, space aliens?

"That's what we thought at first. Mary knew, but she wouldn't say what they was. She just said they was part of a guv-mint experiment gone wrong." The coal on her cigarette glowed brilliant red as she took a vicious drag.

"And you've been waiting all this time for the truth to come out?" Jason tried to keep skepticism from his voice.

Ruby shook her head. "No. Mary told me at least one of them creatures lived and grew up. I been waitin' for them devils to walk the earth, like it's written in the Good Book. That's when the End Times come." Tendrils of smoke wove about her wrinkled face and clouded her deathly grin.

Chapter THIRTEEN

FATIGUE dragged at Brent's muscles as he turned onto Apple Street in Middleton. The early afternoon sun dappled through the canopy of maple and oak trees that lined the residential avenue, and his tires splashed through puddles from last night's rain. He'd lived on this street, with its nineteenth-century gingerbread houses, for over a year now. But today, everything was different. Even here, in this familiar place, the world seemed distant and transformed, full of uncertainty and doubt.

He pulled into the driveway of his garage apartment, closed gritty eyes, and rested his forehead on the steering wheel, willing the world to vanish. He flinched when a fist thumped on his window and muffled words brought him back to reality. The hand thumped again, and this time he recognized Gary's voice.

"Hey, you gonna sit there all day?" Gary glanced at his wristwatch and then gazed up the driveway.

Brent sighed, swiped his palms over his face, and stepped from the car. "Sorry. I just kind of zoned out for a minute. You want to come up and keep me company for a while?"

Gary tilted his head toward the house attached to Brent's apartment. "There's Dr. Athair." He waved as Brent's landlady jogged down the sidewalk toward them. "Hi!" He scowled and muttered, "She's got a cigarette in one hand, as always. I don't care if she is your advisor. That's a fucking disgusting habit."

A lump clogged Brent's throat at the sight of the genuine concern that shone in his landlady's features. It wasn't just that her trim figure and businesslike hairdo reminded him of his mother—she fussed over him, both at school and here, at her home. He blinked back tears and opened his arms to her.

She ran right up to Brent, embraced him, and cradled his head against her breast. "Dear, I'm so sorry. Have you heard anything about your parents?" A faint rasp from years of smoking chafed her syllables.

Brent pulled back and squeezed her hand. "Nothing new. Just what I told you when I called from Ruby's."

She bit her lip and clasped his shoulders with both hands. "Well, with the FBI on the case, I'm sure they'll turn up. They must be just visiting family or friends." After taking a last nervous drag on her cigarette, she flicked it to the street.

Gary stood to one side, scowling at them. "Hey, remember me? I'm the one who got shot."

She held a hand to her mouth. "Oh, my, and I just left you standing there." She tried to embrace him, but he pulled back.

"Ouch. It's still kind of sensitive."

"I'm sorry, Gary dear." She stepped away and scanned him head to toe with clinical efficiency. "How are you holding up?"

"I've been better." He rubbed the bandage on his arm. "I think I'm going to head back to my place and take a pain pill." He glanced at his watch again.

Brent's shoulders slumped. "I was hoping you'd sit with me for a while."

Gary scowled again and seemed about to speak, but Athair beat him to it. "Gary, you do look a little peaked. You run along and take care of yourself, poor thing. It must have been traumatic, being shot. I can sit with Brent."

He rubbed his arm again. "It was good experience for later, when I get assigned to real security jobs instead of just training. Anyway, it's not that bad. I think I just stressed it on the drive here. The doctors said I had amazing recuperative powers."

Her features froze and she blinked. "Really? They noticed that?"

Brent murmured, "I think it was just that ditzy nurse." He rolled his eyes. "Could he have flamed any more if he'd been in drag?"

"The doctor said it too, before you got there."

Brent shrugged. "Well, I'm glad that you're getting better. Come here, you big lug, and give me a hug."

Gary squeezed him with his good arm.

Brent planted a peck on his cheek. "That's better. You go take care of yourself, and Dr. Athair can keep me company. At least until I pass out. I'm way tired."

Gary headed toward his car. "Okay. I'll call tonight. Or maybe tomorrow if the pain pills knock me out." He hopped into his sports car, revved the engine, and sped away down the street. When he turned the corner at the end of the block, he was already talking on his cell phone and steering with his uninjured arm. A pulse of affection warmed Brent's heart at the sight. *That's so like him. Always thinking.* Still, Brent wondered where Gary suddenly got all that energy since he'd just said he was tired.

Athair cast an admiring gaze toward the retreating car. "Already on the phone. He's not going to let a little thing like being shot slow him down. His mind never stops, does it?"

Brent grinned. "Yeah. Sometimes he seems to know what I'm thinking before I do." A wave of fatigue pulled at him, and he steadied himself against his pickup. "I was worried sick when the deputies said he'd been shot."

Athair nodded. "I felt the same way when I heard." Brent swayed again, and she grabbed his arm. "Look at you. You can hardly stand up. You just come right on into my home. You can take a hot bath, and I'll fix you something to eat."

"Thanks, really, but if it's all the same to you I'd rather go up to my apartment. I don't want to impose or anything."

"Like you could impose on me, silly boy," she cooed.

"Well, I'll be more comfortable in my own place too, if that's all right."

"Of course. I wasn't thinking. Let me help you up the stairs. You take a shower, and when you're done I'll be back with some food." She put an arm around him. "Look at you. You're just skin and bones. I can feel ribs."

He couldn't resist flexing his pecs, even though he knew she wouldn't notice. "You sound just like Mom." His voice choked on the last word.

"That's all right. Cry if you need to. I won't tell any of your manly friends."

"I'll be okay. Just let me get my shower."

Twenty minutes later, he emerged from his bathroom, toweling his hair dry and wearing a crisp white robe that ended midthigh, a gift his ex, Matt, had bought for him from the *International Male* catalogue. The homey scents of fresh coffee and stew greeted him.

Dr. Athair stood at the stove in the kitchen alcove, stirring a steaming pot. She gave him a sunny smile. "Do you feel better?"

"More human, yeah. That smells wonderful." He glanced at his apartment, and started to pick up homework assignments that lay scattered across the coffee table. "I'm sorry the place is such a mess."

"Pish and tosh. It's cluttered, but clean. Sit. This beef stew is all warmed up. I'll have a bowl for you in a jiffy." Sounds of dishes clanked in the kitchen. "Say, it's the strangest thing. Dr. Holmes's grandson Clark is missing again."

He scanned the disarray in the living room. "Yeah? He's the wild one, right? He was supposed to be missing last summer, and it turned out he was just in the drunk tank down in Iowa City." He took a pile of books and unread biochemistry journals off the sofa and stacked them under the end table.

"The sheriff says it's probably similar this time. She thinks he's sleeping it off someplace, or spent the night with some friends. According to her, most of the time it's something innocent like that when people seem to be missing."

"I sure hope that's true for my parents." He didn't believe it, though. He sighed, looked over the clutter, and decided it was hopeless to clean up for his landlady. He sagged into the Swedish recliner his parents had given him last Christmas. "I really appreciate your coming over. You didn't have to do this, Dr. Athair."

"Nonsense. What kind of a landlady would I be if I couldn't help out? Plus, you're one of my best students." She appeared from the kitchenette with a bowl of stew, a plate with dinner rolls, and a cup of coffee. "Cream and two sugars, right?"

"Yes, ma'am." He accepted the bowl, and she put the plate and the coffee on top of the August issue of *The American Journal of Microbiology* that sat on the end table next to him. He inhaled the rich aroma of beef and summer vegetables. "This smells wonderful."

"I just happened to make it yesterday, for the weekend. It's nice to have someone to share it with." She eyed the journal. "You're reading the article on *M. vaccae* and enhanced rat performance in mazes, aren't you?"

His face heated. "I confess. It's interesting. I grew up around cows, after all. Their results are just like the ones I thought I'd found last semester. Maybe there was something to it, after all."

"Trust me, it was an anomaly. As to your being smart, it's not from being around cows."

"I didn't say it was. But the research seemed to tie in with some of the projects in the lab, that's all." He slurped a heaping spoonful of stew. "Wow, this is even better than it smells."

"Glad you like it. Wait one minute while I get some coffee for me." She returned to the kitchen alcove, and the sounds of the faucet running and dishes clinking in the sink caught his attention.

Brent realized she was washing a cup, and then remembered the stack of dirty dishes in his kitchen yesterday when he'd left. "Oh my God. You're washing my dishes. Don't *do* that." He struggled to get out of his chair.

She reappeared in the doorway, drying a mug on a dishtowel. "Don't worry, dear. I don't mind. It's nice to have someone to care for." She bit her lip and turned her back.

He hesitated, wanting to comfort her but not knowing what to say. She once told him something had happened, long ago, but she wouldn't be specific, and he respected her too much to pry. "It's... it's nice to have you to care for me, Dr. Athair." The words stammered out, and he felt foolish for uttering them.

She returned and perched on the sofa, her coffee mug cupped in both hands on her knees. "So. If you need to take some time off, I'm sure we can arrange something. Who's taking care of the farm animals?"

"Oh, I didn't tell you. That was the weirdest thing. It was awful. Someone killed the cows last night. You've read about cattle mutilations? It was just like that."

She frowned, and her coffee mug jiggled in her hands. "That's terrible. Did you see who did it?"

"Maybe. It might be the guys who shot at us. They drove off in a fancy car, like a Mercedes or a BMW." He stretched and yawned. "It looked almost like they'd been dissected, or someone was taking samples. There wasn't any blood. They'd excised the soft tissues around the mouth and removed the tongues. On two of them, they'd also removed the udders and the rectum. It was pretty horrible. I'd just milked them a few hours before."

She evaded his gaze and stared at the carpet. "I wonder who could do such a thing."

"The sheriff said he'd never seen anything like it. The vet came and picked them up. He's going to do a necropsy. Maybe that'll turn something up. The FBI agent said it was another clue."

She stood and wandered around the room, putting crooked things straight and straight things crooked. "It's just so bizarre." She stared at a framed photo of Brent and Gary, arm in arm, standing on a bluff overlooking the Mississippi.

They both jumped when Brent's cell phone shrilled. He leaped to his feet. "That's mine. I left it in the bedroom. Maybe there's news from the FBI or the sheriff." He dashed into the other room and snapped his phone open. "Hello?"

"Brent? This is Jason. How are you doing?"

Brent heaved a sigh. "I'm okay."

"If this isn't a good time, let me know. I don't want to intrude."

Brent shook his head and then spoke. "No, that's all right. You said you were going to call. You know what, though, I'm not really up to talking to you tonight. Maybe tomorrow?"

"Whatever you say. But I just spent a couple of hours with Ruby. She's got the most amazing story, and a scrapbook. Did you know she used to work at Grange Station, along with your mother?"

"Ruby?" He frowned and bit his lip. "No way."

"*Yes* way, man." His voice bubbled with enthusiasm. "She's got old photos and news clippings to prove it. I took a bunch of shots of her scrapbook with my phone. You gotta see it. I'm sure this is all connected, somehow, to your parents' disappearance."

"I still don't get that, even if what you say is true. That was all years ago, if it happened at all." He glanced at the alarm clock on his nightstand. Three p.m. "Where are you, anyway?"

"I just left Ruby's. I'm westbound on Route 64, on the way to Middleton."

"Tell you what. Call me about seven. That'll give me time to lie down, maybe take a nap. I still think all this crap about my mother working here is bullshit, but I admit you've got me intrigued."

"Great, man. I'll call at seven. Talk to you then."

Brent tossed the phone on the bed and returned to his little living room. Dr. Athair stood staring out the front window. "Brent, I think someone may have followed you. There's a strange car parked out front. I saw it drive up when we walked up the stairs from the driveway, and it's still there. Someone's sitting in it, smoking a cigarette."

Brent peered out the window and spotted Purcell's corpulent form huddled in a beat-up Chevy. "Oh, him. That's the redneck sheriff's deputy I told you about. The one who said he was going to be watching me. He's too stupid to worry about."

She frowned. "I don't like it. Your parents are missing, and you've been shot at. Now we've got this thug hanging around. I can call the police, if you want. They'll make him go away."

"Really, he's not worth the trouble."

She pursed her lips, and doubt dripped from her voice. "If you say so." She turned and drained her coffee. "Who was on the phone? Any news?"

"No. Well, not exactly. There's this reporter who's been hanging around the last day or so. He thinks my mother used to work at Grange Station. He says all this crap, my parents, the shooting, the cows, that it's all connected to stuff that happened twenty years ago. He's nuts. But now he says he has evidence."

She quirked an eyebrow. "Evidence?"

"Yeah. You remember Ruby's? We stopped there when you came to my parents' Fourth of July picnic last summer."

She nodded, her eyes wary.

"Well, he says *Ruby* used to work at Grange Station too, and that's where she met my parents. Apparently she's got some kind of scrapbook that proves it."

"Sounds pretty tenuous to me. You know, *I* worked at the University back then. Don't you think I'd remember meeting your mother if she was here?" She frowned, "Not to speak ill or anything, but Ruby didn't seem the type to be working at an advanced scientific laboratory."

"Well, wasn't Grange Station a hospital back then too? Maybe she was a janitor or something?"

"Maybe. Just what kind of evidence is she supposed to have?"

"Dunno. Jason—that's the reporter—Jason says he's photographed pages from her scrapbook. He's coming over later tonight to show me. Who knows? Maybe it'll tell us something about where my parents might be. If nothing else, it'll keep my mind off things."

"Do you think that's a good idea, dear? You've been through a lot, and you don't know this person, do you?"

"He's nice, actually." He almost told her they'd spent last night in the same hotel room, but didn't feel like explaining how that happened, and she might think they'd had sex or something. "Hey, I really appreciate the stew and the companionship, but I'm kind of tired."

"Of course." She gathered the dirty dishes. "You said you wanted to take a nap, and here I am chattering away." She carried things to the kitchen and called out, "If you get lonely, just give me a ring. I'm going out to dinner with Malcolm, but I should be home by eight."

"Say hi to him for me. How's he doing?"

"We're celebrating tonight. His big cyber security grant from Mercedes-Benz came through."

"That's great." Brent let his features relax into a smile. "Just don't let him hack into the computers on my truck, okay?"

"If you don't have a built-in cell phone, you're probably safe." She gave his hand a squeeze. "Look at the time! I've got to run"

After she left, reality closed in again. Jason might be crazy, but Brent had known Ruby all his life. If she did know something, it'd be trustworthy. He looked out the window. A wispy tendril of smoke rose from Purcell's car, along with the muted sounds of his radio. The strains of Elvis singing "(You're the) Devil In Disguise" blended with the wind whispering through the trees.

He crawled onto the sofa and surrendered to exhaustion.

Chapter FOURTEEN

RACHEL wrinkled her nose at the stink and avoided stepping in the dried-up cakes of manure that littered the cow pasture. She snapped her head to one side and slapped at the flies that dive-bombed her face. "How much farther, Sheriff?" She stopped and blew her nose.

Watkins paused and looked over his shoulder. "Maybe a quarter mile into yonder woods, Agent. You doin' okay?"

"I think it's the clover. I must be allergic." She blinked gritty eyes and peered ahead. It was at least another thousand feet to the thick woods that surrounded the pasture. "I thought Iowa was farm country. Why all the woods around here?"

"The hills is too steep for the big combines and harvesters. Makes it unprofitable to farm, so a lot of the land has gone back to scrub. The Amish have bought a lot of it up south of here. They still farm the old-fashioned way, with horses."

"So what were the Hydes doing here if they weren't farming?" Her nose threatened to explode from internal pressure, like an overinflated tire. She held her fist to her upper lip and suppressed the sneeze, then wiped the snot onto a wad of handkerchief.

"They were hobby farmers. Kept a few cows for the milk. Farmed about ten acres for oats and beans, and grew vegetables for canning. He had a part-time job at a computer firm up in Dubuque."

"Yeah. The forensic accountants said they were just kind of hand-to-mouth. Not much money, and their kid is on scholarship at the college... where is it again?"

"Collier University. It's private and pretty expensive, from what I hear. Mostly spoiled rich kids from back east and eggheads on scholarship." He paused as they reached the fence. "The gate's locked, and we ain't found the key. Think you can climb it?"

"I'll manage." She coughed and spat nasty-tasting phlegm before climbing over the creaky gate. "What made you look all the way out here, anyway?"

"We didn't have much to do while your crime scene guys went over the farmhouse, so one of my deputies brought his hunting dog out here. He's been trainin' him as a cadaver dog. Anyway, he took off a-runnin' across the pasture."

The fence teetered and creaked as she clambered over it, careful to not catch her slacks in the barbed wire at the top. "Smart move, Sheriff. Looks like you turned up evidence we might have missed altogether."

"Maybe. More like we was lucky. There's gotta be scent trails all over this place. The hound just found the strongest one, and it led to what we found in these woods." He pointed. "Watch out for the poison ivy."

She veered away. "Where? It all looks like weeds to me."

"See these plants with the kind of greenish-red leaves? The leaves grow three-to-a-stem. That's it."

She snuffled her nose. "God, they're all over. I hate working a crime scene in the country. Give me a smelly warehouse in a big city any day."

That earned her a grin. "You just got to be careful, is all. Your clothes should protect you for now, but the poison will cling to the surface of your pants and your shoes. You might want to wash 'em good before you wear 'em again. Use soap and plenty of hot water and wear gloves when you touch 'em."

She stared at him. "You're kidding, right?" She shuffled alongside him as he led the way through brush.

"No, ma'am." He frowned. "Uh, you're walkin' in some right now."

"Jee-sus!" She hopped to one side. "It's friggin' everywhere."

"Yup. Like I said, just don't touch your clothes with bare hands before you wash 'em, and you'll be fine."

"Great." She slapped at another fly. "It feels like all kinds of creepy-crawlies are climbing on me. Let's just get this over with."

They plodded on in silence for another ten minutes. Sweat dripped from her brow and burned her eyes, and the humid air crowded about her like a moose with bad breath. The forest glowed with flecks of sunlight, and the leaves rustled under her feet. At least the fetid scents of rotting foliage replaced the stench of cow shit.

She stopped at an abrupt clearing in the thicket. It was perhaps thirty feet wide and twice as long, with a few discouraged shrubs scattered about the knee-high grass. A dead tree, branches crumpled in skeletal remains about its gray trunk, dominated the middle of the glade. Crime scene tape encircled the tree, and several numbered flags, bright orange and the size of Post-it Notes, marked where the investigators had found evidence.

She wiped her nose while circling the tree. "I see you've already had a team in here."

"First thing we did after we found it." He gestured. "There's blood splatter on this side, right here."

"Shit." The coppery smell of blood mixed with the rot of the forest. Something wet and disgusting had turned the dirt at the base of the tree into a reddish-brown slurry. "Looks like blood. A lot of it. Maybe enough for two hits, right here."

"That's what the team thought too. Hard to say for sure, what with all the rain, though. They also found two 9mm shell casings, at eight and eleven." He pointed to two of the evidence markers. "No bullets. From broken branches and disturbed ground cover, we think that they dragged the body, or bodies, through the woods off to the east. There's a dirt access road about a hundred feet from here. The rain washed away whatever tire tracks might have been there, though."

"So no substantive clues."

"Wouldn't quite say that. First, about a hundred feet up the access road, we found a pickup belonging to Ephraim Zimmerman. He owns this land and lives about a half mile down the road. He seems to be missing too; leastwise, he's not answering his phone or his door. Second, we found three clear footprints in the dirt at twelve." He pointed to an evidence tag under a heavy clump of red-green leaves. "They're from a pair of Reebok Sporterra Extremes. The ISBI forensic team says they can ID the owner, if we can find a suspect to test against. Finally, we found a box of 9mm hollow points hidden under some underwear in young Hyde's dresser, back at the farmhouse. Someone had wiped the fingerprints off the box."

Her head jerked around at that. "Really? Anyone in the house have a permit for a weapon?"

The sheriff shook his head. "Nope. No handgun permits, and no handguns found either. They had a couple of hunting rifles and a shotgun. Don't need permits for those, though."

She nodded. "Stranger and stranger. Why wipe the prints off the box?" She paused to wipe the drool from her nose. "You sent blood samples off to the lab?"

"Of course. Preliminary report says it's from two sources, both male. The blood type of one matches your DB from the drug raid. Also matches the missing Mr. Zimmerman, from his military records."

"Really? Any positive ID?"

"We're working it, checking around to see if Zimmerman had a dentist. No X-rays from when he was in 'Nam, and no luck so far with locals."

"Well, let me know. What about the other blood sample?"

"Same type as Chuck Hyde. We've got tissue samples from razors and combs for both Zimmerman and Hyde. We'll have the results of the DNA comparisons in a week or so."

She nodded, and then exploded with a sneeze and a hacking cough. "Thanks, Sheriff." She scanned the glade through bleary eyes. "I needed to see the scene for myself. Pictures just aren't the same as the real thing."

"I agree, although there's not much to do here."

"Well, at least I saw it. Thanks for taking the time, Sheriff." She gave the scene a last scan, hands on her hips, and sniffled. "Let's head back before my head explodes from these damned allergies." She hadn't taken more than a dozen steps when her cell phone shrilled. She scowled, flipped it open, and snarled, "Morrison here." *This better be good.* Her back straightened when she recognized Montel's supercilious tones.

"Agent Morrison. Where are you?"

"At the Hyde farm, sir. We've found what looks like another crime scene. Blood splatter from two sources, both male, and two 9mm shell casings. The blood's probably recent, but the rain screwed up some of the evidence. Blood types match the Green Island DB and Chuck Hyde. We'll have DNA evidence in a week or so."

"Huh. I'll see if I can speed that up. Which lab did they use?"

"Don't know, sir. Just a second." She touched the sheriff's arm and raised an eyebrow. "Where'd they send the tissue samples?"

"ISBI labs in Davenport."

"You get that, sir?"

"Yes. Anything else, Agent?"

She sniffed, coughed, and avoided another patch of poison ivy. "No, sir. The team is just finishing up at the farm. We won't have anything concrete from there for a while."

"Right. I've set up an office in Middleton. The head of the Political Science Department is an old colleague of mine, and he lent space. How soon can you get here?"

"Uh, maybe an hour, a bit more, probably. Sir, shouldn't I be here, where the investigation is? There are some significant new developments."

"I think we can trust the team to handle that without you, Agent Morrison. The nexus of our investigation has moved here, to young Hyde, just as I suspected."

She frowned in confusion. What was he talking about? He couldn't know about the ammunition they'd found. Not yet, anyway. "Sir, I don't understand."

"While you were out stomping around in the country, I issued a National Security Letter and accessed young Hyde's cell phone records. He's been a busy boy."

"A National Security Letter, sir? But this is just a missing person case, or at worst a drug case. How—"

He interrupted, "I'll decide what's national security and what's not, *Agent*. Is that clear?"

"Perfectly." She dabbed at her nose with a soggy handkerchief and longed to scratch her legs. She was sure that poison ivy boils already festered under her slacks.

"All right, then." He paused, and the sound of a deep breath oozed over the phone. "At precisely 9:19 last night, someone used the web browser on Brent Hyde's mobile phone to illegally access a brokerage account for Security National Bank in Dubuque. According to tower records, the call originated from his parents' farm, or within one hundred yards of that location."

"What? You think there's security fraud involved?"

"I'm sure of it. At 9:21, the person using this cell phone transferred ten million dollars to a numbered account in a bank in Jamaica. It'll take us at least twenty-four hours to get the information on that account from the government down there, and I'm betting by then the trail will be cold. But it's clear to me that this is all connected to this transfer."

She frowned and stopped at the fence. The stench of the manure reminded her of the cows. "Maybe. But what about the mutilated cows? How does that tie in?"

"Who knows?" he snarled. "It's a trivial thing, anyway. Maybe it's just a diversion."

The fence creaked as the sheriff climbed over. She held up a finger to tell him to wait. "Look, sir, I agree this is important new evidence, but I've got some loose ends here I'd like to tie up." She was thinking of burning her clothes and taking a long shower, but he didn't need to know that.

"Agent Morrison. I need you here, as soon as possible. I'm certain that Brent Hyde's guilty of embezzlement, and perhaps the murder of his parents as well. The crime scene you just reported to me is just another piece of evidence against him."

"But why kill his parents? And why use his own cell phone to do the transfer, and then try to hide it in an offshore account? He had to know we could track the transaction back to his phone."

"Maybe he's stupid. Who knows? As to his parents, maybe they found him stealing the access codes to the bank's brokerage account and wouldn't go along with the crime. Or maybe they were all in it together, and this kid got greedy. I just know we need to close the noose around his scrawny neck, and you're the person to do it. So get here, now."

The phone went dead, and she hung her head.

When the sheriff spoke, she lifted her eyes to see his sympathetic features. "Micro-managing bosses can be nasty. Anything I can do to help?"

She sighed. "Help me over the fence, will you? And keep in touch. See if you can track down that ammunition. Meantime, I'm off to Middleton."

His eyebrows crawled up his head. "Middleton? Why there?"

"Probably a wild goose chase." When she hopped down from the fence, her foot caught and she slipped. The sheriff's strong hand gripped her arm and saved her from falling, but one foot landed in a ripe pile of manure. "Fuck! What's next?"

The sheriff gave her a wry grin. "Looks like you've stepped in it now, Agent."

Chapter FIFTEEN

THE shrill of his cell phone woke Brent from a deep sleep. He groped his pockets and then recalled that he'd left the damned thing in the bedroom. "Shit." It rang again, and he staggered from the sofa into the other room. "Yeah?" A cough shook his lungs, and something thick and disgusting clogged the back of his throat.

"Brent, this is Jason. Are you all right? You don't sound so good."

A light evening breeze fluttered through the oak tree outside his bedroom and scattered the early evening sun on his bedroom wall. He squinted against the wavering patterns of light and shadow. "I'm okay. I was sound asleep." He rubbed his eyes and blew a deep breath out his lips.

"Hey, I'm sorry. We don't have to do this now if you need to rest."

"I'm awake now. Don't worry about it. I'll be all right." He dug sleep out of his right eye with a finger while peering at the clock on the nightstand: seven sharp. At least this guy was punctual. "So, you want to come over here?"

"Or we could meet someplace. A restaurant, maybe?"

Brent yawned and stretched. "If you don't mind, I think I'd rather just do it here. I could order pizza or something."

"I promised I'd feed you, remember? How about I bring Chinese? Lo mein and twice-cooked pork okay?"

"That'd be great. Maybe some Szechuan chicken too."

"I'll get some egg rolls while I'm at it. You're still on Apple Street, right? Like the directory says?"

"Right. It's the garage apartment."

Jason chuckled. "Got it. Donchya love Google? Sure makes the reporter's job easier. Shouldn't take more than thirty minutes and I'll be there."

Brent tossed the phone back on the bed and headed to the bathroom, where he took stock in the mirror. What stared back at him would be sure to get him voted off the island on any TV reality show: bedroom hair, raccoon circles under bloodshot eyes, and a huge sleep wrinkle on his cheek. Plus, his mouth tasted like he'd been chewing on pig shit. Stale pig shit. Charming.

He stripped off his wrinkled T-shirt, brushed his teeth, and attacked his face with a hot washcloth. A slug of fatigue still stuck like a wad of glue deep in his brain and dulled his thoughts, but at least he felt more human. He stepped back into the bedroom, dropped to the floor, and did twenty quick pushups, perched on the points of his fingertips and toes. When he bounced to his feet, he added twenty knee bends.

The brief wake-up calisthenics helped to dispel some of his weariness. He eyed his cell phone and clicked it open to send Gary a text message.

hey, how ru? miss u

Just as he pulled a fresh T-shirt from his dresser, the doorbell rang. He held the shirt in one hand and padded on bare feet to answer. The gangly reporter stood on the landing, gripping bulging plastic sacks that smelled of ginger, garlic, and jasmine.

An easy smiled pulled at Brent's lips. "Hi, Jason. Come on in."

Jason blinked and blushed. His eyes focused on Brent's torso and then lurched away to stare at the floor. "Hi. Uh, I brought food."

"So I see. Come on in and put it on the kitchen table." He slipped his T-shirt over his head and ran fingers through his hair. "Sorry. I know I look like something from *Rocky Horror*."

"You look great. Better than I look at my best." He started pulling cartons out of the sacks. "They were out of lo mein, so I got both white rice and brown rice, plus a six-pack of Tsingtao. Hope that's okay."

"It's perfect. I could use a beer." Brent pulled plates and beer glasses out of a cabinet, and two sets of chopsticks from a drawer. "You need a fork, or you want chopsticks?"

"Chopsticks, of course. Wow, you've got your own? Fancy."

"I learned how to use 'em last year, when I was a freshman. Growing up, fried catfish and smashed potatoes were about as exotic as Mom ever got, but now I really like Chinese." He inhaled and a smile tugged at his lips. "That smells truly fine. Just what the doctor ordered." He hesitated for a moment, and then lit a couple of votive candles and put them on the table along with the plates, glasses, and chopsticks. "Dig in."

The mixture of delicate spices and searing peppers combined with the tang of the beer to flush the fatigue from Brent's system. They ate in silence, in the golden light of the setting sun that streamed through the open windows. A chorus of cicadas serenaded them, accompanied by the gentle rustle of the wind in the trees.

Brent chased the last scrap of chicken off his plate and then leaned back and examined his companion. The guy's face was too narrow, his nose was so big he looked cross-eyed, and he'd be laughed off *America's Next Top Model* with that unruly mop of curls. On top of that, he needed a shave, and he was so skinny he could use a Cheerio as a hula hoop.

He was about the sexiest guy Brent had met in years. But memories of his ex Matt churned a deep hurt in his chest. Gary was right: men were toe jam. Love 'em and leave 'em. "Tell me about Ruby."

A smile lit up Jason's face, and his eyes glimmered in the flickering glow of the candles. "She told the wildest story about Grange Station, back twenty years ago when it was a hospital. I think she believes it, but memories are tricky things." He leaned forward. "The story isn't as important as what was in her scrapbook. She's got photos of herself and another person, standing in front of where they worked together." He pulled out his phone. "Here, look. She says that's your mother."

Jason accepted the phone and peered at the image. "It's kind of hard to tell." He flicked his fingers across the screen, and the faces grew larger. "Yeah, I recognize her, all right. That's my mother." He frowned and looked up at Jason. "Where was this taken?"

"At Grange Station. One of the buildings there was surrounded by barbed wire and had a full-time military guard. Ruby's husband was an MP stationed there right before he retired and they started their store."

"That doesn't make any sense. Why would there be a military guard outside a children's hospital?"

"Because the hospital was cover for something else, that's why." Jason slid his chair around to be next to Brent and reached for his phone. "Look, here's a news article she had in her scrapbook." He flipped through pictures and held it out to Brent.

He peered at the photo and recognized his mother and another woman. "I can't make out the caption. What's it say?"

"It says they're DARPA employees of the quarter." Jason's voice rang with triumph.

"And that proves what, exactly?"

"DARPA. You know. The Defense Advanced Research Projects Agency. They invented the Internet, and who knows what else. It's a top secret agency that develops military technology. This is from a newsletter for Grange Station, and your mother and this other woman were DARPA employees of the quarter for their research."

"You're saying my mother worked on military technology. At a children's hospital." He raised his eyebrows. "That makes no sense."

"Look, I tracked down Collier budgets from back then. Dr. Holmes, and the Stillwell-Holmes Institute for Research in Epigenetics, had a multimillion dollar contract from the Department of the Army back then. They lost it a couple of years later, and a whole bunch of the Grange station shut down. I'm telling you, the hospital angle was all cover-up." He looked stubborn, and his voice held conviction.

"But my mother doesn't know anything about science. She homeschooled me until I was sixteen, when I knew more science than she did. She tried to tell me that the Earth's shadow caused the phases of the moon, for God's sake!"

"She may not know astronomy, but she earned a master's degree in experimental psychology from Northwestern about two years before this photo was taken."

"I don't believe it."

"Meike Hilda Zeigler. That your mother?"

Brent flinched at hearing his mother's given name. "She never used her real name, from her German grandmother. The only reason even I know about it was that it was on my FAFSA when I applied for financial aid."

"She used it when she got her master's degree. I've got a photo from the Northwestern yearbook showing her in a behavioral science lab with one of her professors, one Sonja Athair. It's the same face as in the photo with Ruby that you just identified."

This was too much. The world swirled about, and breath shuddered in his chest. "What? Dr. Athair was my mother's professor? They *knew* each other and didn't *tell* me?"

Jason gripped his hand. "I know this is tough, Brent. But this part of the story hangs together, and Ruby's scrapbook is just another nail in the… well, just confirms it. I've got tons of documentary evidence that what was going on in that lab was something the government wants hidden. That's why I was wanting to talk to your mother, to find out what she knows about DARPA and Grange Station."

An incipient headache pounded in his forehead, and Jason's voice seemed to come from far away. He pushed a deep, cleansing breath out of his mouth, just like his father taught him when hunting, right before taking a shot at their prey. He shoved back, stood, and shook out his arms before pacing around the table. "This is just crazy," he muttered. He stopped to stare at Jason. The poor guy's face twisted into an impossible combination of determination, remorse, and sympathy. In that instant, Brent believed. He collapsed onto the sofa. "How is this related to my parents' disappearance?"

"God, I wish I knew. But just when I start looking into this, shit starts happening. Like my Deep Throat contact."

"Your what?"

"I've got this source that's been sending me text messages. All I was working on was this local story about kids disappearing from Grange Station. Sort of a boogeyman urban legend that's been going around these parts for years."

Brent nodded. "I remember. Counselors at the Boy Scout camp next to Grange Station used to scare us with it. What's that got to do with all this?"

"Nothing, near as I can tell. I was just looking into the history of Grange Station for origins of the legend, kind of a human interest story for the *Shopper*. Then I started getting these text messages. Little cryptic tweets giving me hints about what to look for and where. That's how I found the stuff on the DARPA contract, and how I connected your mother to a graduate student named Meike Hilda Zeigler at Northwestern."

"So you've got someone feeding you information? Why don't you track *them* down?"

"I tried. He's using a prepaid cell phone. No way to trace the owner." Jason peered at him. "Shit, man, you look tense. I took a massage class at the vo-tech last summer. Let me rub your shoulders." He jittered behind the couch, like a squirrel looking for a nut. "Hold still."

Brent started to squirm away when fingers dug into the back of his neck and shoulders, but his muscles responded with instantaneous, glorious release. "Oh. That feels nice." He leaned into it.

"That's it. Just relax and let the tension work out. Wow, your back's coiled up worse than a Gordian knot. Good thing I'm not Alexander."

"Very clever." He leaned back and relished the tendrils of pleasant repose that oozed down his spine. "Man, you're good at this."

"You just need to know what buttons to push." He worked the neck a few seconds longer, and then mused, "Ruby's scrapbook gives more leads. The woman in the picture with your mother, for example. Mandy Geary. I bet we can track her down and find out what she knows."

"Mmmm." Brent closed his eyes and hoped Jason didn't notice that one part of him wasn't relaxed at all. He shifted his jeans to a more comfortable position. "So you still haven't said how this is all connected."

"Yeah. Well, first I start looking into the history of Grange Station. Then I get all these anonymous tips, pointing to military research and your mother. *Then,* the very day I try to contact her, bang! She disappears. Even more, my source texted me last night and said you were in danger. That's why I went to the farm, to warn you."

Brent leaned forward and let Jason reach inside his T-shirt to get at his back. "The text came from the same source that sent you the other information?" Jason's fingers kneaded at the sides of his lower back and worked even more remarkable magic on his latissimus dorsi.

"Yeah. The same prepaid cell." He stopped the blessed massage. "Feel better? You're looser now."

"Yeah. Thanks. That was incredible." He kind of hoped Jason *would* notice the romantic effects of his massage, after all.

Jason avoided his glance. "Sure. My pleasure." He slipped onto the opposite end of the sofa, as far from Brent as he could get. "You know what we should do next?"

Brent let a languid grin play across his lips and waggled his eyebrows like Groucho Marx. "I can think of a thing or two we might do."

Jason stayed focused on the twenty-year-old mystery. "I think we should track down some of the names in Ruby's scrapbook. There's that woman, Mandy Geary. We should also try to find Ruby's husband's CO with the MPs, Lieutenant somebody. I don't remember his name. Then there's a guard who worked in that research building she mentioned: Aston Minock. Who knows what we'll learn from them. I tell you, I'm convinced there's a cover-up of all of this going on."

Before Brent could answer, a fist pounded on the door and a man's voice shouted. "Brent Hyde. FBI. Open up!"

Chapter SIXTEEN

BRENT jumped to his feet, romance forgotten and hope swelling in his chest. "Maybe the FBI has news about my parents." He rushed to the front door and flung it open, where he recognized the female agent from this morning, Rachel somebody, in the dim light from the street. She stood a few inches behind a tall, gray-haired man, dressed in an impeccably pressed black suit, whose narrow features and sharp eyes reminded Brent of a greyhound.

"Mr. Hyde." He flashed his ID and slipped it back in the pocket of his suit before Brent could read it. "I'm Agent Montel Strorm. I believe that you've met Agent Morrison. May we come in?" He pushed inside without waiting for permission.

Brent, eager for news, gave way. "Yeah, sure." Agent Morrison nodded to him as she passed, her face grave. Worry flashed in him. "Do you have news on my parents? Do you know where they're at?"

Strorm turned and raked his gaze over Brent, as if he were examining a new strain of the Ebola virus. "Nothing specific yet. We've got some leads we'd like to discuss with you, though." He turned to face the little living alcove and glowered at Jason. "I recognize you. You're Mr. Killeen. That… *reporter.*" A sardonic smile twisted his lean features. "Fancy finding *you* here."

Jason stood and offered his hand. Strorm just stared at it. After a beat, Jason pulled out his cell phone, opened the recorder app, and held it up. "That's correct. I'm Jason Killeen, sir. Please speak up so my phone will pick up your voice. Would you mind repeating your name, so I can be sure I get it correct?"

The little smile on Strorm's lips tightened. "Certainly, Mr. Killeen." He held his badge out for inspection. "That's Special Agent in Charge Montel Strorm. Should I spell it for you?"

Jason glanced at the badge and ID and nodded. "I've got it. Thank you." He set his phone on the coffee table, the recording app visible and running.

Strorm turned on his heel and scanned the room. He stepped to the kitchen table, dragged a chair to a position opposite the sofa, and sat at stiff attention while pulling a notepad from his suit coat pocket.

Rachel pulled her badge from her purse and offered it to Jason without speaking, but he smiled at her and nodded. "I recall meeting you earlier, Agent Morrison. Nice to see you again."

Brent motioned for Rachel to sit in the easy chair while he sat on the opposite end of the sofa from Jason. "So, what can you tell me about the leads?" He tipped an eyebrow at Strorm.

Montel's eyes narrowed in Jason's direction. "We don't do business in the presence of the press."

Brent's throat tightened in irritation. "He's a friend. I'd like him to stay."

Montel leaned forward and nudged Jason's phone with the end of his automatic pencil. "No recordings. This is strictly off the record. Do I make myself clear? You can stay only if you're here as Mr. Hyde's... *friend*. Understood?"

Jason picked up his phone and pressed the screen. "Understood." He lounged back and crossed his legs. "Now, the polite thing to do, the *professional* thing, Agent Strorm, would be to inform Brent what brought you here this evening. What are you doing to find his parents?"

Montel looked like he'd bitten into an apple and found Jason inside. "I'll ask the questions, Mister. You're here as a courtesy to Mr. Hyde."

Brent kept his voice even and spoke to Rachel, ignoring Strorm. "I *would* like to know the status of the investigation. It's been more than twenty-four hours, now."

Rachel's eyes shifted to her boss. She licked her lips as if to speak, but he beat her to it. "What can you tell us about your father's employer, Mr. Hyde?"

"His employer? They're just a little computer services outfit. They customize payroll, billing, and other software packages for local businesses. They do some desktop support too. My dad's in the programming end of the company."

Montel nodded. "He works full time for them, then?"

"Well, no. He's basically on-call. Some months he'll work full time, but usually it's around twenty hours a week. He does a lot of the coding at home, but the customizing always requires interaction with the customer. What's this got to do with their disappearance?"

Montel leaned forward. "What kinds of customers does he deal with?"

Brent shook his head, frowned, and let impatience show in his voice. "I have no idea. I remember a company that did janitorial services, and a big real estate agency in Dubuque. I'm not sure what else. Really, I don't see where this is going."

"How about brokerage firms?"

"Maybe. Dad doesn't talk much about his work." He paused, and surprise raised his eyebrows. "You think one of his *customers* kidnapped my parents?"

Montel flipped pages back in his notebook. "Cox, Inhofe, and Associates was one of the companies using programs your father customized. They're an investment firm." He glanced up and raised his eyebrows. "Ever hear of them?"

"Yeah, sure. They're one of the regular sponsors of the local high school's sports teams. I didn't know Dad worked with them."

"Uh-huh." Montel consulted his notes again. "Last night at 9:21, someone hacked into one of their brokerage accounts and transferred ten million dollars to an off-shore account." He glanced up. "Quite a coincidence, wouldn't you say? Right when you're parents disappear, someone steals ten million dollars from one of his customers."

Shock thudded inside Brent's chest and shuddered out his throat. "You're saying my father *stole* that money and then ran off? I don't believe it."

Montel leaned back, and a compact smile twisted his mouth. "No, it seems unlikely your father was involved. At least, not directly."

"If the theft happened at 9:21, he'd been missing nearly three hours, at least." The room seemed to whirl about him. Brent squeezed his eyes shut and rubbed his temples. When he opened them, Montel's gray stare bored into him. He confronted the cold gaze with one of his own and challenged, "If someone hacked into the system after he disappeared, they must have taken him someplace and forced my dad to tell them how. Can't you trace their location from their IP address?"

"Of course. Strange you should ask that."

This whole conversation was just weird. Brent paused and gave a silent count of three to control the anger and impatience that roiled within his mind. "Why is that strange? You're not making sense."

"It's strange, because we did trace the hacker. He used a cell phone."

Brent frowned. "A cell phone? You mean the web browser on one of those prepaid jobs? I guess that would be untraceable, then. But couldn't you still figure out from the towers where they called from?"

"It wasn't a prepaid phone. And yes, we can and did trace the approximate location from the towers."

Brent avoided rolling his eyes. "So you're done, then. You know who stole the money, where they were at, and that means you've maybe got a clue about the location of my parents." His face heated. "Why the fuck didn't you just come out and tell me, instead of putting me through all this bullshit?"

For the first time, Montel's smile seemed genuine. "The problem, Mr. Hyde, is that the hacker's location was, as nearly as we can tell, your parents' farm. And the criminal used *your* cell phone. I thought perhaps you might help us understand how that happened?"

Brent's chest deflated like a punctured inner tube. His hands trembled, and his voice quivered. "My phone? They used *my* phone? That's impossible." His hands pressed against his jeans pocket to reassure himself the device rested in its usual place. "I always carry my phone in my pocket. There's no way any hackers used my phone to steal that money."

Montel purred, "Indeed. If no one else could have done it, then you see our dilemma."

"Yeah, I guess. You think maybe the people who shot at us somehow tapped into my phone?" He pulled it from his pocket and stared at it, wondering what other sabotage might lay hidden inside.

Jason snorted. "They think *you* did it, Brent. If I were you, I wouldn't say anything more to them." He glared at Montel. "Is Brent a suspect or not? If he's not, I think you should go."

Confusion and fear mingled to fog Brent's thoughts. He barely understood Montel's next words, although there was no missing the man's sneering intonation. "Mr. Killeen, I remind you that you're here as a courtesy. Right now, Mr. Hyde is a just person of interest in our investigations. Since he's not a suspect, he's obligated to cooperate with our investigation. As are you."

Jason snapped, "Oh, I'll cooperate all right." He stood, walked behind the sofa, and placed his hands on Brent's shoulders. "Is there anything else? Do you have any information at all on the whereabouts of Brent's parents, or was this just a sadistic little fishing expedition?"

Brent reached up and touched Jason's hand, grateful for the anchor of the reporter's reassuring touch. He glanced at Rachel. Her face remained impassive, but her eyes brimmed with compassion.

She gave him the slightest nod, as if to say everything would be all right. "Brent, would you be willing to let us have your cell phone? It's possible that someone hacked into it and used it without your knowledge. Our computer forensic investigators might be able to find traces."

Montel snorted. "That's most unlikely, Agent Morrison."

She didn't look at him. "How about it, Brent?" She held out her hand.

His hand still gripped the device. When he looked at it, all he saw was danger, as though an old and fun friend had betrayed him. "Take it. I'll get another tomorrow. It's got to be infected with a Trojan or something." He slid it across the coffee table toward her.

The barest of smiles bent her lips. "If it is infected, our team will find it. They're the best." She pulled what looked like a baggie from her purse and slid the phone inside using a pen.

Montel stood. "That's all for now, Mr. Hyde. Don't leave town without contacting us. We'll know, and it won't be good for you."

Brent thought about Purcell outside, watching, but didn't trust his voice to speak.

Jason squeezed his shoulders and asked, "What about the search for Brent's parents? So far, you've just come here and accused him. Are you doing anything to, you know, actually look for them?"

Storm sniffed. "If you're a reporter, Mr. Killeen, you should know the Bureau doesn't comment on ongoing investigations." He scanned the apartment again. "Gentlemen, I'm sure we'll be back in touch. We can find our own way out." He gave a curt nod in Brent's general direction, turned on his heel, and marched to the door. Rachel rolled her eyes at his back and winked at Jason before she followed him out.

When the door slammed shut, Brent inhaled a shuddering breath. "What the fuck was that all about? I can't believe my dad had anything to do with that theft."

"That business about your cell phone is even weirder." He paused and then mused, "Of course, they could have been lying about that."

Brent twisted his head to look at him. "You think? They can do that?"

"Yeah. They have no obligation to tell the truth during an investigation. If a mere mortal like you or me lies to *them,* we go to jail for obstruction of justice. If the cops or the DA lie to us, though, well, they're just doing their jobs. They can use lies and tricks and even threats to get evidence against suspects. It sucks, but that's the way it is. Different laws for the cops than for the rest of us." Jason circled around and sat in the easy chair.

Brent frowned and thought for a moment. "So you really think they suspect me?"

"I'm sure Strorm does. Rachel is another matter." He tapped a finger on the chair. "Suppose for a moment they were telling the truth about your cell phone. It doesn't really make sense. I mean, if you're bright enough to hack into a secured computer system, why be so dumb as to do it from your own phone? It's not like you couldn't have done it anonymously any number of ways. If the cell phone story is true, it's got to be a setup of some kind."

"I don't see how it can be true. But how about my parents? It didn't sound like they're doing anything to find them." His face heated with anger. "I should have pushed them harder on that."

Jason touched his hand. "Don't beat yourself up. They were only here to test their theory that you stole the money. I think you convinced at least Rachel you didn't. After all, she took your phone." He paused for a moment. "It's still early in their investigation. We don't know what they learned about the cows, for example."

"I forgot about that." Brent swallowed an angry lump in his throat and fought back tears. "I feel so fucking helpless. I wish I could do something."

"For now, your best bet is to rely on Rachel and the FBI. What we *can* do now, though, is figure out whether or not this is connected to the Grange and what your mother and Ruby found there twenty years ago. I think we should check out the people from Ruby's notebook." He pulled out his cell phone. "Let's see if any of them show up on a Google search."

Brent watched without much hope as Jason spoke the name Mandy Geary into the phone's search engine. "That's the woman from the picture?"

Jason nodded. "That was too easy. I've got a hit, from the KCRG TV website." His eyes widened. "Jee-sus. Mandy Geary's dead, from a single gunshot wound to the head. Her daughter found her body this morning in her trailer, near Lost Springs, Iowa. Police have no suspects." He looked up. "This has got to be all connected. We've got to go there and check this out."

Brent jumped to his feet. "Let's do it. Anything's better than sitting around here."

Jason shook his head. "It's too late to learn anything tonight. Tomorrow morning's soon enough." He fiddled with his phone. "Where the fuck is Lost Springs, anyway?"

Chapter
SEVENTEEN

JASON shivered in the chill night air as he descended the steps from Brent's garage apartment. Purcell's patrol car still squatted under a tree across the street, and a gentle breeze carried the soft twang of a country-western song his way. An ironic grin tugged at his features when he caught the lyrics: *I fought the law, and the law won.* The red coal of a cigarette glowed from where Purcell must be sitting, watching him. Jason thought about accosting him, but decided the deputy wasn't worth the effort.

He circled his van, inspecting it to make sure no one had vandalized it. Not that he thought Purcell would do that, but you could never be too careful. When he eased into the driver's seat, he glanced at the mess of wadded up reporter's notes, crushed soda cans, and discarded junk food bags that littered the interior. In contrast, Brent's apartment had been tidy, with just a few stacks of scientific journals on an end table. His mouth turned downward when he thought about the two of them riding together to Lost Springs in this rat's nest. He glanced at the clock on the dash. After eleven. If he spent an hour or so at the car wash, he could make it halfway presentable.

The engine coughed and wheezed before it started. He slipped it into gear and headed across town, but less than two blocks later, without warning, his lights flashed off and the engine quit running. He fought with the suddenly powerless steering wheel to pull to the side of the street, rolling to a stop behind a Volvo station wagon. Trees arced overhead like the buttresses of a cathedral, hiding the faint moonlight in flickering shadows. Except for an occasional upstairs night light, the windows of the homes lining the avenue were dark and silent.

"What the fuck?" He pumped the accelerator and cranked the engine, but it wouldn't fire. "Jee-sus." The gas gauge said three-quarters full, so that wasn't it. It was like the starter suddenly failed.

He pulled the hood latch and stepped out of the car, but his phone rang before he could do anything. When he glanced at the caller ID, he didn't recognize the number. "Yeah? Who the hell is this?"

"Jason, is that the way you talk to all your sources?" The voice gurgled with electronic distortion, masking even the gender of the caller.

He recognized the source he'd come to think of as his Deep Throat. "Oh, it's you. You were right about Brent being in danger. Thanks for the warning."

"I'm afraid that was just the beginning. More is to come before this is over. Who were those people at his apartment tonight?"

A shiver skittered down Jason's spine. "How'd you know about that?"

"Just answer the question. Who did they say they were?"

"The FBI. They had all kinds of wild-ass accusations that Brent stole money from one of his father's business clients. They were complete jerks. Well, one of them, anyway. The female agent didn't say much."

A throaty laugh bubbled from the phone. "FBI? How... clever of them."

"You sayin' they weren't Feds? I got the badge number of the woman. I can check."

"Oh, I'm sure they are both with the FBI." Another chuckle. "Too. It's their *other* masters who are being clever."

He rolled his eyes. "So why did you call me? I've kinda got a situation here."

"You mean with your van? Don't worry. It'll work when I'm done with you." The caller sighed, as if taking a deep breath or maybe a heavy drag on a cigarette. "Look inside the left rear wheel well on your van. Tell me what you find."

Jason frowned but knelt and ran his fingers along the rough surface. A gasp escaped his lips when his hand encountered a rectangular box, about the size of a pack of cigarettes. He tugged, and when it came free he peered at it in the faint light. Heavy magnets attached to one side, and a small antenna protruded from one end. "What the fuck is this? It looks like a bug."

"It's a tracking device. That oafish sheriff's deputy parked across from Brent's apartment put it there tonight, while you were inside."

"Well, thanks. Maybe I'll stick it on a cross-country semi and let him follow that."

"Put it back. If you take it off, they'll just plant another one. Better that you know it's there. You can remove it later, if you need to lose them. Meantime, it doesn't hurt anything."

"I don't like the idea of being bugged. I'm not sure it's even legal. First amendment, and all, you know."

That got him a snort from his caller. "I doubt they are too worried about what's legal. And if they are, well, that FBI agent could just issue a National Security Letter. No judicial review, nothing but his letter, and then his surveillance is perfectly legal."

He shrugged, and then realized Deep Throat couldn't see the gesture. "Whatever."

"Did you put it back where you found it?"

Jason balanced the device in his hand for a moment and then repositioned it in the tire well with a sudden movement. "Yeah. I guess you're right. Better a bug I know about than one I don't."

"I knew you were a smart boy."

"Gee, thanks." He stood and leaned against his car. He watched while a Honda Civic puttered by and pulled into a driveway in the next block. "I'm glad Brent's okay. His boyfriend got shot, though."

"That was accidental, I assure you. He's... important, in his own way."

"So why are they after Brent? You know, besides the disappearance of his parents, there's more than one dead body associated with this case."

"They're after Brent, but he's not physically in danger right now. At least not from them." The voice paused. "More than one body, you say? I only knew about one, a not so innocent victim, I'm afraid. What other bodies do you know about?"

"There was one found in a drug raid near the Mississippi River, not far from Brent's farm."

"That's the one I knew about."

"The other one is a waitress down in Lost Springs. Mandy Geary."

Brent could swear he heard a faint intake of breath at the other end. "Mandy Geary. I haven't heard that name in a long time. How did she die?"

"A bullet in her brain last night while she slept, according to the news."

The voice gurgled, "Interesting. What makes you think she's connected to this?"

"She worked with Brent's mother twenty years ago, at Grange Station. I found an old photograph of them together." He stopped and licked his lips. "She gets shot just when I start investigating. That's a coincidence, and I don't believe in coincidences."

"Like I said, you're a smart one."

"Yeah. Not smart enough to get to her while she was alive."

"You say you traced her from an old photograph? Impressive. You have justified my faith in you, Mr. Killeen. May I ask? Who are your other sources?"

"You know I can't tell you that. I'll protect them, same as I protect you."

"Of course. Your ethics and all." Another sigh bubbled forth. "Mandy Geary. If they are going after her, you may be in danger too, Mr. Killeen. It might be a good thing to have that ham-handed deputy close by, after all."

"I already figured out I might be in danger. Getting shot at was kind of a hint. But having that jerk around won't make me feel any safer. Shit, I think he'd just as soon kill me as spit on me."

"He might, but the person he's working for plays a more subtle game. Or at least he used to."

The trees rustled in a gust of wind, and Jason shivered. "I don't get it. This is all connected to some of kind of super-secret military research crap from twenty years ago, right? That DARPA contract you told me about. But why is it coming to a head now?"

"There are those who hope to profit from that research, of course."

"But it looks more like the Gerion Group wants to cover it up, not profit from it. Otherwise why kidnap Brent's parents, or kill this Mandy person?"

"You speak of the Gerion Group like it was a person, with desires all its own."

"Well, it's not a person, it's a corporation. But that doesn't mean the owners don't have desires and plans."

That annoying, all-knowing chuckle erupted again. "Owners? Really? You think anyone *owns* a big corporation like the Gerion Group? It's owned by fifty state pension plans, dozens of banks, insurance companies, and mutual funds. Thousands of people own it. So many different people own it that no one owns it."

"That's stupid. Of course the stockholders own it and control it. Who else?"

"Ah, well, you've identified the nub." Another sigh. Jason was sure now the caller was stopping to take a drag on a cigarette. "Ownership isn't control, and control isn't ownership. What *matters* is control. That's what people lust after. Control and power. All that money, all those resources. That's power. Unlimited power, since those who control it really aren't answerable to anyone. Least of all the *owners.*"

Jason frowned. "So what? You're saying that there's an internal battle for control of the Gerion Group? And the factions are *killing* people? I don't believe it."

"Please, Mr. Killeen. Don't disappoint me now. The evidence is right there, in plain sight, if you'd only look." Another sigh. "Follow your leads. One side wants to cover up events from twenty years ago. The other side thinks they can use those events to bootstrap themselves into power. Trust no one. Stick by Mr. Hyde and that friend of his, Mr. Dixon. Use your brain to figure this out. You don't have much time." Deep Throat paused, and a hiss of static filled the moment of silence. "Your van will work now." The phone went dead.

Jason scowled and swore. "Bastard. Tell me what you fuckin' know; don't play games with my head." He stuffed the phone back in his pocket and slammed into the driver's seat of the van. Without much expectation, he cranked the engine. It turned over at once and hummed as if nothing had ever been wrong. "Bastard."

He glanced at the button on the rearview mirror that activated the van's built-in cell phone. A memory nibbled at his brain, something about using mobile networks to hack into a car's internal computers. The electrical engineering department had gotten a big grant from Daimler-Benz on automotive security systems. Maybe that was it. He'd drop by tomorrow, if he had time, and ask them. For sure, Purcell wasn't the only one who was screwing with his car.

He stared into the dark street and thought about his source's words. Follow the leads. Stick with Brent *and* that asshole Gary. That's what Deep Throat said. The bastard had been right so far. He pounded on the steering wheel and tried to calm himself. *As God is my witness, I will get to the bottom of this.* He knew what he had to do.

He jerked the van into gear and lurched forward toward the car wash.

Chapter
EIGHTEEN

RACHEL strode down the polished white corridor of the Stillwell Research Center until she came to a sign announcing the "Otis P. Strong Microbiology Laboratory." Someone had taped a cartoon underneath showing a fat rodent lounging in an enormous mound of trash with the caption, "Rat's nest? *Rat's nest?* Of *course* it's a rat's nest! What were you expecting?" A smile tugged at her lips as she surveyed the disarray on the other side of the glass wall. It was as though a thousand researchers, each with an OCD obsession for tiny vials of colored fluid, had jammed their individual collections into this one room. Despite the wide lab benches, expansive windows, and blinding white color scheme, the overall impression was of hopeless chaos. Graduate students, clad in stained white coats, huddled amidst the bottles, microscopes, computer screens, laser printers, and nameless liquids bubbling through miles of glass tubing.

She took a deep breath and pushed into the room. Memories of her high school biology lab made her expect formaldehyde, ether, maybe ammonia or other putrid odors, but only a faint burnt-sugar scent lingered in the air. She paused next to a young woman who sat peering into a microscope. "Excuse me, ma'am."

The woman pushed a strand of dangling, greasy hair behind one ear, but otherwise did not acknowledge Rachel's words.

She cleared her throat and tried again. "Excuse me, miss? I wonder if you could tell me how to find Dr. Athair?"

No response. Rachel thought perhaps she was hearing impaired, so she touched the woman's shoulder. The tech finally jerked her gaze away from her equipment, and her watery, myopic eyes scanned Rachel from head to toe. "Who are *you?* This is a closed lab. You shouldn't be here." She scowled and turned back to her microscope.

Rachel gripped her arm until the technician looked up. "I'm Special Agent Rachel Morrison, FBI." She pulled her ID card from her shoulder bag and held it up. "I have an appointment with Dr. Sonja Athair, and her assistant said she'd be in this lab."

The woman peered at the ID. "FBI? What's the FBI want with the Dragon Lady? You gonna arrest her?"

Rachel kept her voice steady. "I'm not going to arrest her. I just need to ask her some routine questions. Can you please tell me where I can find her?"

"Sure. She's over at the Q24 pyrosequencer."

"And where would that be, Miss...." Rachel paused to read the woman's nametag, "Uhlferts?"

"On the other side of the lab." Uhlferts waved a hand at the far right corner of the room. "Look for a big white box with a blue hood. You can't miss Dr. Athair—she's the Dolores Umbridge clone."

Rachel wondered if she'd wandered into another world. "Who?"

"You know. From *Harry Potter*." Seeing Rachel's blank look, she rolled her eyes. "Geez, what planet you *from*, anyway? Think June Cleaver, if that helps." Uhlferts turned back to her microscope. "Now if you'll excuse me, I got work to do before my three thirty class."

Rachel trudged in the direction Uhlferts had pointed, where she found an attractive older woman reading an array of numbers and letters scrolling across a computer screen. "Dr. Athair?"

The woman glanced at Rachel, and then her face split in a wrinkled smile. She pressed a key on the console, and the screen froze. "You must be Agent, uh, Fredrickson, was it?" She held out her hand.

"Special Agent Rachel Morrison, ma'am." She returned Athair's limp handshake and showed her ID. "Is there someplace we can talk?"

"There's a faculty lounge just down the hall. We should have some privacy there." She pronounced "privacy" with a short *i*, like a Brit, even though her speech burred with a flat Iowa twang.

When they were in the corridor, Athair asked, "What was this about again? One of my students?"

"I'd just like some background information about Mr. Brent Hyde. You're his landlady, right?"

"Yes. I'm his advisor too. Here we are." She held open a door marked *No Admittance* and glanced inside. "Good. It's empty. Please have a seat. Would you like coffee or a soft drink?"

"I'm fine, thank you." Rachel perched on the edge of an overstuffed leather armchair and cast her gaze over the Danish modern décor. The room was large enough to hold a dozen or more people without feeling crowded. A window filled one entire wall, looking out onto the parking lot. An abstract painting, all swirls of brilliant greens, yellows, and blues, covered another wall. Incomprehensible scribbles and diagrams crawled across a whiteboard hanging next to the door.

Athair stood in a small kitchenette in the corner, where an espresso machine buzzed, grinding and brewing her coffee. "You sure you don't want a cup? This is the best coffee you can get in Iowa. Dr. Holmes has a cousin who imports the beans from their plantation in El Salvador."

Rachel permitted a thin smile to form on her lips. "I'll pass for now, thank you."

"Your loss." Athair settled into a matching leather chair opposite Rachel, leaned back, and sipped her steaming brew. "Thanks. I needed a caffeine break." Her expression turned from sybaritic to serious. "Is this about Brent's parents? Is there any news?"

"We're still looking. You'll understand that I can't say more."

She nodded. "Sure. You can't discuss an active case. I'll do whatever I can to help. Poor Brent is beside himself."

"You've spoken to him since they disappeared?" Rachel pulled out her phone. "You won't mind if I record our conversation?"

"Go ahead. Less chance for error." She took another gulp of coffee. "I brought Brent some stew when he got home yesterday and sat with him for a while."

Rachel rested her elbows on her knees and held her phone in both hands in front of her.

"He doesn't live in your home?"

"No, in the apartment above my garage. I rented it to him last year, when he was a freshman."

"So you can see his comings and goings?"

"I guess. Not that I keep track of what he does. None of my business."

"So you don't know exactly when he left for this last visit home?"

Athair frowned. "I didn't say that. He mows my yard as part of his rent. He finished that about three in the afternoon, two days ago. I remember because I was just leaving for a movie. *The Black Swan*. You should see it. Really remarkable performances."

"But you didn't see him actually leave?"

"No. But he said he was going to take a shower and then head out. I imagine he left in the next thirty minutes or so. His pickup was gone when I got back, but that was around six thirty."

Rachel nodded. "I understand you called the local sheriff that evening, to see if they had any information about accidents. You were looking for Brent's parents?"

"That's right. I called some local hospitals too. A friend of his phoned about the time I got home and asked me to check things out. Brent was worried, and it's unlike his parents to just disappear like that."

"So you knew his parents?"

"Casually. I met them several times when they visited. We went out to dinner once or twice here in town, and they invited me to a family picnic at their farm last July Fourth."

"What kind of relationship did Brent have with his parents?"

Athair scowled and leaned forward. "A happy, healthy one, as far as I can tell. What are you getting at, Agent Morrison?"

"You have no reason to think there was any conflict between them?"

"None. Are you implying that he *did* something to them? I don't believe it."

Rachel ignored her questions. "How about financial problems? You're his landlady. Was there ever a problem with the rent?"

"Absolutely not." Athair leaned forward, and her voice carried conviction. "This is a stable, loving family. By all evidence, the family finances are sound."

Rachel kept her voice steady, while wondering how Athair could know about the family finances. *May as well ask.* "What evidence is that?"

The older woman's husky voice tensed, and her eyes crinkled with impatience. "I'm on the college scholarship committee. We make families file a financial statement when students apply for aid, a FAFSA." She frowned. "I've already said more than privacy laws permit. You probably need a warrant before I can be more explicit."

Before Rachel could ask another question, the door swung open and a tall man with a hawk's nose, flowing gray hair, and brooding eyes strutted into the room, his immaculate white lab coat streaming behind him. Athair rose to her feet and faced him. "Aaron, how are you? Any word on Clark?"

He cocked an eyebrow at her. "He's still missing, the little twerp. But thanks for asking, Sonja." He walked to the kitchenette, and the coffee machine buzzed again. A heavy sigh passed his lips. "I swear, he's no better than his mother. Not too bright, irresponsible, inconsiderate, especially after all I've done for the two of them."

Athair *tsked* at him. "I'm so sorry, Aaron. You deserve better."

"Well, it is what it is. I can't live their lives for them." His gaze landed on Rachel, and his eyebrows went up. "I thought I knew everyone who worked here." He stuck out his hand. "Professor Aaron Holmes. I run this lab."

Rachel stood, accepted his handshake, and showed him her ID. "Special Agent Rachel Morrison, FBI, sir."

He blew on his coffee and then remarked, "Ah, that explains it. Are you doing a background check on someone? Maybe for our DARPA project out at Grange Station?"

Athair saved Rachel from having to respond. "She's investigating a missing persons' case—the parents of one of our students. Brent Hyde."

He shook his head. "Brent Hyde? That name's familiar."

Athair glanced at Rachel before she spoke. "He works in my lab. You may have seen him around. He's often here with his friend, Gary Dixon?" She turned to Rachel. "Gary works for Grace Development, the company that manages the security here and at Grange Station."

Rachel nodded. "Interesting. I thought he was just a trainee...."

Holmes interrupted her. "Ah yes, I recall Mr. Dixon quite well." He sipped his coffee and seemed to gather his thoughts. "His superiors at Grace Development think very highly of him, very highly indeed. I recall speaking to Mr. Dixon just last week. Well spoken, well built, and quick witted. Excellent stock. Now *he's* someone a father could be proud of," he simpered as he took a sip of coffee. "You say his friend's parents are missing?"

Rachel nodded. "Yes."

He peered at her. "And the FBI is involved. That's… interesting." He paused for a gulp of coffee. "Do you suspect foul play, Agent, uh…."

"Morrison, sir. I'm afraid I can't comment on an open investigation."

He gave her a smug little smile. "Well, then, I guess that answers my question, doesn't it? If you didn't suspect foul play, why would you be investigating? Do you have any leads? You must, or you wouldn't be in my labs, disrupting our important research."

"I'm just trying to get some background information on young Hyde, sir."

Athair said, "Brent's a Stillwell Scholar, Aaron. He's worked in my epigenetics lab for over a year."

His lips turned up, and he beamed at Rachel. "Well, if he's a Stillwell Scholar, then I can tell you he must be a fine young man. We have the highest standards."

Athair's gaze stayed locked on Rachel. "I personally nominated him, Aaron. You remember: Brent Hyde."

His face froze for an instant before he nodded. "Quite. And now his parents are missing, you say? I do hope that doesn't interfere with his studies in any way. Will he need financial assistance? I'm sure I can arrange something."

Rachel glanced at her phone to be sure it was still recording. "Why would you think he needs financial assistance, sir?"

He rolled his eyes. "You did say his parents were missing, didn't you? Isn't it customary for young people to get assistance from their parents? I know my deadbeat daughter and her knucklehead son Clark expect that from me, and they're adopted, not even genetically related."

Rachel blinked. "Your grandson is Clark Holmes, sir? I understand he's missing too. I know local law enforcement is working on the case."

Holmes shrugged. "I'm sure he's off drunk someplace, too inconsiderate or inebriated to contact anyone. In any case, if Mr. Hyde needs financial help, I'll be there for him. It's the least I could do for Mar... for his parents." He took a quick sip of his coffee. "Surely they haven't abandoned him. Foul play, you say? Any suspects?"

Rachel kept her voice steady, even as her eyes inspected his expression. "I didn't say there was foul play, sir." She turned to Athair. "Thank you for taking time to talk to me. Your assistant has my card. If you think of anything else, no matter how trivial it might seem, please call me."

Athair's features had paled, but her expression remained calm, controlled. She quirked her lips, glanced at Holmes, and then looked down. "I'll be sure to do that, Agent Morrison. Brent is special to me... to everyone here who knows him."

Holmes clasped an arm around Athair's shoulder. "All our students are special. If you need any help, Agent Michelson, just give me a call. I can pull strings in Washington if needed. The Director of the FBI is a personal friend of mine, and so are both our senators."

Rachel resisted the temptation to correct him about her name. "Thank you, sir, but I don't think that will be necessary." She nodded to both and escaped back into the hallway, where she leaned against the door. *How did that asshole know Mary Hyde's first name? Athair knows more than she's telling too.* Rachel clenched her jaws and marched out of the building, more determined than ever to get to the bottom of this case.

Chapter
NINETEEN

BRENT closed his eyes and tried to relax in the backseat of Jason's van. Gary sat next to him, his fingers tapping on the armrest, matching the rhythms of the alternative rock that pulsed from the radio. The steady thump of the tires against the expansion joints on the old two-lane highway fought against the insistent drumbeat from the speakers. The throbbing behind his eyes added to the cacophony of cadences in his head. The song transitioned from the clangor of Linkin Park's "Waiting for the End" to the lament of Coldplay's "Clocks." His heart tried to find synchronicity in the sounds, but there was none.

He opened his eyes when the radio's volume diminished and Jason's voice called from the front seat. "You guys doin' okay back there?"

Gary leaned forward and answered, "We're fine. How much farther?"

"GPS says about ten minutes. I've been thinking we should stop at the restaurant where she worked, to see if we can pick up any local gossip."

Gary shrugged and looked out the window. "Whatever."

Brent turned his gaze to the endless fields of corn that lined the highway. Ancient glaciers had scraped the land flat here so that the rows of tasseled plants stretched to infinity. He leaned his forehead against the window and let his breath fog the glass. Worry about his parents still hovered over him. In fact, it was becoming familiar, in the same way the gap left by a missing tooth becomes familiar to one's tongue. Their absence was part of his reality, plowing furrows into the contours of his being.

The van slowed as it entered the village of Lost Springs. A cheery sign, surrounded by a colorful splash of flowers, welcomed visitors to "Iowa's Carnation Capitol." A row of well-kept homes, all white with black trim, gave way to a block of ornate Victorian brick storefronts that constituted the commercial district. Jason pulled into a diagonal parking space and announced, "Here we are. Floyd's Pig Shack. You think maybe it specializes in barbecue?"

Gary's voice dripped with scorn. "Sounds delicious. Just what I'd like for a fucking midmorning snack."

Brent ignored both of them, climbed out of the van, and stretched. The fresh country air filled his lungs, and he caught the scent of bacon wafting from the restaurant. Sunlight warmed his face as he scanned the street. Half a dozen beat-up pickups were parked nearby, and an elderly man with a grizzled white beard sat dozing on a park bench in front of Floyd's. Two dogs of indeterminate breed romped on the sidewalk before disappearing around a corner, their tails swishing in canine glee. Otherwise, the street was vacant. He turned to Jason. "What's next? Do we just go in and start asking questions?"

Jason shook his head. "That won't work. We order coffee and chat first, friendly-like, and hope they warm up to us. Come on." He pulled the door open and stood to one side while Gary and Brent entered. As they passed, he whispered, "Sit at the counter."

Gary shuffled inside and slouched, elbows on the polished surface, with a bored expression on his face. Jason detoured to the cash register, and Brent followed him. Someone had taped a photo of a smiling, overweight woman in a waitress uniform to the back of the register. A sign pasted to a jar underneath read, "In loving memory of our neighbor and coworker, Mandy. Her daughter Brenda Ann requests friends make a donation to the Lost Springs Humane Society in lieu of flowers."

Brent opened his wallet and added a twenty to the fives and tens in the jar. "That's so sad. I'm sure her daughter must miss her." He thought of his mother and blinked back tears.

Jason added another twenty. "She has a nice smile." He touched Brent's arm. "Let's sit."

Brent took the stool next to Gary, who tilted an eyebrow at the photo. "That the old lady we read about online?"

Jason slipped into the seat next to Brent and nodded. "Mandy Geary. She looks like someone's grandmother. Why would anyone do something like that to a nice old lady?"

A strawberry blonde waitress, middle-aged and with red-rimmed eyes, wiped the counter in front of them. "It's just awful. You boys friends of the family?"

Brent read the name Cindy stitched in elaborate embroidered script on the bosom of her uniform.

Jason shook his head. "No, we didn't know her at all. We just saw the news story about her death on TV, up in Middleton. It's awful that anyone could do something like that, but to an old lady... well, it just breaks your heart, that's what it does."

Brent blinked. All traces of New Jersey had vanished from Jason's speech, replaced by the flat, nasal twang of the local dialect.

Cindy pulled a wad of lacy handkerchief from her apron and swiped at her eyes. "We're all in shock. We ain't never had no murders here."

Jason shook his head. "What's the world coming to?"

She sniffed, and a smile quivered on her lips. "I saw you boys make a donation. That's real good of you, what with you bein' strangers here and all."

Jason nodded. "It was the least we could do, and it's for a good cause."

"Poor Mandy. She did love animals." She blinked back tears. "I took Puddin, her cat. The poor thing's just been cryin' his little heart out, he misses her so. Just as things was lookin' up for her too."

Brent thought he could see Jason's ears perk up, like a dog around a bone. "How's that, Cindy?"

She leaned forward and spoke in a loud whisper. "She told me she was gonna come into big money, just any day." Her voice returned to normal as she wiped the counter. "Poor Brenda Ann—that's her daughter, Brenda Ann. She didn't know nothin' 'bout it, though, so maybe she was jest whistlin' Dixie."

Gary squirmed on his seat. "I could use some coffee."

Guilt flooded Cindy's features. "What am I thinkin', flappin' my jaw when I got customers. I'm so sorry." She turned, pulled three cups from a shelf and a carafe from a burner. While she poured, she asked, "You boys need a menu? Moe can still fire up the griddle if you want pancakes."

Jason poured sugar into his steaming cup. "I could use one of those donuts I saw over by the register."

Brent chimed in with, "Me too."

Cindy turned to Gary. "How 'bout you, son? What'd you do to your arm, anyways, you poor thing?"

Gary's lips emitted a little *hmph.* "I got shot." His lip curled when he looked at the donuts. "Just coffee for me."

"Oh, hon, bless your little heart. Seems like folks is getting' shot all over the place. What happened?"

Jason's gaze followed her as she loaded glazed donuts onto two plates. When Gary didn't answer, he spoke. "It happened the same night poor Mandy was killed. Somebody took potshots at us on Brent's parents' farm, up by Bellevue."

"Anybody else git hurt? I don't recall hearin' about that; we've all been so stirred up about what happened to Mandy."

Brent shook his head. "No. Except my parents are missing. I came home for the weekend, and they were just gone."

She *tsked* while she served them. "I'm so sorry to hear that. You know, though, my folks went on a second honeymoon a couple years back and didn't tell nothin' to nobody. They jest took off to Texas without a never-you-mind. I didn't even know they was gone 'til I got a postcard from Brownsville. Maybe your folks is jest on vacation someplace?"

"I hope so. The FBI sure doesn't have any clues on where they might be, or who shot at us, for that matter."

"The FBI, you say? They'll find 'em, you'll see. But that's not like here. Somebody snuck into Mandy's trailer and shot her, right between the eyes, poor thing. Whoever done it stole a big tip she got that very night, right from her purse. They took a photo from her dresser too. And them big-city cops from Clinton, they's about as useless as tits on a boar, excuse my French. They ain't got no idea who done it."

"Both of these cases are a mystery, that's for sure." Jason peered at her from over his coffee mug. "Strangest thing, Cindy. A friend of Brent's parents told us that his mother and Mandy worked together, years ago, at Grange Station."

Cindy frowned and bit her lower lip. "You mean that old hospital for them re-tarded kids, up in Middleton?"

"That's the one."

"Funny you should mention that. Mandy and me was talking about that place jest a coupla weeks ago. And Brenda Ann—did I mention that's Mandy's daughter? Brenda Ann told me yesterday that the photograph what's missin' was of her momma and some of her friends, from back when she worked there. She said it was somethin' her momma always kept close by, in her bedroom. Anyways, that was way back, a-fore she got herself preg... well, before she had Brenda Ann and moved herself here."

Jason tipped his head. "Really? You say Mandy mentioned the hospital recently?"

The bell over the door jangled, and an older man in overalls and a crisp denim shirt sauntered inside. He nodded to the waitress and spoke in somber tones. "Mornin', Cindy. Sorry to hear 'bout Mandy." A chair squeaked against the floor as he pulled it out and sat at a table.

"Be right with ya, Mort." She turned back to Jason. "Yeah. Let me chew on that while I take care of old Mort. Don't go 'way." She grabbed a mug and the carafe of coffee and hustled to Mort's table.

Gary rolled his eyes. "That old bat isn't going to tell us anything. This is a waste of time."

Jason glowered at him. "Don't talk like that. I like her. She's genuine, and she cares about her friend."

"Don't tell me how to talk, you little...."

Brent put a finger to his buddy's lips. "Shhh. Be nice, now. I know your arm hurts, but Jason's helping us. Let's follow his lead." He stared into Gary's golden eyes and wanted to hold him, to make his sore arm better, just like Gary had held him after Matt left. His arm must have hurt bad. That must have been why he was being so grumpy.

"Whatever." Gary hunkered over his coffee and scratched at a rash on his wrist.

Brent and Jason munched on their donuts in silence, but Brent watched Gary from the corner of his eye. Brent thought again about giving him a hug, but decided the locals might not like the idea of two men embracing.

Cindy started a fresh pot of coffee brewing before she returned to where they sat. "I been thinkin' 'bout what Mandy said. Back in the '90s, there was this TV show 'bout this real smart guy. He was raised to be a super soldier or somethin', but he escaped and went around doin' good deeds while this evil scientist chased him. He was so smart he could fool doctors into thinkin' he was a surgeon, or trick the cops into thinkin' he was FBI. He could fool anyone into thinkin' he was anything."

Brent frowned. "Do you mean *The Pretender*?"

"That's it! It's on late-night reruns now, on channel nine. That actor, he was real good-lookin'."

Jason's eyes twinkled. "He was indeed. I remember the show well. Does this have something to do with Mandy?"

"Oh, yeah. I never thought much about it at the time, but I mentioned to Mandy about how Billy Edwards looks just like the guy on that show. Billy teaches third grade at our school here in town, jest down the street? Anyways, Mandy told me she thought that show was based on real life."

Brent diverted his attention from Gary's profile, squinted at her, trying to follow her meandering chain of thought. "You mean Mandy thought this Edwards person was like the Pretender?"

"No. Bless your heart, ain't you payin' attention, hon? I said they *looked* alike, is all. But Mandy said that she worked at a military hospital with a little kid like in that show. He had his own special school, where they learned him how to fire rifles and build bombs. Crazy stuff."

When Jason spoke, a hint of New Jersey reappeared in his accent. "You mean she said Grange Station was that kind of place? A military experiment to breed super soldiers?"

"Well, she never said for sure where it was. But that's the only hospital she ever talked about workin' at. 'Ceptin' she always said that Grange place was for re-tards, so I never gave it no mind. But now, with all these people gettin' shot, and the po-lice not havin' no clues 'bout nothin', ya gotta wonder. I bet it's jest like that Area 51 place, where they got them flyin' saucers and space aliens hid, 'cept it's right here in Iowa."

Gary rubbed his eyes and yawned. "Right. It's all a government conspiracy. They're covering up space aliens, breeding super soldiers, and building a secret NAFTA superhighway."

She nodded at him. "You got that right. It's all part of that there New World Order. Reverend Chambers says it's a sure sign the Rapture is soon to be upon us, praise the Lord." She gave them a narrow look. "Is you boys saved? I can ask the reverend to say a special prayer for you at the meetin' tonight. You're welcome to join us."

Jason put a bill under his coffee cup. "Thank you, Cindy, but we've got to be on our way. Tell you what, though. Ask the reverend to pray for Brent, Gary, and Jason, will you?" He added a second bill. "That's for the plate at tonight's meeting, okay?"

Gary rolled his eyes again, but Brent tipped an eyebrow at him and shook his head before he turned back to Cindy. "Thank you for your prayers. And we'll say one for Mandy."

"Bless you, son." She pulled out her wadded up hanky and dabbed at her eyes.

Once they were outside, Gary turned to Jason and snarled, "What the fuck was *that* about? Don't tell me you're a Jesus freak?"

"As it happens, my parents are Jewish, and I'm more or less an agnostic."

"All that conspiracy crap is bullshit. Super soldiers, my ass."

"Look, I don't agree with her conclusions, but we still confirmed the connection between Mandy and Brent's mother. We've also got a second person saying there was a military connection back then with Grange Station. That's something."

"I don't believe anything that old biddy said." He spat. "*Pray* for us. That's the way these hicks insult you. Or are you too stupid to figure that out?"

The corners of Jason's mouth turned down. "I think she was trying to be nice, so I was nice back by respecting her and her beliefs. You might, you know, try it sometime."

Brent ignored them and waited next to the van for Jason to unlock the doors. As he glanced across the street, he spotted Purcell's cruiser. The portly deputy sprawled in the front seat, smoking a cigarette. A sardonic smile twisted the man's lips, and he stroked his brow in a two-fingered salute directed at the three of them.

A chill shivered down Brent's spine as he recalled the threats from the FBI agent last night. Maybe there was something to this conspiracy crap after all.

Chapter TWENTY

BRENT woke from a catnap as Jason's van bounced to a stop in front of his garage apartment. He rubbed his face with his palms and then squinted out the windows against the midafternoon sun. A smile tugged at his lips at the sight of Dr. Athair kneeling at her rose bushes with a floppy polka-dot hat shading her eyes. She tossed a merry smile their way, stripped off her gardening gloves, and headed down the driveway.

Gary glanced at his watch and sneered, "It's about time we got back. I've got a doctor's appointment in less than twenty minutes." He rubbed his arm. "I hope I get rid of this damned sling."

Jason's jaw muscles writhed, and he seemed about to speak, so Brent interrupted. "I hope so too. Do you want me to go along?"

Gary shook his head. "I'll be fine. But I need to leave now if I'm going to make it across town to the doctor's office. I should be back in a couple of hours at most." He slipped out of the van and trotted to his sports car, parked on the street in front of them. "Hey, Dr. A. Good to see you. Gotta run!" He blew a kiss her way, jumped into his car, and sped off before she could respond.

Brent clambered out of the backseat, slammed the door, and stretched. When Jason got out and joined him, Brent cocked an eyebrow at the reporter and remarked, "Thanks for taking us to Lost Springs, but I'm not sure how much we accomplished."

Jason shrugged. "Every bit of information, even negative information, is useful."

Dr. Athair's husky alto chimed in. "Spoken like a true scholar." She stuck out her hand. "I don't think we've met. I'm Sonja Athair."

He accepted her hand. "Jason Killeen, ma'am. Pleased to make your acquaintance." A wry grin creased his lips. "I'm afraid I'm just a reporter, though, not a scholar."

"Pish and tosh. Reporters gather evidence, form hypotheses, and reach conclusions, just like scientists do." She turned her smile on Brent. "How are you this afternoon, dear? You look more rested."

"I'm good, Dr. Athair. Still no word on my parents, though."

She ran her fingers through his hair. "You poor thing. I'm sure they'll turn up soon." She glanced back up the driveway. "Why don't you two boys come on up to the house? I made chocolate chip cookies this afternoon. I'll fix us a fresh pot of coffee, and you can sit a spell. How's that sound?"

"I'd love that." He turned to Jason. "She has the best coffee."

"That's what comes from knowing people who own a coffee plantation in El Salvador." She chuckled. "Come on, then. I've got something to show you besides cookies."

Brent and Jason followed her up the driveway, through the side door, and into her kitchen. The scent of cookies and flowery air freshener failed to hide the lingering, stale odor of thousands of cigarettes that permeated her home. Sunlight speckled through the frilly drapes at the windows and bounced off the bright yellow walls and the dark oak cabinets. Her fingers fluttered toward the colonial dinette in one corner, where a stack of cookies rested on a plate. "You boys just have a seat while I get things started."

Brent lounged back and relaxed, while Jason perched in his chair as his gaze stayed glued to their hostess. He cleared his throat and asked, "So, what kind of doctor are you, Sonja, if you don't mind me asking?"

She threw him a cheery grin. "Always the reporter, I see. I'm a professor of applied psychology and neurosciences at the university."

Brent chimed in, "She's one of the best teachers I've ever had. She's also a world-famous researcher in epigenetics."

Jason blinked. "That's what you told me about at Ruby's, right? Two-faced cows? Stuff like that?"

Dr. Athair flounced back to the table with a manila folder in one hand. "Brent, what have you been telling this poor child? Two-faced cows, indeed." She reached out and squeezed her student's hand. "Epigenetics studies heritable changes in gene expression caused by mechanisms other than changes in the underlying DNA. Two-faced cows, or chickens with two beaks, are just examples. I specialize in more subtle behavioral changes."

Jason nodded. "You know, I'm pretty sure that's word for word what Brent told me. I'm not sure I understand it, but that's what he said too."

Her eyes sparkled. "It's an old field, but one that has increasing importance. Dr. Holmes is the real pioneer. His work on epigenetics and behavior continues to be groundbreaking." She opened the manila folder which she'd placed on the table. "But I wanted to show you something, Brent. I searched the online archives of the *Collier Clarion* from over twenty years ago. Look what I found." She shoved a printed copy of a microfiche from the student paper across the table toward him.

Brent scanned it, with Jason peering over his shoulder. "This is an article about my mother! It says she's a new research associate from Northwestern joining Dr. Holmes's project."

"Look at the date," Jason whispered.

"Twenty-two years ago." Brent's breath caught in his throat as whatever doubt he'd had before evaporated. "How can this be? Why wouldn't she tell me?"

Dr. Athair stroked his hand. "Honey, I don't know. I'm sure she had her reasons. According to the article, she was going to work at Grange Station. I'd just started working here on campus back then, over in Stillwell Hall where my labs are now. That must be why I don't remember her being here."

Jason's gaze bore into her, and his voice carried certainty. "That's another confirmed source. We've got to believe she worked there." He dropped his eyes to the article. "I thought Grange Station was just a hospital back then?"

She shook her head. "No, there's always been an agricultural lab out there too. It's still active, even though the hospital closed years ago. For some reason, the whole installation is secured: no one gets in without authorization."

Jason's eyes narrowed. "A secured agricultural lab? What are they working on? Germ warfare?"

She paused to munch on a cookie. "I don't see how. Last I heard they were studying *M. vaccae*. There's some kind of psychology experiment going on there too. I remember seeing a classified IRB agenda item about a year ago. That's really unusual."

"IRB?" Jason pulled out his phone. "You mind if I take some notes? What's IRB?"

Brent jumped in, glad to able to contribute something. "It's the Institutional Review Board. It has to approve all research involving human subjects." He turned to Dr. Athair. "But I've never heard of an IRB meeting being classified."

She nodded. "I haven't, either, but this one was. I seem to recall this was another Army contract. Maybe they're doing PsyOps research or something."

Jason narrowed his eyes. "What they're doing now isn't the point. It's what they were doing back then." He tapped his forefinger on the table. "I think we need to go out there and check out the older part, the hospital where Brent's mother worked."

Athair frowned, and for a moment her face turned cold and calculating before it relaxed back into their charming hostess. "I don't think you can get in. The security's really tight. *I* can't get in, and I've been with Dr. Holmes for twenty-four years. Besides the Army, that lab has contracts with several big agribusiness companies, and they're sensitive about trade secrets."

Jason shrugged. "Hey, they let me in last spring, for a report I was doing. It's not impossible. It just took a couple weeks to get approved. Besides, I'm not interested in growing tomatoes shaped like cubes or making goats give milk that they can weave into bulletproof vests. I just want to get into the older part, into building three."

Athair's face paled. "Where did you hear about the goat project?"

Jason scowled at her. "You mean they're really doing that? It was all over the news a few months back. I thought it was on a par with Elvis sightings or space aliens in the *National Enquirer*."

Brent pressed his fingers to his temples and closed his eyes. "Will you both wait a minute, please? I'm having a hard time taking this all in." He took three cleansing breaths and then gazed at Dr. Athair and Jason. "Okay, I know you both want to help. Let's stay focused on what we can do to find my parents, okay?"

Jason's voice was soft but determined. "I still think we need to figure out what happened back then. It's the only real lead we've got."

Dr. Athair nodded. "I have to agree."

Brent blinked and looked back at the old newspaper article. "Look, I'm not disagreeing. But what should we *do*? I mean, like now?"

Jason's finger tapped against the table again. "Dr. Athair, if we can't get in the active research station, how about the old hospital? Maybe there's something there."

She pursed her lips. "I can't imagine what would be there." A frown wrinkled her forehead. "I suspect you can get in that part of the Grange, though. There were some homeless people camped out there a year ago, and I don't think they ever did much to secure the place afterward. In fact… Brent, do you remember I told you about Clark Holmes?"

"Yeah. Did he ever turn up?"

"Not yet." A grim smile twisted her lips. "I think they haven't checked all the drunk tanks and fraternity houses yet. But his girlfriend said she last saw him at the old part of the Grange two nights ago. They were out for a thrill, or something."

Brent nodded. "It figures. That place is, like, the local haunted house. It's where the kids go on a dare, the scary place with ghosts. The Boy Scout camp counselors even told stories about the boogey man there." He rolled his eyes. "I'm not surprised that idiot Clark would take a date there. He's got real class."

"Now, dear, if you can't say something nice…." She stood and headed back to the counter. "Does everyone want coffee?"

Jason nodded, and Brent said, "Sure." He turned to the reporter. "Where did Ruby say my mother worked? Which building?"

"Building Three."

"And she said there was some kind of secret lab in the basement, right?" When Jason nodded, he continued. "All right, then. I want to see that lab. At the very least, it'll confirm Ruby's story. Maybe I'll be able to tell something from the lab layout too—what kind of research they were doing."

Athair returned to the table with three cups of coffee. "That place has been closed twenty years. I doubt that there's anything to learn from going there."

Jason stroked his chin. "You know, I don't see how it can hurt, and it might help." He dumped three teaspoons of sugar into his coffee and clinked his spoon against the mug. "I'd like to see it myself."

Athair's eyes widened, and she murmured, "It might not be safe. There was some kind of violence there last spring, with all those homeless people."

Jason shook his head. "I covered that story. The homeless people basically got attacked by some redneck yokels from town." His eyes narrowed. "Did you mention Clark Holmes? I think he was one of the ringleaders, and his parents pulled strings to keep him out of trouble with the law."

Decision firmed in Brent. "We're going there. It's where all the trails seem to lead." At least he was doing something positive, instead of waiting for someone else to act.

Jason agreed, "It's settled. You want to leave now?"

"No. I want to wait and bring Gary along." He dropped his eyes. "I hope you don't mind."

Jason frowned, seemed about to speak, but then stopped. His mouth turned down, and when he finally spoke, the words stumbled past his lips. "Bring him. I didn't mention my call from my source last night, did I?"

Brent raised his eyebrows. "No. What'd they say?"

Athair gaped at Jason and spoke at the same time as Brent. "What source?"

They stopped, stared at each other, and then she giggled. "Fill us in, Jason. Tell me about your source."

"I got started on this story because of a lead from an anonymous caller. I don't know who it is." He paused, looked her in the eye, and she nodded. "So far, this source has been reliable. He—or she, I'm not sure which—warned me about Brent being in danger the other night, when he got shot at. So anyway, I got this call last night, and Deep Throat—that's what I call my source—says to stick tight to Brent and Gary. Both of them."

She blinked, but her face was impassive. "Well, Gary does have security training. That company he's with, Grace Development, is supposed to be first rate. Maybe that's a good idea. Isn't he weapons qualified, Brent?"

"Yeah. He's black belt karate too. If there *is* any danger, he'd be good to have along."

Jason nodded. "He was quick on his feet at the farm when we got shot at too." His gaze swapped back and forth between the other two. "So we wait until he's back."

The need to act pressed on Brent. "But we go tonight. I want to see what's there." His eyes dropped again to the old newspaper story, and worry about his parents swamped him once more.

Chapter TWENTY-ONE

KIMBALL reveled in darkness.

He lounged in the back of his van and inhaled the aroma from a goblet of Alexander Valley Cabernet Sauvignon. The wine exuded a sweet, oaky nose with an undercurrent of spices: cedar, plum pudding, and perhaps a dash of fruitcake. He sighed, grateful for the sybaritic distraction while waiting for his target. He excelled at waiting.

His half-lidded eyes never left the monitors arrayed in front of him. The fuzzy images from the infrared cameras revealed a dusty parking lot, partially filled with beat-up cars. The heat signature from the nearby apartment complex glowed in the near distance. He'd opened the windows in the front seat of the van, and the lethargic sounds of a working-class neighborhood after bedtime fluttered through the darkness. A cat yowled in the next block, a dog barked, and a breeze whispered through the discouraged shrubs that littered the apartment entrance.

A van rattled into the parking lot, and Kimball leaned forward. He drew a careful sip from his wine glass before placing it on top of the rack of equipment in front of him. The sign on the side of the van read, "Middleton Shopper." Waiting was over.

He snatched up a small device, the size and shape of a television remote control, and pointed it at the vehicle. A skinny young man with a shaggy mop of hair stepped out of the driver's side. Kimball's fingers danced over his device as the man pointed his car keys at the door. When the lights flashed and the vehicle chirped, the man turned and slogged toward the apartment complex.

A grin pulled at Kimball's features. The device in his hand glowed for a moment, and then the screen flashed, "*le signal a reçu. sauf?*" He pressed the button marked "*oui*," and picked up his wine glass. Just to be sure, he'd wait another thirty minutes. Meantime, he slipped headphones over his ears and scrolled through his MP3 files. *Seigried Idyll.* Perfect.

WHEN the lush tones of Wagner's gift to his second wife faded to nothingness, Kimball removed the headphones and stretched. He slipped latex gloves onto his hands and flexed his fingers. His gaze flashed over his monitors one last time. A fast-food wrapper skittered across the parking lot, but he was alone. The apartment windows all gaped dark and empty, with no heat signature of a hidden face peering into the night.

Waiting was over.

Kimball slid the side door open and stepped outside. He scanned the exterior once more before he tugged the door closed. When it clicked in place, he paused to inhale the darkness. He wrapped the night about himself like a homeless person clings to a billionaire's discarded overcoat. The amber glow from a single street light marched in ragged rows of light and shadow across the scattered vehicles. The stench of weeks-old scraps of garbage moldering in the bottom of a dumpster fouled the air. He glanced up as wings rustled overhead. *Too late for a bird.* A shrug twisted his shoulders, and he wondered for a moment if bats scoured the night with him.

Without hesitation, he strode to the van. One hand aimed what was much more than a television remote control. He pressed a button. The vehicle chirped, the lights flashed, and the doors clicked open. His eyes narrowed in grim pleasure as he slid into the passenger seat.

The glow from the screen on the more-than-a-remote was enough for him to locate the diagnostic jack underneath the dash. In seconds he'd placed a tiny transponder, smaller than a USB jump drive, into the receptacle. When the display on his not-remote screen flashed, "*raccordement confirmé,*" he exited the van, relocked the doors, and ambled to his waiting vehicle. His eyes scanned the parking lot and the blank windows of the apartments, like a raven looking for mice. *Good. No sign of detection.*

Confidence welled inside him. This was almost too easy.

Two miles away, he stopped in the parking lot of his motel and crawled into the back of his van once more. With a few quick mouse clicks, he confirmed his connection with the other car's onboard computer. One by one the critical systems lit up: ignition, brakes, steering, accelerator, GPS. No need to follow the vehicle: the GPS would tell him where it was at any time, any place. If needed, he could disable the car, or even crash it by locking the brakes and steering.

As he shut down his computer systems, a flashing alert in the task bar caught his eye: two unread messages. He hesitated and then clicked on his e-mail program. Both missives were from Montel. The first, with a red exclamation next to it in the folder listing, demanded an immediate meeting. He scowled when he read the second.

Verloc. Urgent we meet at once. I'm in your hotel suite now. Where are you? Critical you respond soonest.

Just like that asshole to not bother to sign it. He pulled out his BlackBerry. No voice mail, no text messages. *What the fuck is so piss-urgent that he has to have a face to face instead of calling? He knows better than to jiggle my elbow when I'm on the job.* He tapped his forefinger on the mouse for a few moments before keying in a reply.

Lock on target secured. ETA to hotel five minutes. KV

While his systems shut down, he checked the Beretta in his ankle holster. *I don't trust this asshole any further than I can piss into a hurricane.* With the half-empty bottle of cabernet sauvignon in hand, he locked his van and headed toward the hotel.

He traipsed on heavy feet through the empty twelve-story atrium and into the glass-enclosed elevator, which whisked him to the tenth floor. The suites on this floor all had picture windows that faced onto the balcony that ran around the atrium. Curtains hid the interior of his suite, a dozen steps to his right, but a golden glow from the interior told him the lights were on. He hesitated at the door and caught the theme for Fox News from the television. He rolled his eyes and opened the door with his key card.

Montel lounged in the easy chair, an open bottle of Jack Daniels on the end table next to him and an ice-filled glass of whiskey in his fist. He glared as Kimball entered the room. "Where the fuck you been, dickhead?"

Kimball glanced at the open briefcase on the coffee table and the half-empty bottle of booze. He ignored Montel, but didn't miss the bulge at his shoulder that hid his weapon. *Jesus, it's the middle of the night, and this cocksucker still has a coat and tie on. His ass is so tight he must use tweezers to pull the shit out.* He retrieved a clean glass from the bar, poured himself a generous helping of wine, and settled into the sofa. He inhaled the delicate scent and took a luxuriant sip, letting the spicy liquid roll over his taste buds while he closed his senses against the blare of the television.

Montel leaned forward, his face white and his jaws rippling. "Answer my fucking question." He flicked off the television and tossed the remote toward the coffee table. He missed, and it tumbled to the floor.

Kimball gazed at him through slitted eyes. "I've been doing what you hired me to do. I've placed a bug on the reporter's vehicle. I followed the targets to Bumfuck, Iowa, earlier today, but the electronics will provide more effective use of my time."

"I want you sticking fucking close to them. You need to be ready to fucking take them out if I fucking call."

Kimball let a relaxed smile reveal his teeth. "Really, Montel, your profanity isn't very imaginative tonight. Do you know more words than 'fuck'?" A languid chuckle escaped his lips as his employer turned purple.

"If you like breathing, you'll be more respectful. Assfuck." He swilled whiskey and then refilled his glass.

Kimball decided he'd pushed his employer far enough, at least for now. "What brings you here tonight, Montel? I thought you didn't want any connection to my activities."

"I'll ask the questions, asswipe. Why did you waste time planting a bug on that twerp reporter's car? I've already *got* a bug on his car."

"You mean the one that oaf in a sheriff suit put on his van? The target found that one less than an hour after he placed it." He smiled when Montel turned even redder. "Anyway, what I did was better than a bug. I can take control of the vehicle whenever I want, through the transponder I left in the maintenance jack." Let Montel chew on that.

Instead of admiring his work, Montel snapped, "Don't sound so smug. The control systems for that brand link into the commercial cell phone network. It's about as secure as Times Square on New Year's Eve. We can control it without your crappy transponder."

Kimball sneered. "It would have been nice if you'd told me that. I don't have access to NSA resources like you do."

"I tell you what you need to know, you worthless prick. In the future, when I say jump, you ask 'how high?' You got that?"

Kimball sighed. "I got it. So what's so bleepin' urgent tonight?"

"There's been a change in status. We've uncovered evidence of another set of players out there."

Kimball's eyebrows wrinkled his forehead. "Another set of players? You mean besides the FBI and me?"

"Yeah. We think there's a rogue group in Gerion management trying to stage a hostile takeover of the company."

"And this affects me how?"

"We think they're after the same targets as you. We just don't know what they plan to do with them. We had an undercover agent watching the farm where you snatched the Hyde woman. A neighbor named Zimmerman." Montel paused to swirl his whiskey. "He's dead. Shot through the forehead."

Kimball savored another sip of wine. "Really? Tell me more."

"Looks like he got whacked in the woods near the farm, along with the Hyde woman's husband. Probably happened about the time you snatched her. Anyway, both bodies got dumped in Bear River. Zimmerman's stiff turned up that night at a DEA drug raid."

"Interesting." Kimball sniffed at the wine. "Any idea who had the contract?"

Montel swallowed whiskey and exhaled. "I've got a pretty good idea. The company's working on some defense contracts here at the university. The group behind the takeover seems to have hooks deep into that project."

Kimball gave a little laugh. "What? Some military ass-hats are thrashing about? DIA, maybe? Excuse me for the terror in my heart. They couldn't gather intelligence on a preschool birthday party if it was written up in the New York Times."

"Not DIA. Not even company security. We think they may be deploying assets from the project itself."

"Project assets? You mean weapons? Anything I need to be aware of?"

"Just stick to your targets like a fly on shit." Montel dug through the briefcase and handed Kimball a file. "The project's outside town, at a place called Grange Station. If they go there, text me at once."

Kimball opened the file and paged through the contents. "This is the site? Grange Station, you said? All I see is a bunch of cows, some kind of agricultural research crap, and some old, boarded up buildings."

"There's more than meets the eye. That's still an active research station, except it's mostly underground."

"So the cows are just a cover?"

Montel grunted and poured more whiskey. "Just watch out. This kind of intra-company fight can unleash all kinds of nasty shit. If the Gerion Group looks weak, other multinationals might get involved, fighting over the spoils like hyenas. The last time *that* kind of corporate warfare happened, the whole world economy tanked. If we screw this up, who knows what those greedy fucks will do." His face sagged, and weariness seemed to ooze from him. "I know this is just a job to asswipes like you, but don't fuck it up. There's too much at stake. If you get caught, they won't hesitate to squash you, assuming I don't get to you first." He lowered his head and massaged his eyes.

Kimball leaned back and savored his wine. "Under the circumstances, perhaps I should renegotiate my contract. Maybe get some hazardous duty pay."

Montel's head snapped up at that. "How's this for fucking hazardous duty pay, you dumb fuck. You screw this up, and I'll turn you over to this billionaire I know. He's got a special hospital he keeps in Thailand. Seems he gets his rocks off on butchering guys like you. He likes watching the expression in their eyes as he saws off body parts." He finished his whiskey and stood. "*Don't* fuck up, and we'll talk about a bonus you can put in the bank. *Do* fuck up, and you'll live a short and very painful life." He stormed out of the room, slamming the door after him.

Kimball leaned back and flipped through the folder Montel had left. A corporate takeover opened new opportunities, maybe new customers for his services. Perhaps the other side would even give him a contract on Montel. That would be a job he'd enjoy.

Chapter TWENTY-TWO

JASON squinted against the glare of headlights and edged the steering wheel to the right. When the oncoming pickup whizzed past, gravel spattered against the van and gritty clouds of dust obscured his view. Not that he could see much. The terrain undulated left and right, up and down, in hairpin turns and over steep hills. It was like driving on a roller coaster track, except that instead of soaring skyward the path snaked through a murky morass of trees and dense brush.

Gary twisted in the passenger seat next to him. He scratched at his leg and then pulled a pistol from the holster hidden in the small of his back, under his shirt, and removed the magazine.

Jason rolled his eyes. "That's, like, the tenth time you've done that since we left for Grange Station. Are you afraid the bullets will fall out or something?"

"It doesn't hurt anything to check."

Brent leaned forward from the backseat and spoke over the rattle of rocks against the tire wells. "Do you really think we need that? It kinda creeps me out. This place is supposed to be abandoned, after all."

Tension coiled in Gary's voice as he muttered, "We've been shot at, and you think we shouldn't be armed?"

Jason tapped the brake as the road narrowed to cross a one-lane wooden bridge. "Well, I'm glad he's got it, even if we don't really need it."

Gary glared at him. "What makes you so sure we won't need it?" He slipped it back into the holster and turned away to stare out the window. "Didn't that guy, Clark what's-his-name, disappear from here a couple nights ago?"

Brent chimed in. "Clark's an idiot. Everyone thinks he's off in a drunk tank someplace." He leaned forward and squeezed Gary's shoulder. "I'm glad you're along. I feel safer with you here."

That earned him a quick smile, even though Gary then snorted and jerked his shoulder away. "Watch my arm, will you? Besides, you just said I creeped you out."

"No. It's the pistol that does that. I mean, Dad and me, when we go hunting we use shotguns or a deer rifle. But a pistol? That's different."

A wry grin tugged at Jason's lips. "You mean a pistol is for human prey, right?"

Brent's image in the rearview mirror nodded at him. "I guess. I mean, I know that's not entirely true. But that's what it feels like tonight." He paused. "Like I said, I'm glad you've got it. But promise me not to use it unless you have to, okay?"

Gary's snort was even more derisive than before. "Gee, I was planning to blow away the first person we saw. Didn't Dr. Athair say there was homeless folks out here? They'd make good target practice, don't you think?" Jason glanced over, and Gary's eyes glinted at him. "What you think, buddy boy? You could write it up as an exclusive."

"Like I said, I'm glad you're along, and I feel better that you're armed." He slowed as the headlights flashed on a "No Trespassing" sign mounted on a rusty chain-link fence. "There's a wide spot in the road up ahead. Somebody want to check the GPS and see if we're close?"

His phone cast a ghostly gleam against Gary's face as he stroked the screen. "This looks as good as anything. Building Three should be about three-quarters of a mile that way." He pointed at an angle to the fence.

Jason nodded. "Assuming the Google Earth aerial photos were accurate, and we picked out the right buildings from the old newspaper stories." He pulled the van close to the fence and off the gravel. The engine dieseled for a couple of seconds before it rattled, coughed, and died.

Gary laughed. "Good job. Now anyone out there will know we're coming."

Brent hopped out of the backseat. "There's no one out there, except maybe some high school kids. We're more likely to scare them than the other way around."

Gary jumped out and ran to the fence. "There's an opening here, and a footpath. It looks like it's pretty well-travelled." The leaves jittered in a light breeze, and moonlight danced through the forest and speckled the scene.

Jason climbed out and clicked the key fob to lock the car. "Like Brent said, probably high school students." He turned on a flashlight and beamed it over the fence.

"Hey, what you think you're doing?" Gary snarled. "Turn that damned thing off. If there *is* anyone out there, we don't want to be targets."

Jason clicked it off. "I guess we can see by the light of the moon. It's brighter than I'd expected." He stuffed the light in his back pocket, just in case. "So, Gary, you've got the phone with the GPS. You want to lead us?"

"I wouldn't have it any other way, buddy boy." He bent sideways and stole through the fence and into the gloomy shadows. "Come on."

Jason let Brent go first, while waiting for his eyes to adjust. The sickly sweet odor of vegetation mixed with humid night air. As he strode down the path, leaves from the thick underbrush seemed to reach out and rub against his bare arms. Low-hanging branches grabbed at his shoulders and scratched his face. Vines coiled about his ankles like worms, or maybe snakes. He hated snakes. In fact, he hated the woods. He could swear that a thousand creepy-crawly bugs were already scampering up his pant legs and hiding inside his shirt. No doubt they'd be drilling into his body and leaving nasty little red welts under his skin before long. He shuddered and hugged himself. *Stay focused. One foot in front of the other. Don't fall.*

Brent came to an abrupt stop in front of him and Jason almost tripped. "What's up?" He rolled his eyes at his melodramatic whisper and tried again, in a normal voice. "What's up, guys?"

Gary waved a hand, and his voice hissed. "Shut up." He leaned forward, and Jason could swear he *sniffed*, like a cat or dog.

Jason forced down the giggle that bubbled in his throat.

Gary muttered, "Someone's had a campfire up ahead. Recent too. Not more than a couple of days ago."

Jason peered into the darkness. "Really? Where? I don't see anything?"

The moonlight shimmered in Gary's eyes when he turned to face them and point. "About a hundred yards that way. I can smell it."

Jason sniffed, but caught only the odor of rotting leaves. "I don't smell anything."

"It's there. I can smell blood too." He pulled out his handgun. "Be quiet."

Gary and Brent padded ahead, and Jason followed, watchful of snapping twigs and slapping branches. The path meandered up a steep hill to a small clearing. His two companions slid down an embankment, and Jason hesitated. It was only about a five foot drop, but it looked enormous. He squatted down and slid on his seat to the bottom. When he stood, he slapped at his clothes, and leaves, branches, and other detritus fluttered to the ground. He imagined tarantulas and baby rattlesnakes slithering off his skin and shuddered, before noticing the other two were about thirty feet ahead of him. He hastened after them and promptly twisted his ankle. He slammed into the trail with a thud and a sharp stinging pain on his hand. "Fuck me!"

In seconds, maybe microseconds, Gary was at his side. "I said shut up," he whispered.

Jason sat up and blinked. "I'm fine, thank you. No broken bones. Just a skinned palm." He stood and brushed himself off. "How did you *move* so fast?"

Gary glared at him. "Training." He pointed to the trail. "There's a sidewalk. Think you can walk on that without falling over your feet?"

Jason glanced down. Sure enough, the crumpled remains of an old, half-buried walkway lay hidden under the vines and dead underbrush. "I think so."

Brent's feet whispered through the underbrush, and he pulled at Jason's wrist. "Let me see. Are you sure you're all right?"

Jason snatched his hand back. "I'm fine. Are we there yet?"

Gary scowled at them. "I told you guys to be quiet. There's someone out here with us, watching."

Brent shrugged. "I heard something too. Sounded like a small animal to me, maybe a squirrel."

"It's no squirrel." He scratched his cheek with the barrel of his pistol and whispered, "Stay close, and don't make any noise. The buildings are only about fifty yards in front of us."

Less than thirty feet ahead, Gary stopped and cocked his head. He held up his palm. "Stay here. I'll be just a second." He crouched low and scuttled into the brush.

Jason peered after him. "Jesus, where did he go? He just disappeared."

"He's good at this, you gotta admit. I can barely see him myself."

As if from nowhere, a dark figure coalesced out of the darkness about twenty feet in front of them. He knelt, picked up a handful of soil, sniffed it, and then seemed to lap at it.

Jason's stomach tightened. "Shit. Who is that? And did he just *taste* the dirt?"

"I think it's Gary."

The figure stood, cocked its head as a breeze trifled with the leaves and odd scents roiled the air. In an instant, the shadowy figure rushed through the gloom, and Gary stood at their side. Rage flared in his whispered words. "Can't you guys be still for even ten seconds? Shut your fuckin' pieholes."

Jason opened his mouth to speak, but Gary held up a hand and he thought better.

Gary turned and scuttled forward, stopping at the ragged remains of an old hedgerow. When Brent hunkered down and crab-walked after him, Jason did the same, feeling like an idiot and silently cursing his sore ankle.

Gary's instincts apparently held true. They stopped when the forest opened into an abrupt clearing. Moonlight bathed the scene before them. In the middle distance, a two-story brick building squatted under the stars. Weathered planks boarded up the windows, and hoary vines crawled up the sides. Wooden steps sagged up to a rust-stained door.

The sign above the door was legible even in the flickering moonlight. Building Three.

Jason gasped and gripped Brent's shoulder. A man skulked along the wall of the building. He wore a long coat that billowed about his lean frame. His hair glimmered wild and white, snarling about his head like an albino Medusa's cap. His breathing whisked through the night air like bat's wings, wheezing from the gaping hole of his mouth.

His eyes were the worst. At first, Jason thought perhaps he had no eyes, only empty sockets that opened deep into his skull. But then he shifted, or perhaps the light shifted, or perhaps the evil inside his soul seeped out, and a dim green light lit those hollow orbs.

Jason trembled and looked away, but had to look back. This time, the man was just a man, with a haggard face, ragged clothes, and gloves with no fingers. He slid along the building, up the stairs to the entrance, and inside. Insubstantial as the promise of a dream, he vanished.

The wind carried an odd scent. Jason wrinkled his nose. He'd smelled that once before. He'd been writing an exposé about conditions at a slaughter house, and the stench had permanently seared its way into his psyche. He gagged and swallowed bile. Somewhere nearby, something was dead.

Chapter
TWENTY-THREE

JASON'S stomach roiled when the wind shifted and the stench of putrefying flesh wafted through the woods. He tried to kill the smell by pressing a finger hard against his upper lip. His hand hurt from where he'd skinned it, and he still imagined that bugs crawled over his skin and drilled little holes into his flesh. His arm itched, and he wondered if he'd gotten into poison ivy on top of everything else. He stared ahead and muttered, "I've got a bad feeling about this."

Jason glanced to his right where Brent emerged from the gloomy shadows. "Same here. There's something dead nearby." He made a sour face and pinched his nostrils together.

A small laugh erupted from Gary, on the left and just inside the cover of the trees. "Keep breathing normally. The smell will numb your olfactory nerves, and you won't notice it after a minute or so." He spoke in normal tones, and his gaze stayed focused on the clearing. He scratched his arm with the barrel of his gun.

Jason's nostrils clenched against the odor, but he took the advice and breathed in through his nose. "So I guess we don't have to be quiet anymore?"

That earned him a sneer from Gary. "You never *were* quiet, klutz. From the sounds that old guy made when he went inside, he went down a hall, closed a door, and then his footsteps faded out. If I can't hear him, he can't hear us."

Brent nodded. "That's what I heard too."

Jason flinched when, without warning, Gary crouched low and raced across the clearing to the building. Once there, he stood with his back to the wall, next to the door, and held his weapon pointing at the sky.

Irritation at the sudden movement turned Jason's mouth downward. "What the fuck's he doing? And what gives? I didn't hear a thing. You guys got super powers or something?"

Brent peered across the clearing at his friend. "He's casing the joint." He spoke in an overdone imitation of Edward G. Robinson from an old gangster movie, and then his tone returned to normal. "Trust me, I don't have super powers. But when we'd go hunting, my dad trained me to listen. I mean *really* listen. You city boys just don't know how to do that."

Gary had edged up the steps, where he inspected the door, pulled it open, and stepped into the dark building. A moment later, he reappeared in the doorway and waved them forward.

Brent trotted toward him, but Jason hesitated. His ankle still hurt from where he'd fallen, and this place still smelled like zombies could jump out at any instant. He sighed and hobbled to the steps where the others stood.

Gary rolled his eyes. "Look, if this is too much for your delicate constitution, you could just wait for us in the van." He reached down and scratched his leg before he turned back to face the interior.

Jason's face flushed. "I'm staying," he muttered, but Gary had already stalked off, followed by Brent.

The steps creaked and sagged under Jason's sneakers, and the door's rusty hinges resisted his push. He paused to examine the heavy padlock that hung on the unlatched hasp. The shackle glinted in the moonlight, as if someone had recently severed it with bolt cutters. *I guess that explains why this place is unlocked.* He pushed inside, where dust motes floated in faint columns of moonlight. The rays from Gary's flashlight roved over the interior. The second floor overlooked the entryway, and the starry night glimmered through a shattered skylight. Filth and broken floor tiles heaped at the edges of the corridor, while animal droppings, leaves, and dirt covered the rest. Near the stairs, the beam hesitated on a pile of discarded beer cans, a mattress, and used condoms.

Jason sighed, and the stench didn't seem so bad. Maybe his olfactory glands really were getting used to this. He clicked on his flashlight just in time to see something with wings flutter from a corner of the room and escape out the skylight. "Charming. I hope that was a bird and not a bat."

Gary's light traced a line down the hall. "He went this way." Without another word, he strode down the corridor, with Brent following.

A fly buzzed at Jason's head, and he waved it away. "How can you tell?"

Brent turned his head and answered, "There's a path. I can see where he walked. If you can't see it, just follow us. Stick close so you don't get lost."

Jason limped after them while he cast his light back and forth across the floor. Something with tiny claws skittered away, and red eyes shone at him from under a pile of leaves. "What the fuck's that?"

Gary's indifferent voice answered, "Rats." He stopped and held his ear to a door. "This is where he went. I don't hear anything on the other side." He stood to one side, his back to the wall, his gun at the ready, and pushed the door open.

The light from the flashlights bounced off the walls and reflected in shadowy waves of illumination across the three young men. Jason glanced at the other two and then pushed forward to stare into the chasm behind the door. Stairs descended into a Stygian darkness. Foul odors and faint animal chittering rose from the depths.

Brent pulled him back. "You're making a target out of yourself. Suppose he's armed?"

Adrenalin prickled in Jason's fingers. "Oh. I didn't think of that."

A tight little smile twisted Gary's features. "I did. Apparently he's not armed. Or not there. Down we go."

Jason scowled. "Wait a minute. Why are we following this guy? I thought the idea was to figure out what went on this building twenty years ago. Shouldn't we check out what's up here?"

Brent had already started down the stairs. "From Ruby's story, the secret stuff was all in the basement. That's what we need to check, whether that old homeless guy is down here or not."

Jason slapped another fly away from his face. "Are you sure you've thought this through?" No answer. He shrugged and followed the bouncing flashlight beams.

The stairs ended in a broad corridor with rusty armored walls on each side. Windows, their thick green glass smoky with dust and age, opened into impenetrable rooms. His two companions were already at the far end of the corridor, pushing open what looked like a bank vault door. "Wait up."

Gary vanished to the other side, but Brent waited. "You're limping. Are you okay?"

"I'm fine. I just twisted my ankle." He slapped at more flies. "Shit, this place is filthy with these fucking things."

"They're attracted to dead meat. We're getting close to whatever smells." He held the door and motioned for Jason to go ahead.

Gary had stopped about thirty feet ahead of them. His flashlight pointed down a side opening in the corridor. Brent trotted up to him. "What did you find? Oh…. Fuck." He and Gary disappeared around the corner.

Jason stumbled forward and stopped where he'd last seen his companions. Gary's flashlight beam held Brent like a spotlight. He knelt beside a pit filled with what looked like an enormous pile of rotting dinosaur excrement, covered with flaps of cowhide. A pasty white material filled the pit and congealed at the edges of the putrid flesh. Flies and other disgusting bugs flittered about him. "What the fuck is that?"

Brent turned a stricken face to Jason. The cold light turned his features pallid, and his eyes glowed like saucers. "It's a lye pit. And those are cows. Or what used to be cows."

Jason looked again. Was that an eye that stared at him? And those weren't ropes coiled in the depths. They were intestines. He stepped closer, and a rat skittered away. "Fuck. That's disgusting."

Brent stood and backed away. "They're pretty decayed, but I can tell that someone cut them up, just like the cows at home. They've excised their sexual organs, their udders, and removed their lips and tongues."

The sour taste of vomit burned at the back of Jason's throat. "Why would anyone do that?"

Gary circled around behind the pile of rotting flesh. "Get a load of what's behind the pit."

Against his better judgment, Jason followed Brent to the other side of the alcove. Something glistened in the rays of his flashlight, something not human. It had a head, and arms, and legs, but it looked deflated, like someone had let all the air out of a full-sized blow-up doll. It wore clothes too: sneakers, blue jeans, and a letter jacket from Middleton High School. Gary pushed at it with the toe of his shoe, and it slumped into sudden perspective. A human skeleton coalesced out of the muck, with ribs, a skull, and purple and blue goo where it should have flesh. Jason peered closer and spotted a dozen tiny, hairless creatures nestled where the *person* should have a stomach: babies suckling on a mother rat.

He rushed back to the main corridor, and sour vomit spewed and splattered onto the grubby tiles. Someone held his head and steadied him.

"You gonna be all right, man?" Brent's voice oozed calm.

"I think so. God, did you see that?" Another spasm gripped him, and he dry heaved. "Fuck." He pushed deep breaths in and out. "Okay. Okay." He stood and leaned against the corridor. "I'm not going to be sick again, but after seeing that I don't think I'll ever be *all right* either." Jason pulled out his handkerchief and swiped at his face.

"If you're done hurling, it's my turn." Brent leaned forward, put both hands on the wall, and spewed. "I wasn't ready for that."

Jason cast a reluctant glance back into the alcove. "How long you think he's been dead?"

Brent shrugged. "Hard to say. The decomposition's pretty advanced, but with the rodent infestation it could be as little as a couple of days." He shuddered and wiped his lips with his sleeve.

Gary stood watching with his hands on his hips, and laughing. "You two pansies about done?" Before they could answer, he spun on his heel and flashed his light down the corridor. "Who's there?" Footsteps pattered, and an amber glow shone from around a bend in the corridor. A door slammed shut, and darkness returned.

Jason stared. "What the fuck was that?"

Gary gave him a grim look. "I don't know, but I'm going to find out. Brent, did you catch the name embroidered on that letter jacket?"

"I was too busy not hurling."

"Clark Holmes. And that homeless guy led us right to him."

Brent's eyebrows went up. "Dr. Holmes's grandson? Shit. You think the homeless dude had something to do with it?"

"Or else he knows who did it. He led us right here, no turns. And then he ran off. He's not going to get away from me." Gary checked the clip in his weapon and then stalked down the corridor.

Jason raised his eyebrows at Brent. "What do we do?"

He bit his lip. "We can't stop him, and I can't let him go alone. You can stay here, or go back to the van if you want. But I've got to go with him." He sped off in the direction Gary had gone.

Jason paused, then muttered, "I've got a bad feeling about this." He glanced one more time at the horrors in the alcove before he raced into the darkness after Brent.

Chapter
TWENTY-FOUR

JASON'S ankle throbbed as he ran down the dark corridor. He rushed around a corner and almost collided with Brent and Gary, who had stopped before what looked like a pressurized hatch on a submarine. A dim red glow emanated from a bulb recessed in the wall overhead, and faded crimson letters painted on the wall read, "Danger! No Admittance!"

Brent peered through a porthole in the metal door and whispered, "There's a lighted corridor on the other side. It looks empty."

Jason frowned. "Why the fuck are there electricity and lights here?"

Gary pulled out his cell phone, and its pale glow illuminated his face as he glanced at the screen. "According to my tracking program, we're pretty close to the parts of the Grange that are still operational. Since they're using this for dumping biological waste, it makes sense that they'd have lights in these utility tunnels. They might not even know how far they extended the power."

That didn't sound quite right to Jason, but he decided to wait for more data before arguing.

Gary's light flashed ahead, tracing a line through the debris on the floor. "The homeless dude went right by here." The beam continued, and then stopped on a low, rusty pressure door about thirty feet ahead. "His trail leads there."

The latch on the metal door clanked as Brent tested it. "It seems to be locked."

Jason peered down the corridor where Gary's flashlight still pointed. "How can you tell his trail ends there? I don't see a thing. And I thought this place was abandoned."

Gary twisted his light to shine into Jason's eyes. "His tracks are plain enough, if you've got the brains to look. Even you can see that this place isn't abandoned." His voice dripped with sarcasm.

Jason shielded his face with his hand. "I for sure can't see anything if you blast that damned flashlight in my eyes." He thought for a moment. "I think Ruby mentioned underground utility tunnels running all through the old Grange Station. Maybe that's what these are."

Brent nodded. "That makes sense. There are tunnels underneath the campus in town. They have power cables, and pipes for steam in the winter and chilled water in the summer. We used 'em to string fiber-optics to the lab's greenhouse last summer."

Gary's eyes narrowed as he inspected the walls and floor. "That could explain how that homeless colony survived out here in the winter. They'd just hide out underground."

At last, this was something almost familiar to Jason. "Just like the abandoned subways back home. I did a story on homeless people living in them for my high school newspaper."

Jason squinted as the beam of Gary's flashlight raked across him. It paused, and then passed down the wall to the metal door. "Whatever. That's the only way in." He strode off, held his ear to the door, and then jerked at the knob. It clanged open, and yellow light from the interior flooded the hallway. "Looks like this is the way he went." He ducked his head and disappeared on the other side.

Jason limped after Brent to the open door, which led onto a narrow platform with a metal grate for a floor. Steel rungs protruded from the rough concrete walls, leading downward into a dark hole in the grating and upward to the shadows beyond the bare bulb overhead.

Gary gripped the metal rungs, and his lithe form disappeared into the depths, reminding Jason of a lizard scampering on a basement wall. Brent heaved a sigh and followed. As they descended, their lights flicked on to illuminate the downward path, into a twisty morass of pipes and cables.

Jason rubbed his sore ankle, winced, and clambered onto the rungs. The cold, rough metal bit into his palms, and a clammy updraft cut through the thin fabric of his T-shirt. When his head disappeared below the metal floor, the light on the landing clicked off. The darkness above propelled him downward, and illumination followed as he descended, flashing on then off with his progress. Enormous, convoluted pipes surrounded him, and it seemed as though he descended into the metallic bowels of the worm Ouroboros. From somewhere in the distance, a steady *drip, drip, drip* echoed.

It seemed to Jason that the rungs went on forever, but eventually he reached the bottom, where he skipped the final few steps and landed with an echoing clang and a throb in his ankle. Brent waited there for him, on a grated walkway that hovered over a stagnant channel of water. Gary was already forty feet away, down the passage. An amber light flashed off as he walked, and another, further along, flashed on. Jason imagined they must be motion-activated, like the lights in the freezer cases at Walmart.

He shuddered and peered into the serpentine waters under their feet before looking back at Brent. "I see we've found the River Styx. How far down are we? A hundred feet? Two hundred?"

That got him a laugh from Brent. "I counted the rungs. I'd say we're no more than twenty, maybe twenty-five feet under the level where we entered. Make it thirty-five feet underground altogether."

Jason nodded. "Right. So it just *feels* like the Ninth Circle of Hell." He glared at Gary. "What's Nimrod up there doing? Looking for Cerberus?"

Brent's teeth glowed in the yellow light, and his belly laugh reverberated against the concrete walls. "Either that, or the Minotaur. He's following the homeless dude's tracks, of course. Come on." He trotted away.

Jason muttered a curse. He had no choice but to follow.

Every hundred feet or so, the corridor divided into two or more branches. Gary never hesitated, although as nearly as Jason could tell he chose at random. After a half an hour, the three paused at another low, rusty door.

Jason's breath huffed as he panted. "Tell me, how the fuck are we going to find our way back? I'm totally lost."

Gary cocked an eyebrow at him. "Unlike you, I came prepared. I've got an inertial tracker strapped to my ankle." He pulled out his phone and exposed the screen. "See? It's got a Bluetooth connection to my phone, and keeps track of the turns we've made since we lost GPS signal."

Jason peered, and, sure enough, a green line snaked across the screen. "You can follow that? A ball of string would have been better."

"We don't have a ball of string," Gary sneered. "Besides, this is more reliable. No one can cut it." He placed his ear against the door. "I don't hear anything on the other side. Stand back."

Brent held up his hand. "Wait a minute. Listen."

Jason concentrated. The black water underneath the grate, the steady drip, and the rough concrete walls reminded him of a cave. A silent cave. "I don't hear a thing."

Gary hissed and held up his hand. "Shut up, you idiot." He tipped his head and then cocked an eyebrow at Brent. "Footsteps." It wasn't a question.

Brent nodded and whispered. "They're pretty far back, maybe at the first turn. You think they're following us?"

"I don't think it matters. It's just one person. I say we go ahead."

Jason looked from one to the other. "There's someone down here following us? While we're following God knows who. Maybe the guy who did... did... whatever happened to the dead kid in the letter jacket. Are you guys fucking crazy? We need to get out of here."

Gary's eyes narrowed. "If we go back, these damned automatic lights will announce our approach to whoever's there. If he *is* following us, that gives him the advantage of surprise. He'll know we're coming and can ambush us." He scowled. "By my reckoning, we're pretty close to the agricultural lab, the part of Grange Station that's still active. Our best tactical choice is to go ahead. There's got to be an exit someplace—another ladder upward, maybe. Besides, we came here to explore." Without waiting for an answer, he waved them back, gripped his gun, and pushed on the door.

The hinges creaked, and the door opened to more blackness. Something rustled in the distance and then fell silent. Gary crouched low, held his weapon in both hands, and stepped into the room. Jason jumped when yellow ceiling lights flashed on, brighter than before. Gary pivoted like a radar antenna, scanning the room. "Clear."

Brent stepped inside and stopped. "What is this place?"

Jason peered over his shoulder and breathed, "Files. This could be what we've been looking for." His gaze ranged over the room. "There must be twenty or thirty file cabinets in here." He surged forward, his sore ankle forgotten in his eagerness to explore.

Brent ran his hand on the front of one cabinet. "It looks abandoned, like they're dead files. Maybe they're just old personnel files."

Jason shook his head, and his voice quivered with excitement. "I don't think so. Look at those." He pointed to steel rods that ran the length of the cabinets, top to bottom, padlocked in place. "That's how the military used to secure secret files. Those hasps at the top are welded in place, and that's heavy-duty steel in the sides and the drawers. And look here. This one's even got a combination lock built right into the drawer." He nodded. "These aren't just any old files. Someone went to a lot of trouble to keep whatever's here secret."

Gary circled the room as if looking for someone to shoot. "So what's next? We can't take thirty fucking file cabinets with us." He stopped by a sturdy-looking metal door at the rear of the room. "The homeless dude went this way. Our best bet is to follow him—keep the forward momentum."

Jason frowned. "Let me look around first. Maybe I can figure out which files we need to look at. We came here to get information, right? Not to chase after some poor old tramp." He wandered through the rows of cabinets, looking at their sides and shuffling through the debris on the floor. "I was in a file room at Camp Dodge for a story on the National Guard. They had an index taped to the side of one of the cabinets. Look for something like that."

Brent rattled a padlock on one of the cabinets. "This is pretty rusted out. I think I might be able to pry this loose if I had a crowbar."

Gary snorted. "I can shoot it off, if you'll tell me which one you need in." He paused, a sour look on his face. "I saw some tools in an alcove back a hundred feet or so. Let me check and see if there's a crowbar." He glared at Jason. "Assuming there's really anything here worth looking at."

Jason scanned the room. "I know there's an index someplace. There's got to be. Maybe it fell onto the floor...." His gaze landed on a plastic envelope half hidden under the nearest cabinet. "I bet that's it." He stooped down and picked it up. The scratched and filthy surface obscured what was typed on the paper inside. He walked to the brightest part of the room, and, with the same care an obstetrician uses in the delivery room, he pulled out a flimsy, dusty sheet of paper. "This is it, all right." He held it in the light and peered at the faded typing. "See if you can find a cabinet labeled eight. It looks like there are technical reports on research inside that one." He paused and glanced at Brent. "Jeeze, there's a whole slew of them by your mother, Mary Hyde."

Brent's eyes widened. "I still can't wrap my head around her working here. I've got to see these reports." He walked to the far left and inspected the first two cabinets. "They look like they used to have numbers painted on them, but they're illegible now."

Jason looked around. "That one's number ten. And the one two down is twelve. So *this* is the one I want." He rattled at the padlock and bar. "Can you open it?"

Gary stared at him as if he'd suddenly sprouted an extra head. "Maybe you aren't such a doofus after all. Let me get that crowbar." He ran from the room.

Brent held out his hand. "May I see the list of reports?"

Jason handed it to him. "Sure. Be careful, though. It's almost like tissue paper."

Brent's eyes grew wide as he inspected the titles. "Jesus. She was doing research with Dr. Holmes and Dr. Athair. There's a whole series of reports on reinforcing epigenetic expression through psychological conditioning." He stopped. "I'll be a cow's ear. I want this one." He pointed.

Jason read over his shoulder. "*Epigenetic Traits induced by exposure to a novel strain of Mycobacterium Vaccae and Behavioral Conditioning in Human Males.* Sounds like gobbledygook."

"It could explain a lot. *M. vaccae* is common in cows. I just read an article about how infection with a rare strain improved rat performance in mazes. I even thought I found the same thing in Dr. Athair's lab last semester. Fuck knows what they were working on twenty years ago, but I want to read that report."

Gary tromped into the room. "Stand back." He wedged the crowbar between the cabinet and the rod. "This the one you want opened?"

Jason nodded. "That's it."

Gary grunted, and his muscles flexed. Veins bulged in his neck while beads of sweat popped on his forehead.

Brent frowned. "Don't hurt yourself."

The metal shrieked and tore. The rod and padlock flew across the room and clattered against the wall.

Gary grinned. "Piece of cake."

Jason rushed to open the middle drawer and flipped through the files. "This is it." He opened a thick folder. "This looks like the report you wanted."

Brent snatched it from his fingers and thumbed through the pages. "God, look at this. There's a whole section about how they infected the children here with *M. vaccae*, and then gave them psychometric tests that proved they had higher IQs." He paused and scanned another page. "Geez. There're sections about improved stamina and more acute senses too. Here's one on operant conditioning to reinforce epigenetic responses. This would be cutting edge stuff, even today. I can't believe they were doing this kind of research twenty years ago, let alone that my mother was involved."

Jason scowled. "Did I hear you correctly? They experimented on *children*? You're right. I can't believe they did that."

Brent glanced up, and his eyes grew wide. "Oh. Of course you're right. I was just caught up in the results. It's completely unethical."

Jason snorted. "I'll say. No wonder they want to cover this shit up. Even if they had the parents' consent, the *kids* can't consent. Fuck knows what this might have done to them."

Gary looked from one to the other. "The kids here didn't have parents, right? No parents to give consent. No one to give a fuck about the poor little bastards." He shook his head. "Brent, your mother would never have done anything like that." He stopped and stared into the back of the room. "We seem to have attracted attention."

Jason looked around but saw nothing. "You mean that guy following us?"

"No. I think he's still five or ten minutes away. But the guy we've been following is headed back this way. I recognize his gait." He pulled his weapon from its hiding place at his back and crouched behind a cabinet. "Don't just stand there like targets. Hide!"

Chapter
TWENTY-FIVE

JASON huddled between two filing cabinets and waited. Brent sat with his legs crossed on the floor next to him, absorbed in the technical report his mother had written and apparently indifferent to his surroundings. Jason recognized the metallic swish as Gary checked his clip for what seemed like the zillionth time. Gary had positioned himself at the back of the room, out of Jason's sight and near the rear door.

Jason's sore ankle throbbed, and he shifted and stretched when the leg started to cramp. Brent muttered something unintelligible under his breath as he inspected a page from the report.

Gary hissed, "Shhh! He's coming."

In the stillness, Jason's heartbeat thudded in his head, and the rustle of Brent turning a page in the report seemed as loud as the roar of a helicopter. The faint trickle of water in the corridor blasted his senses as if it were Niagara Falls. But still he heard no sound of the homeless man's approach, despite Gary's assurances.

Then something from the back of the room clicked. Jason held his breath. Rusty hinges squeaked. Faint shadows marched across the cabinets, and hoarse breathing rasped from somewhere close. It seemed to bubble up from the depths of a chest ravaged by disease. A thin voice whimpered, "Who's there? Who's been chasin' a poor old man?"

Gary rapped out, "Show yourself. We won't hurt you."

Command powered his voice, and Jason almost stood and put his hands up. *Where did he learn to do that?* He remembered his high gym teacher, an ex-Marine, who used his voice to compel obedience in the same way.

Jason dared to peak around the corner of the file cabinet. Shadows shrouded the rear of the room where the door now stood open.

Then, like Michael Myers stalking Jamie Lee Curtis in *Halloween*, a wizened figure coalesced out of the gloom: first his eyes, glowering in the light, then his snowy hair and pasty features, and finally his wraithlike body. He limped, and he leaned on a haft of pipe, using it as a makeshift cane. "Why you boys followin' old Aston? He ain't never hurt you."

Aston. That name was familiar. Jason tried to dredge up where he'd heard it. Something to do with the Grange....

Gary stood, his weapon pointed at the old man. "Stay where you are."

Aston halted. "You wouldn't hurt an old fellow, would you? I ain't done nothin'." His voice trembled with an elderly man's whimper. His eyes rolled in their sockets as he scanned the room, the broken cabinet, and the scattered files. "What you boys doin' here?"

Brent stood, still grasping the report in one hand. "We won't hurt you, old man. But we've got some questions, if you don't mind."

Gary grunted. "Yeah, and you're gonna answer too." He circled forward, his eyes never leaving Aston, until they both stood in the same pool of yellow light. He aimed his gun at the man's head and growled, "What do you know about that body back there? The kid in the letter jacket?"

Aston slumped and seemed to lean more heavily on the pipe for support. He took a step forward, and his gaze landed on the open file cabinet and the reports scattered on the floor. "You boys broke that cabinet? Aston's supposed to watch them cabinets. Keep 'em safe. Aston's done good, all these years." He lifted a trembling hand to wipe a tear from his cheek.

Jason decided he needed a better view and stood up. The man's name nagged at his subconscious. He *knew* he'd read it, and recently too. He pulled out his cell phone and opened his notes. *Aston. It was here someplace.*

Gary glanced over his shoulder and laughed. "You're going to make a *phone call*? What kind of fucking idiot are you? There's no signal—"

The old man moved like a rattlesnake, with sudden and lethal intent. He lashed out with the pipe, no longer using it for support. It cracked against Gary's wrist. The pistol clattered away and rattled to a stop near the open door. The pipe slashed again, this time at Gary's knees.

The old man was fast, but Gary was faster.

The pipe swooshed at empty air as Gary danced back. His hand flopped at the end of his wrist, but he didn't seem to notice. He dashed forward and launched a brutal kick at Aston. But the old man was quick, and cunning too. Instead of attacking Gary, he dashed deeper into the room. Before anyone could move, the pipe swung again. This time it slammed into Brent's midsection. He went *whoosh* and collapsed. His head cracked against the floor, and he lay motionless against the wall opposite where Jason stood. As he fell, the report flew from his hands and landed at Jason's feet.

Aston, now agile and rugged, slammed on top of Brent's body as it tumbled to the floor. He grasped Brent's head in both hands. "Stop!" His voice thundered in the room, no longer an old man's weak whine. "Stop right now or I'll snap his neck." The yellow light from the rear door highlighted the crazy old man's face. His eyes bulged in their sockets and blazed with madness.

A cold ball of ice formed in Jason's stomach. Brent was so still, so quiet, so helpless. He couldn't be dead! He'd just hit his head. Jason had to do something, anything to help. He scanned the room, frantic for some way to intervene. His eyes lit on the crowbar, where Gary had dropped it, just a few feet away. Maybe he could use that.

Then he spotted Gary, and the whole scene rose to a new level of the macabre. Gary crouched in a fighter's stance a dozen feet away. His muscles twitched, and a guttural snarl passed his lips. His handsome features were barely recognizable, twisted into a bestial rage. His jaw muscles jumped as if firecrackers exploded inside, and his eyes glowed red and feral. He spoke, and his voice was inhuman, level, mechanical. "Leave him alone."

"Back off. I mean it." Aston's voice coiled with insane fury. He jerked Brent's head again.

Brent's chest rose and fell, and Jason thought he saw his eyelids flutter. He was alive! Hope flashed through him and warmed his cheeks. Hatred for Aston, hot and urgent, thrashed at him. What to do? Maybe Gary would think of something. He was the one with paramilitary training.

Gary took one, then two steps backward. His muscles rippled. His wrist had already swollen to double its normal size. He crouched like a wrestler, arms held wide, and his eyes never left Aston.

Jason remembered to breathe, and memory cascaded through his mind. "Aston Minock. That's it." Pieces of the puzzle fell into place. Maybe there was something there that was a key to this. Maybe knowledge would save Brent.

Gary looked at him like he was insane, but Minock's eyes grew wide until they resembled boiled eggs. "How the fuck you know who I am, boy?"

"You worked here, twenty years ago, as a guard. Ruby told me." Jason watched Aston for a reaction, and hope flared more certain.

Aston's features sagged, like deflated bread dough. "Ruby. I ain't thought about that bitch in ages. Figured she and that asshole husband of hers was dead by now." He cast a wild-eyed glare at Gary and tightened his grip on Brent's head. "Don't you get no ideas, boy. I can snap this one's neck like a chicken wing in nothin' flat, and don't think I won't."

Jason remembered the hostage negotiator he'd interviewed. He'd said to make them see the victim as human, as a person. This had to work. He kept his voice soft, reasonable, like the time he'd interviewed the alleged serial killer in New Jersey. "His name is Brent. Brent Hyde." He pointed at the still form. His chest still moved in and out: he wasn't dead yet, but his eyes were closed.

The old man snorted like a bull. "Like I give a fuck."

"His mother worked here too, back then. Mary. Do you remember Mary?" Jason's heart thudded in his chest. The room shrank around him, until all that was left was Aston's face, his bloodshot eyes, his craggy features. That face became the center of Jason's existence. The face, and the trembling hands holding Brent's life in a fistful of rage.

Aston's features softened, and tears glistened in his eyes. His breath seemed to foam from his throat. "Mary?" he murmured. "Meine schöne Meike." His voice quavered, as though in fear, or perhaps in love, and he wheezed, "He's Mary Hyde's child?"

"Yes, Mary Hyde. You remember Mary, don't you?" *Keep your voice even, soothing. Don't startle him.* He pushed air in and out in calming breaths. *Stay cool.*

"Mary was good to me. I loved her. She told me to—" Aston didn't finish the sentence.

A sharp sound, like someone clapping their hands once, snapped from behind him. Then dead silence clogged the room. A sudden ache drummed in Jason's ears, as if someone had poured molten wax inside them.

His concentration never wavered. His gaze never left Aston's face.

A perfect round hole appeared between the man's eyes. In slow motion, his head snapped backward. Red and white and gray muck splattered against the concrete wall behind him. It dribbled from the filing cabinets and onto the grimy floor. A flat coppery smell penetrated Jason's nostrils. Aston collapsed in a boneless heap behind where Brent still lay, motionless.

Silence roared like an ocean in Jason's skull. He stumbled forward and knelt at Brent's side. A pulse, steady and strong, throbbed against Jason's fingers. His pupils reacted to light. Maybe he'd be all right.

Jason shook his head. Now nails seemed to be pounding into his ears. Voices warbled around him, as if he were underwater. Gary stood with his arms held high over his head. One hand flopped at an odd angle. Gary's gaze, though, was now locked on the doorway.

Jason rotated his head to follow Gary's stare. Everything was still in slow motion. From nowhere, a mighty wind howled.

A fat man stood in the doorway holding a cannon. No, not a cannon, just a big fucking gun. He wore a Smokey the Bear hat, and he was saying something. Jason could just make out the words through the muck in his ears.

"Don't you faggots move. The bossman's comin' for ya. I think he's gonna let me snuff ya, but first he's got some questions. Should be fun, helpin' him *question* you fuckin' faggots." He laughed and spat.

Purcell. It was Purcell. He must have followed them, using the bug on Jason's car. What was he saying now?

"Why doncha try to escape? I'd like that. I got orders not to kill ya yet, but I wouldn't mind blowin' one of your knees out. Hurts like hell." His laughter bounced against Jason's eardrums, and pain throbbed in his head.

Brent stirred. His eyelids fluttered, and he moaned. Jason gripped his hand and whispered, "It's going to be all right." He prayed it was true.

Aston's brains dripped from the wall and left a glistening trail on the floor next to where Gary's pistol had landed.

A desperate plan churned in Jason's mind.

Chapter
TWENTY-SIX

RACHEL rubbed her forehead and stared at the screen of her laptop computer. She was sure she had missed something. Something important.

A knock at the door broke her concentration, and a muffled voice announced, "Room service."

She muttered, "Shit," and then sang out in a louder tone, "I mean, just a minute." She closed her laptop, picked up stray towels, and threw away this morning's newspaper before she opened the door. "Just put it there, on the desk, please."

The young man deposited the tray and lifted the lid off the plate. "Your Reuben sandwich and fries, ma'am. Will there be anything else?" He had spiky blond hair and watery blue eyes. Tattoos of chains coiled about his wrists and peeked out from underneath his starched shirt.

"That's all." She accepted the bill, added a precise 20 percent tip, and signed with a flourish. "Thank you."

"Thank *you*, ma'am. Just leave the tray outside your door when you're done. I'll pick it up later tonight." His teeth gleamed white, and then he was gone.

She sighed, pulled a Coke Zero from the mini-fridge, and sat back at the desk. The fries were too salty for her taste, but the sandwich was on rye like it should be, and the corned beef was excellent. She reopened her laptop and logged onto the SharePoint site the Bureau had established for this case. *Follow the money.* That was always a good idea.

She clicked through folders, looking for the dossier on the investment firm in Dubuque: Cox, Inhofe, and Associates. The preliminary report from the SEC auditor confirmed the missing stolen ten million dollars from their brokerage account, but something didn't seem quite right. A grim smile bent her lips as she scanned the files. Montel must have been busy with his National Security Letters. The folder included incorporation papers, financial statements, and fifteen years of income tax filings, all the way back to the original incorporation date. Besides the two principals, the company had only one employee, a receptionist, and a bare handful of customers. Google Maps street view showed its address was in a strip mall in a run-down part of town. She frowned. It made no sense for this rinky-dink firm to have a brokerage account with ten million dollars in it.

Her eyes widened when she checked the social security numbers for Cox and Inhofe. After a few more clicks, she leaned back and frowned, her fingers templed in front of her face. Her eyes narrowed in grim determination.

She leaned forward and pored over financial statements, following money trails. Two hours later, she stretched and glanced at the clock. Nearly 1:00 a.m. She picked up the phone and dialed Montel's room.

His voice growled from the phone. "Whoever this is, it better be good."

"Sir, this is Special Agent Morrison. I've been looking at the financials for Cox, Inhofe, and Associates. You really need to see what I've uncovered."

"It's late. Can't this wait until morning?"

"I really think you'll want to see this, sir."

He grunted. "Give me ten minutes."

Rachel shuffled through her notes and munched on cold french fries while she waited. She underlined two names on her notes, and then tried a Google search for Aston Minock and found a story from a year ago that identified him as a homeless vagrant. A similar search for Meike Hilda Zeigler came up blank. She put a question mark on her notes next to those names.

When Montel rapped at the door, she rushed to let him in. "I'm sorry to bother you, sir, but I think I've uncovered something pretty big." She stopped and stared. He wore an immaculate white shirt, a suit, and a tie with a perfect knot. His slacks hung with a knifelike crease that broke just above his glossy shoes. He had groomed his gray hair to perfection, and it looked like he'd just shaved.

She swiped a snarl of hair from her forehead and tucked her stained T-shirt into her sweatpants.

He perched on the sofa and turned an icy stare in her direction. "So dazzle me, Agent Morrison."

"Um, yes, sir." She picked up her scribbled notes and sat next to him. "You must have issued National Security Letters for the financials of Cox, Inhofe, and Associates. I've been following where they led."

He nodded. "That's the investment firm young Hyde stole from, right?"

She blinked. "I don't know that he stole from them, sir. In fact, I don't think he did. But I got to thinking. Why does this little one-horse outfit in Dubuque, Iowa, have a brokerage account with ten million dollars in it? Their only employee besides the principals is a receptionist, and they only have sixty-three clients."

"There are rich people everywhere, Agent Morrison."

"Yes, sure. But these clients aren't rich locals; they're all out-of-state corporations. And this little firm has handled billions in transactions for them over the last fifteen years."

His eyebrows crawled up his forehead. "Billions, you say? I admit that gets my attention. Do tell me more."

"Yes, sir. I started by checking out Cox and Inhofe. They popped into existence fifteen years ago when they formed their company. No prior history that I could find. And get this: their social security numbers are *sequential*, and issued on the same day."

He examined his fingernails and yawned. "Coincidence. Maybe they were friends and applied for the numbers at the same time."

She couldn't keep the exuberance out of her voice. "There's more. Neither one has a driver's license—at least not in the US. They don't have a credit history. None, zip, nada. The only address on file for either of them is a PO Box. They're completely off the grid."

"It sounds like they want to stay anonymous." He paused. "I admit that's unusual, especially as they are running an investment firm that handles significant transactions. Are you sure about all this?"

She handed him a sheet of notes. "I'm sure, sir."

His lips turned down as he scanned the scribbled diagram at the bottom of the paper. "What's this? A schematic for a plate of spaghetti?"

"Sir, like I said, Cox and Inhofe only have sixty-three corporate clients, all out of state. I traced those companies, and then I traced the owners of those companies, and so on. I found out they own each other, like that worm that eats its own tail."

He nodded and murmured, "The Worm Ouroboros."

She gave him a quizzical look and then continued. "Yeah, I guess. Anyway, they're all a closed loop. They own bits and pieces of each other. Everything tracks back to just these three companies." She handed him another page of notes with a sense of triumph.

He glanced at it and then peered at her. "Summarize your findings, please. How does this connect to our case?"

She took a cleansing breath. "As nearly as I can tell, the ultimate source of all the funds that Cox and Inhofe handled is the first company on that list, Granville Pulp and Paper. All the preferred stock for *that* company is held by the CEO of the Gerion Group, and he's also chairman of the board of GP&P. Their sole business seems to be financial services provided to... the Gerion Group. I didn't have the time for a detailed analysis, but it looked like about a third of the funds stayed with Granville Pulp and Paper, and the rest moved out and through these sixty-three shell companies."

"Interesting. Are you suggesting he funneled funds from Gerion to Granville?"

"I'm not a forensic accountant, but it sure looks that way."

"And you say the CEO of the Gerion Group did this, defrauded his own company. Why do you think he would risk that, Agent Morrison?"

"Who knows? Maybe it's a tax scam for the Gerion Group. Maybe you're right and he's stealing. Maybe it's something else. But it's clear that this huge multinational corporation is somehow tied to Cox, Inhofe, and Associates, and they're trying to cover things up by passing the money through all these shell companies." She paused and held his eye. "Now, I ask you, why would they let a freelancer like Charles Hyde at their books? Doesn't that sound risky, even stupid?"

A momentary smile bent his lips. "An excellent question, Rachel. Why, indeed?"

Her breath caught in her throat. "There's more, sir."

"Do tell? Go on." He leaned back and draped an arm over the back of the sofa.

"The second company on the list, Brownfield Biologics, is even more interesting. Its address is another PO Box, right here in Middleton. It seems to have received about a third of the funds siphoned from the Gerion Group. Care to guess who's the CEO of this company?"

"Please don't play games, Rachel." His voice caressed the words, bantering, playing with each syllable. "Just tell me what you know."

She shoved another sheet at him. "The CEO is Dr. Aaron Holmes. I met him earlier today. He's in charge of some kind of big DARPA research project here at Collier University. Some of his other projects are funded by, get this, the Gerion Group, and have been for years."

"Interesting. You said there were three companies?"

"Yeah, but I need to tell you more about this company first. The original incorporation papers—also from fifteen years ago—for Brownfield Biologics lists five stockholders, and the Iowa Department of State doesn't show any changes in ownership since then. One is Sonja Athair. She's another hotshot researcher at the University. Two others look like dummies, nonentities with one share each, just to fill out the required number to incorporate. But the fifth one is none other than Charles Hyde, Brent's father. He owns 20 percent of the company."

Montel closed his eyes and frowned. "Really? So Hyde is tied into this money laundering scheme, or whatever it is, and has been for what? Fifteen years, you said?"

"That's right." She grinned in triumph. "You see why this is significant. This changes the whole scale of the investigation. It even occurs to me that the missing funds from the brokerage account might be a setup, a distraction."

A smile toyed with his lips, and she wondered if his face might crack. "You have a suspicious mind, Rachel. I like the way you think." He leaned forward and peered at her. "This is excellent work. Just out of curiosity, who are the other two owners for this company? What is it, Brownfield something?"

"Brownfield Biologics, sir. Aston Minock is one of the listed names, owning one percent of the company. There's a news story from a year ago that identifies a man with the same name as a homeless vagrant camping out at Grange Station. Don't know that it's him, but the name's not exactly common. The last person is someone called Meike Hilda Zeigler, with twenty percent of the initial stock. I couldn't find any record of her at all."

"Uh-huh. Maybe she's a German national. In any case, we'll have to follow up on both of them. What else do you have?"

"Nothing more on Brownfield Biologics. But the third company, Grace Development, might be the most interesting of the three. Beyond Delaware incorporation papers, I can't find anything on it except a website."

He frowned. "Pray tell, how is finding nothing interesting?"

"I did an IP trace on the location of the host machine for the website. It's in Langley, Virginia." She couldn't keep the thrill of discovery out of her voice.

His eyes narrowed. "From that I infer that you deduce it's a CIA front organization?" His eyes turned to slits, and his tongue flicked at his lips. "Still, it seems careless of them to host their website at Langley."

"I used the authority of your National Security Letter to get all the way to Grace Development, but not inside. What does that tell you?"

"Excellent point. Rachel, you've done good work here. Really good." He stroked his chin and gazed at her as if she were a butterfly he was about to impale on a display board. "Tell me, if I order you to arrest young Hyde and close this case, what will you do?"

She tipped her head back, and surprise fluttered in her stomach. "Sir, there's no basis for arresting him. We're onto something much bigger here. There might be billions in embezzlement. Tax fraud. Maybe more."

His voice was hushed, not quite a whisper. "You didn't answer my question, Rachel."

She scowled. "I'd take an order like that upstairs, sir. All the way to the Director, if I had to."

He sighed. "I was afraid you'd say that. What I'm about to tell you is classified. More than Top Secret. Do I need to remind you of the penalties for disclosing matters of national security?"

"I know the law, sir." She wondered where this was headed.

"Very good, then. We have a bigger mission here than a missing person or two, Rachel." His phone shrilled, and he frowned. "Excuse me. I have to answer that ring."

He whipped out his iPhone and stood. "Strorm here." He listened for a few seconds, and his face paled. "What's the tactical situation? Uh-huh…. It's a stalemate, then. You're sure they're not injured? Just a moment."

He put his phone down, rubbed his eyes, and muttered, "Shit, shit, shit." He pursed his lips and put the device back to his ear. "Okay, Verloc, it's vital that the two targets not leave that site. Got that? It's also vital that they aren't damaged, at least until I get there. Understand?" The person on the other end must have said something annoying, because his face turned sour and he rolled his eyes. "No, he's just in the way, expendable. Same goes for that obnoxious little reporter. I only care about the two primary targets." He listened again and then nodded. "All right. Remember your orders and don't get creative. I'll be there within the hour."

He stood. "Rachel, come with me. I'll brief you on the way."

She pulled on her sneakers and stood. "Where are we going, sir?"

"Grange Station."

Chapter
TWENTY-SEVEN

BRENT'S head throbbed in cadence with each beat of his heart, as though his brains and arteries were suddenly too large for his skull. His arms fumbled against slimy concrete when he tried to sit up, and agony exploded in his gut.

Gentle fingers stroked his brow, and a soothing voice murmured, "Take it easy. You've had your breath knocked out of you. Just lay here for a moment."

He opened his mouth to speak, but could only cough. Sour vomit burned at the back of his throat, and saliva flooded his mouth. He managed to croak out, "Oh God, I'm gonna be sick."

"Here, I'll help you sit up."

He knew that voice. It was Jason. He struggled to a sitting position, with Jason doing most of the work. The room spun around him, and noxious outhouse odors fouled his nose. When the room stopped gyrating, he spotted the homeless man sprawled nearby, in a puddle of blood and gore. At first, it looked like his head had sunk into the floor. Brent gulped and tried to concentrate. The back of the homeless guy's skull seemed to be missing, and his head was... shaped wrong, squashed somehow. Sudden spasms convulsed Brent's body as he tried to retch, but only a thin trickle of bile came out.

Jason wiped Brent's mouth with a handkerchief. "That's it man, let it out."

Brent gasped and looked again at the bloody corpse. "What the fuck happened?"

Gary's voice came from across the room, but it faded in and out like someone was twirling his volume button. Why was he way over there, instead of here, helping? "He slugged you, and then tried to use you as a shield." He paused and nodded toward the doorway. "Then Deputy Dawg over there showed up and blew his brains out."

Brent's head wobbled on his neck, and he blinked bleary eyes. He recognized the file room. The gruesome body belonged to the homeless guy. He got that. But why was Gary holding his arms up, like a gangster in a bad movie? Why did his hand flop at that weird angle? And who the fuck was Deputy Dawg?

Gary peered at him and then spoke again. "We need to check him for concussion and broken ribs."

A surly voice from the doorway sneered, "What, the girly-boy's hurtin'? The little faggot couldn't stand a little bump on his head?"

Brent turned to inspect the speaker. His muscles resisted with ponderous inertia, like a battleship in heavy seas, and the room wavered about him. A fat man with an enormous gun and a Smokey the Bear hat stood in the door. Brent concentrated. The name came to him. "Deputy Purcell."

The officer's eyes gleamed, and his voice spoke in a falsetto. "Officer Purcell." He scowled, spat, and waved his gun at Gary. "You. Get over there by them two. No funny stuff."

Gary nodded. "Can I lower my hands?" Without waiting, he dropped them to his sides. "I still want to check his injuries." He moved across the room on cat's feet.

Purcell shrugged. "I don't give a rat's ass what you do, as long as you don't pull no funny stuff."

Gary knelt next to Brent, and his good hand gripped Brent's chin. "Follow my finger."

Brent had to concentrate, but his eyes seemed to work. "Do I pass, doctor?"

Gary touched his cheek. "You're doing fine." He glanced at Purcell. "I need to check his pupils. I'm going to use the penlight in my shirt pocket."

Purcell leaned forward. "Move nice and slow-like, so I can see what you're doin'."

Gary showed him the light, then flashed it into Brent's eyes.

Brent blinked, dazzled for a moment by the flash.

Gary seemed satisfied. "Good. Your pupils react. We'll need to get you checked out, though, to be sure you've not got a concussion."

He turned back to their captor. "I'm going to check his ribs next. He got hit pretty hard by that pipe."

He turned his back on Purcell, leaned forward, and pressed on Brent's midsection. "How's that feel?"

Brent grunted. "Sore, but I don't think anything's broken." He took a deep breath. "I'm feeling better. Thanks."

Gary reached out with his good hand and squeezed Brent's fingers. "My heart stopped when that asshole hit you. I couldn't stand it if… well, I should have done a better job protecting you." His eyes flicked to Jason, then to something behind them, near the homeless guy's ruined head.

Jason's glance followed Gary's, as if it meant something to him. But then he reached out and touched Gary's wrist. "I don't like the way that looks, man. It's all swelled up, and it shouldn't bend at that angle."

Gary shrugged. "I'm pretty sure it's dislocated, maybe broken." His gaze turned to Jason. "Looks like you're the only one of us that's still operational."

Jason nodded, and he whispered, "Understood." He turned to face Purcell. "Since we're doing first aid, I'd like to wrap Gary's wrist, to help reduce the swelling. There's a ruler behind that file cabinet that might serve as a splint." He nodded in the direction of the bloody corpse.

"No way, faggot. You stay right there."

Jason's lips thinned. "Look at me." He held out his skinny arms and exposed his wraithlike torso. "You're saying you're fucking afraid of *me?* You've got a *gun,* for God's sake. Besides, you could break me like a toothpick anytime you wanted."

Gary laughed. "And you called *us* faggots. What does that make you, if you're afraid of this sissy?"

"I ain't afraid of nothin'." Purcell scowled and waved his weapon at them. "Go ahead and play nurse, faggot. If your sissy boyfriend there needs his wrist looked at, go to it. You can't do nothing to me, no how." He lounged back against the doorjamb and grinned.

Brent frowned. Gary and Jason seemed to be up to something, but he couldn't quite figure out what. He rubbed his forehead and moaned.

Gary settled next to him and wrapped an arm about his shoulder. "I need you to lie down. I want to check your ribs again." He looked up. "That is, if Mr. Big Shot with the gun will approve."

Purcell waved his weapon and snarled. "You faggots don't worry me none. Just stay on that side of the room."

Brent resisted. "My ribs are fine. Really. They feel a lot better."

Gary's eyes flashed at him, and his soft voice cut with the slightest edge. "I need to you lie down." He gave a gentle push and helped Brent to a prone position.

Behind them, Jason fumbled with something near the homeless man's body. Gary squatted next to Brent, on the balls of his feet, and probed his stomach with his good hand. He was now facing Purcell. He kept his head turned down, as if looking at Brent, but his eyes never left their captor. His muscles tensed, and his breaths came in short, controlled bursts. A chill gripped Brent's core. *He's planning something. God, don't let him be hurt.*

Jason crouched next to a filing cabinet, and his voice rapped out, "Hey, you! Officer Wiggum. Drop your gun now or I'll shoot!"

Brent lifted his head and goggled in the direction of the shouted command. His heart froze at what he saw. *Where the fuck did Jason get that gun? And what the hell! The fucking safety's still on the damned thing! What the shit does he think he's doing?*

Purcell's weapon roared, and sparks flared off the metal cabinet as his first shot ricocheted harmlessly into the concrete block wall. Jason's eyes tried to pop out of his skull as he struggled with the trigger on his weapon. Nothing happened, of course. Brent wanted to scream at him to flip the safety, but no sound would come out of his mouth.

Gary, though, attacked. He sprang across the room as if launched from a rocket. A karate chop landed on Purcell's gun arm, and the sound of bone snapping filled the room. The man's face turned purple, and a meaty paw swung, but Gary was fast, far too fast for the lumbering deputy. The fist went wild and missed. Purcell stumbled and whirled to face Gary.

Jason howled, "Why won't this fucking thing *shoot?*"

Brent scrambled to his feet and staggered toward Jason, toward the gun. The muscles in his legs quivered, and he couldn't think, couldn't speak, couldn't *move*. The room undulated about him, and chaos rattled his thoughts.

Purcell and Gary circled each other, like a bear in the circus and his trainer. Sudden as lightning, Gary rushed forward. He balanced on one foot and powered a sideways kick into Purcell's knee. When his sneaker met bone, another crack resounded in the room. Purcell collapsed to the floor, where he rolled about screaming in agony. Gary kicked him in the throat, and the screams ceased.

Brent leaned against a filing cabinet and panted. The room whirled around him. "What the fuck? Is he dead?"

A satisfied smile twisted Gary's lips. "No, but I bet he wishes he were." He marched across the room and snatched the gun from Jason's hands. "You know, these things work better if you turn the safety off." He held it up and clicked the switch. "Like that. You're lucky that fat-ass idiot missed. If it'd been me you'd pulled that stunt on, I'd have blown your head off."

Jason sagged against the cabinet. "Is it over?"

Gary punched him in the shoulder and laughed. "You bet. Gutsy move, goin' for the gun. I just wanted you to distract him while I made my move. But when you point at someone, you gotta be ready to shoot."

Jason's eyes rolled in their sockets and came to rest on the homeless man's body. "That could have been me." A shudder shook his body, and his voice trembled.

Brent peered at him. "Have you ever fired a gun before?"

"Once, back in New Jersey. On assignment with a cop. His didn't have a safety." His face turned ashen. "Fuck. I could have been killed."

Brent shook his head. "What were you thinking?"

Jason's mouth turned down as his gaze bore into Brent. "I was thinking both of you were hurt. I was thinking that if we were going to get out of here, it was up to me. I saw Brent's gun on the floor, and I decided to go for it. I figured, what's the worst that could happen?" He looked at the puddle of brains on the floor. "I think I'm going to be sick."

Gary tugged on his wrist and something popped. He grimaced and sneered, "God, you're such a fucking pansy." He scanned the room. "We need to get out of here. Purcell said his boss was coming, whoever the fuck that is. We're not in very good shape for another battle." He headed into the hallway and paused. "Come on. Let's hustle, men."

Brent looked from Jason to Gary and back again. "I don't care what he says. You're a hero, man, going for the gun like that."

"Maybe. Or maybe I'm just dumb. Do you need help walking?"

"I'll be fine." Jason held his hand anyway. His solid grip was comforting and felt just right, somehow. Brent gave Jason's fingers a gentle squeeze, and they fled back into the depths of the labyrinth that coiled underneath Grange Station.

Chapter TWENTY-EIGHT

JASON pushed outside Building Three and heaved a sigh of relief at being free of the oppressive darkness. He searched the clearing for his two companions and wished the others had waited for him. Moonlight cast a scintillating glow through the canopy of trees where Brent waved to him from the shadows. Jason's ankle ached from when he'd twisted it earlier, and their recent dash through the tunnels hadn't helped. He grimaced and hobbled toward Brent, careful to avoid the gaps in the broken sidewalk.

Gary huddled in the brush behind Brent. The clip in his gun gave a metallic swish as he checked it yet again. He stood erect and rotated full circle while he held his weapon in a double-handed grip. He muttered, "I could swear I heard footsteps in front of us when we were in the tunnels."

Jason limped up to them and paused to catch his breath. He thought for a moment about how Gary held his weapon and then frowned. "I thought your wrist was broken?" He moved closer and inspected Gary's arm. "What gives? It's barely swollen."

Gary jerked away and snarled, "Don't touch me, creep." He holstered his gun and rubbed his wrist. "I guess I must have just dislocated it. I pulled on it when we were back in the tunnels, something popped, and it stopped hurting." He reached into his sleeve and scratched his arm. "Damned arm itches like the devil, though. Something must have bit me."

Jason stared at him and, despite himself, anger flared. "That doesn't make any fucking sense. It was twice normal size. I saw."

Brent's fingers brushed Jason's arm. Even his gentle touch and calm voice didn't ease Jason's irritation. "Things were kind of hectic back there. I don't remember it being swollen. Maybe it was a trick of the light or something?"

Gary stomped off. "Don't matter. It's fine now, just a little stiff. Let's get out of here."

Jason scowled and started to speak, but Brent squeezed his hand and whispered, "It's not worth it. Let's just get out of here. We can talk later, okay?"

Jason took a deep breath. Streaks of blood smeared across Brent's handsome features and matted against his blond hair. Sudden guilt replaced Jason's anger. "Okay. How are you doing?"

"I'm still a little shaky, to be truthful." He glanced down at the dozen or more bulging manila folders he'd scavenged from the file room. "Would you mind helping me with these?"

Jason reached out and accepted a thick bundle. He squatted down to tamp ragged edges of papers back inside while he asked, "What's all in these files, again?"

"Mostly these are old technical reports, some by my mother and some by other researchers. They all have to do with the effects of this novel strain of *M. vaccae* on animal and human subjects. It's brilliant science, even though some of the results are pretty horrible."

Jason stood. "You said they experimented on children."

"Yeah. They told the mothers they were providing free medical care, which they were. But they were experimenting too." He frowned. "I can't believe my mother was involved in this. I know she'll have a good reason."

Jason couldn't think of an answer to that. He looked down the trail. "I can't see Gary. Can you?" Jason strained his ears, but only picked up the rustle of the breeze through the treetops.

Brent peered into the blackness. "No, but I can hear him. We should head out." He hesitated. "I'm still a little woozy. Will you hold my hand while we walk?"

"Sure. But you're more likely to keep me from tripping than I am to help you."

That earned him a smile. "But you're my hero. I'll never forget that." Brent tugged at his hand and pulled him forward. "Come on. Gary's already way ahead of us."

Despite everything, Brent's touch sent a thrill up Jason's arm. "Be careful. Your boyfriend up there might hear you and beat me up."

Brent gave him a puzzled look. "You mean Gary? He's not my boyfriend. We're just good buddies. He helped me when I got to Collier last year and my ex dumped me in the first week of classes." He tugged at Jason's hand. "Come on. We need get out of here."

Jason let Brent lead him through the darkness while he contemplated what he'd just learned. Maybe there was hope for him with Brent after all.

When they arrived back at the van, Brent gave his hand a quick squeeze before releasing it. Gary stopped pacing, put his hands on his hips, and sneered, "Where the fuck have you two been? Let's get out of here."

Jason fished in his pocket for the keys and pushed the button to unlock the doors. "Where to now?" He settled into the driver's seat and waited while Brent and Gary tumbled into the backseat. "I'd feel better if we took Brent to see a doctor. He's still woozy."

Gary rolled his eyes. "Jee-sus, what a fucking nervous Nellie you are. Let's get out of here and head back to town. We can figure out what to do from there."

Brent leaned forward. "Thanks for thinking of me, Jason, but I think I'll be okay." He tapped the stack of file folders on the seat beside him. "I want to secure these documents, and maybe show them to Dr. Athair. She was here back then. Maybe they'll jog something in her memory."

Jason shrugged. "You're the boss." He turned the key, but nothing happened. "Shit." He tried it again: still nothing. The headlights flashed when he pulled back on the turn signal stalk, so the battery wasn't dead.

Gary's voice rasped at his ears. "What the fuck are you doing? Let's get going."

"It won't start. It's like the battery's dead, except it's not." Jason thought for a moment. "The same thing happened last night, when Deep Throat called me. I thought he'd disabled my car, maybe with the onboard cell phone system."

Gary's features darkened, and his voice boiled with anger. "This has happened *before*? And you took us all the way out here? Why didn't you say something?"

"Look, earlier today I took it to that research group on campus, the one that's studying how to protect the onboard computers in cars from hacking. They gave it a clean bill of health, and they disabled the built-in cell phone. The lead guy, Malcolm somebody, said it'd be safe."

Brent piped up. "Malcolm Wisby. Gary, you know him. He's Dr. Athair's boyfriend. We had dinner with—"

Gary held his hands over his ears and yelled, "Stop it, will you two? Who gives a fuck who checked what or who's dating who. The point is, the fucking car's not working now, and we're trapped out here." He slammed out of the backseat and stomped to the front of the vehicle. "Pop the hood."

Before Jason could pull the latch, headlights flashed on the road, and another vehicle pulled up behind them in the little access drive. A door opened, and a baritone voice called out, "FBI. Hold it right there. Don't move."

Jason twisted his head to look behind them. A slender man approached in the glare of the headlights, his weapon held in a double-handed grip. Another, shorter figure with frizzy hair appeared behind him. Jason nodded at the papers in Brent's lap. "You might slip those under the seat, for protection."

When the armed man came around to the side of the car and peered inside, Jason heaved a sigh. "Agent Strorm. How good to see you again."

The FBI agent's eyes glinted, and he motioned with his gun. "Out of the van. Do it! Now!"

Jason held his hands high and stepped from the van. "We've not done anything wrong, sir."

"The fuck you haven't, you little twerp. All three of you are under arrest for breaking and entering into a restricted facility of the US Government." He tipped his head in the direction of the rusty "No Trespassing" sign. "That's enough to hold you for now. We'll find more reasons later, if we need them." He glanced behind him. "Rachel. Search them, starting with the one in front of the car. He's armed."

Jason felt better when he recognized the female FBI agent's trim figure. She frisked Gary and immediately found his gun, which she slipped into an enormous purse that hung from her shoulder. In quick order, she checked out Brent and Gary. "They're clean, Montel."

He didn't relax. "Read 'em their rights and cuff 'em."

"Is that necessary, sir? I don't think—"

"Just do it," he snapped.

Jason waited while she secured Gary and Brent and recited the Miranda rights to all three of them. Montel herded them toward his SUV while she approached him, cuffs dangling from her hands. He leaned forward and whispered, "We need to talk."

She paused and seemed to fumble with the cuffs before fastening them to his wrists. She glanced in the direction of the black SUV, where Gary clambered into the backseat with the older agent's assistance. "So talk. Make it fast."

"We left an injured sheriff's deputy behind us, in the subbasement of Building Three. He's okay, but he can't walk out on his own. A crazy homeless guy attacked us while we were in there, and Purcell—that's the deputy—he had to shoot and kill him. We found at least one other body too."

The door on the SUV slammed shut, and Montel called out, "What's the hold up?"

Rachel tugged on the cuffs. "Nothing, sir." She pulled him forward and whispered, "We've already called in a security team from the Grange. They'll take care of Purcell, and the dead body too."

Jason started to correct her, to tell her there were bodies, plural, but he stumbled, and her strong grip saved him from falling.

"Careful, there." Somehow, the blend of stern and maternal in her voice comforted him.

He wobbled after her, favoring his throbbing ankle, toward the SUV. Brent stood in the glare of the headlights, head down and shoulders drooping, next to Montel. Jason narrowed his eyes and spotted Gary's silhouette, already in the backseat. He pretended to stumble and again leaned into Rachel, as if for support. "There's more," he whispered. "There's a file folder hidden in the van you need to know about."

Before she could answer, Strorm called out, "Hold up a minute, Agent Morrison." He waved them back, his eyes seeming to focus on something behind them.

Jason swiveled his head, and his muscles sagged at what he saw coalesce out of the shadows. Without warning, a new figure had appeared from the woods behind them, out of nowhere. Jason reflected that the events of the night must have overloaded his fear circuits, since the only thing he could think was *how interesting*. The newcomer was dressed like a commando, all in black. He wore a ski mask and what looked like a Kevlar vest. He brandished a scary-looking machine pistol in one hand, as if longing for someone, anyone, to kill.

Rachel's fingers tightened around Jason's arm, and he squirmed. "That hurts."

She threw a quick glance his way and muttered, "Sorry." Her grip relaxed, but was still firm enough to control his movements. "Shush, now. We'll talk later."

The commando trotted past Jason's van, ignoring Rachel and Jason, and up to Montel. The two exchanged a few muttered words before Strorm turned to face Rachel and Jason. "There won't be room for all of us in my SUV. Rachel, you're going to have to bring young Hyde and the reporter in their van."

Rachel frowned. "Shouldn't your... agent take the suspect's vehicle, sir?" She nodded toward the commando.

"He and I have things to discuss. We'll do it my way, Agent Morrison."

Jason piped up, "My van won't start."

The newcomer laughed, and thoughts of vampires and serial killers echoed in Jason's mind while shivers ran up his spine. When the man spoke, his voice bubbled with the false effervescence of a TV weatherman announcing tornados in the next county. "Don't worry, I took care of that. It'll work now." He climbed into the passenger side of the SUV and slammed the door.

Montel jerked on Brent's cuffs and led him away from the SUV and back toward where Rachel and Jason stood by the van. He gave Rachel a curt nod. "We'll meet at the facility. Follow us. Do you need help securing these two?"

"We'll be fine, sir."

He turned on his heel and stalked away without looking back.

She scowled and cast an exasperated look at Jason. "Okay, kid. Where are your keys?"

"They're still in the ignition."

"Fine. You two get in the back. Here, let me help." She steadied Jason's shoulders while he climbed into the rear of the van, and then repeated the process with Brent. "Can I trust you two guys to be good?"

Jason turned his gaze to Brent, who huddled in the seat, eyes downcast and shoulders slumped. "I'm worried about him, ma'am. He took quite a rap on his head tonight."

She pulled a penlight from the purse that hung on her shoulder and shined the beam first into one eye, then the next. "The pupils respond equally. That's a good sign."

Brent mumbled, "I'm fine. Just a little shaky, is all."

Rachel pulled a keyring from her purse and jiggled it from one hand to the other. "Can I trust you guys? No funny stuff if I take off your cuffs?"

Relief flooded Jason, and he twisted in the seat to offer his wrists. "I promise. You've got my word, if that helps."

"I should know better," she muttered, but then undid both sets of cuffs with a quick gesture. "Just sit back there and be quiet, you hear me?"

Jason rubbed his wrists. "Thanks, ma'am. You won't regret this kindness."

She grunted and climbed into the front seat.

When the engine roared to life, Brent's hand reached across the seat and caressed Jason's arm. Once they were moving, he sidled closer and put his head on Jason's shoulder. He sighed, and his breath warmed Jason's throat when he whispered, "I wonder where she's taking us."

Rachel answered from over her shoulder, "The new part of Grange Station, where Dr. Holmes has his research projects."

Jason furrowed his brow, and a chill tingled out his fingertips. "Why there?"

She shrugged. "Don't ask me. Agent Strorm is in charge, and he's not talking." She paused while negotiating a narrow bridge. "Anyway, I understand there's an infirmary there. We can get Mr. Hyde's head injury checked out."

His reporter instincts nagged at him to demand more details, but Brent snuggled closer and murmured, "Please hold me." He squeezed Jason's hand and added, "My hero."

Jason sighed and stroked Brent's brow while he thought about the files hidden under the seat. Going back into the Grange couldn't be a good thing for any of them. "Agent Morrison, we need to talk. Now. Bad things are happening at those labs."

Chapter
TWENTY-NINE

JASON caught his breath as Rachel pulled into the Grange and slowed for the security gate. "I've got a bad feeling about this place."

She shrugged. "We'll be fine. I understand your suspicions, but from what you told me, your evidence is pretty thin. In any case, if we're going to check it out, how else would we start except by going here?"

He squirmed. "I don't know. But I don't trust Strorm. I don't think you should either."

"Really?" Weariness dragged at her voice. "He's an *FBI agent* and my boss, for God's sake. I *have* to trust him." She stopped the van and rolled down her window as a uniformed guard approached. "I think we're expected, Sergeant."

The man shined a light in her face. "Yes, ma'am. Agent Strorm is already inside. But I've still got to see your ID."

"Certainly." She showed him her FBI identification. "The two in the back are in my custody."

Jason shielded his eyes with his hand when the security guard beamed his flashlight into the backseat.

Brent stirred, and his eyes fluttered open. "Where are we?"

Jason murmured, "At the gate to—"

The guard interrupted him, "You two got any ID?"

Rachel spoke from the front seat. "You've already taken my ID, Sergeant. Surely prisoners in the custody of an FBI agent don't need ID."

He turned his beam back on her face. "Don't look like they're in custody to me. Besides, I gotta have ID. My orders are nobody gets in without ID."

"Don't shine that thing in my face, Sergeant." Her voice snapped with command, and he lowered the flashlight.

"I still gotta have ID."

Brent reached in his back pocket, pulled out his wallet, and offered his driver's license. "Will this do, sir?"

His voice sounded bleary to Jason's ears, but he couldn't suppress a grin as he followed suit. The guard disappeared into the gatehouse, where he scribbled something in his log book and then made a phone call. His gaze never left the van while he listened to the phone.

Rachel turned around and gave them a grim smile. "Thanks, boys. I should have just arrested him for interfering with a federal agent and obstructing justice."

Brent gave her a shaky smile. "It's simpler this way, don't you think?" His voice had a faint quiver, and Jason's breath caught in his throat.

"Are you all right, man?" He stroked Brent's brow. "You feel a little clammy."

His smile was like sunshine. "I'm fine. Really."

The guard returned and handed their driver's licenses through the window. "All right, then. You know where you're going, ma'am?"

"I'm not sure. Where's the infirmary?"

"It's in the basement of the main building, ma'am. Just follow the road to the second building on the right. You can park in the circle drive. I'll let them know you're coming."

"Thank you, Sergeant." She waited for him to raise the gate and pulled on through. When he was out of earshot, she muttered, "Like I didn't just see him call it in. He probably has to check with the friggin' front office to get permission to scratch his ass. Ain't bureaucracy grand?"

Jason found himself liking her, even if she was his captor. "I got the same runaround when I came out here last month to tour the place. Nice to see our tax dollars at work."

She snorted. "Right. Except that I think he's a private rent-a-cop, not DOD. The military would have just taken my FBI ID and not futzed with yours after I told them you were in my custody."

Jason frowned. "He was wearing fatigues. But I guess you're right. The light was too bad for me to see his insignia."

She nodded. "Other than three stripes pinned to his collar, his uniform was bare." She pulled the van to a stop. "Here we are."

Jason recognized the three-story brick building he'd visited earlier. Most of the structure was dark tonight, but the glass-enclosed atrium at the front entrance blazed with light. Inside, Montel stood chatting with Gary and the mysterious third man who'd appeared from the woods. The commando had removed his ski mask and looked ghostly pale in the glare of the lights. Gary must have said something funny, because all three broke into laughter. A balding, middle-aged man in a white lab coat stood to one side, staring at the screen on his cell phone.

Jason turned to Rachel and asked, "Who's that other guy, the commando-type talking with your boss and Gary?"

She shrugged. "You ask a lot of questions."

"I was just wondering if you had a mirror. I wanted to check to see if he has a reflection, now that he's taken off his ski mask."

Brent's mouth squiggled in an impish grin, and Rachel's twitched, but she kept her voice professional. "Very funny. Come on, get going. Let's not keep them waiting."

She slid open the rear doors and waited for them to exit. Brent stepped from the back of the van and made sure the files were still hidden under the seat. He turned to help Jason out and then followed him toward the building. When Jason put weight on his ankle, pain exploded up his leg, and he grimaced.

"Are you all right?" Brent squatted down and pulled up Jason's pant leg. "My God, your ankle's all swelled up like a balloon. How did you manage that hike back to the van?"

Jason grunted. "Badly, and with great pain."

Brent slipped an arm under Jason's shoulder. "Try not to stress it any more. Maybe they've got some ice in the infirmary." The two of them hobbled after Rachel into the cool interior of the lab building.

Gary sauntered over and asked Brent, "How are you doing?"

"I'm better. I rested some on the ride here. Jason's ankle looks pretty bad, though."

Gary rolled his eyes. "Whatever."

Montel cocked an eyebrow at Rachel. "Didn't you cuff your prisoners, Agent Morrison?"

She shrugged. "One of them can hardly walk, with a sprained ankle, and the other one is still woozy from a rap on the head." She nodded toward Gary. "Besides, I see you didn't cuff yours either."

Montel's mouth quirked. He frowned and muttered, "That's different." He waved the white-coated man forward. "This is Dr. Jelnick. He's one of the researchers here, but he's also a board-certified internist. He'll check out the injuries." He turned back to Rachel. "Mr. Verloc and I have a videoconference scheduled upstairs with Dr. Holmes. Will you please assist Dr. Jelnick while he gives our three friends here medical attention? By the time he's cleared them, we should be done."

Rachel scowled and stepped closer to the older agent. Between reading her lips and hearing muffled syllables, Jason understood her hushed words. "We need to talk, Montel. Now. I don't like this at all."

Strorm beamed at her and boomed, "That's excellent, Agent Morrison. You've done really fine work. I'll be sure to put a letter in your file. Now, you help the good doctor with these three. I assure you that we'll finish this thing off tonight."

Her jaw muscles jumped. She glanced at the others and kept her voice low. "You're planning to close the investigation, sir? Do you really think that's wise?"

"Who said anything about closing the investigation? I just said we'd finish our part of it." His voice hardened. "Now, do as I ordered, Agent Morrison."

Her face turned white, and silence stretched between them. At last she spoke. "Very well, sir. I agree they need medical attention, and I won't delay that any further. But I need answers. And soon."

"Trust me, Rachel. You'll have answers and more before the night is over." He turned away. "Kimball, please come with me." The pallid stranger followed, quiet as a ghost.

Dr. Jelnick stepped forward and spoke in clipped tones. "So, which of you has the concussion?"

Brent held up his hand. "I hit my head. Don't know that I've got a concussion."

Jelnick nodded. "All right then. We'll take care of you first." He peered into Brent's eyes and grunted. "You look fine, but just to be safe I want to do a CT scan. Lucky for you, we've got one right here on site in the neuroscience lab." He turned to Jason and continued in the same indifferent tone. "You there, with the bad leg. Stay put. I'll send someone up for you with a wheelchair. Don't try to walk on it. I'll see you down in the infirmary after I've got the CT scan done."

He turned to Gary last. "How about you? You look fit. Any problems I need to look at?"

Gary shrugged and shook his head. "My wrist is a little stiff." He held out his arm, and Jelnick palpated the joint.

"There's a little swelling, nothing bad. Move your hand for me. Uh-huh. Any pain?" Gary shook his head "no," but Jelnick frowned and examined the back of his forearm. "What do we have here? A rash, and this looks like a scar from an old gunshot wound."

"Yeah. I got shot three days ago."

Jelnick's eyes widened. "Three days ago," he mused, and then faced Montel. "Is he one of the—"

Montel interrupted, snapping, "That'll be enough, Doctor. Just tend to your patients and don't ask questions."

The physician blinked and then turned back to Gary. "That rash is a bad case of poison ivy, son. When we get to the infirmary, we'll give you a salve to help with the itch."

Jelnick led Brent to the elevator, and Gary tagged after them, along with Montel and the other man, leaving Jason alone with Rachel. He leaned against the wall and winced. "What's going on here, Agent Morrison?"

She glanced at him and scowled, but then her face softened. "I could try to find a chair or something for you."

"I'll be okay. Really." He inspected her features. "You have an honest face, Agent Rachel Morrison. You've treated us fairly."

"That's my job."

He made a decision. "I trust you. That other guy, Strorm? I think he's a stuffed shirt at best, and a sadist at worst. And the one he called Kimball is just freaky. But you'll do right by us, given a chance."

She tweaked an eyebrow at him. "What's your point?"

"There's more going on here than meets the eye. I told you about the evidence we found of crimes dating back twenty years in this place, maybe more. I don't care what anyone says, I'm not going to let them sweep any of this under the rug. It's too big."

Her eyes narrowed, and she gave him an appraising stare. "I won't stand for a cover-up either, even though it's hard to prosecute crimes that old. Tell me what else you know, Jason."

Before he could answer, the elevator swished open and a perky nurse in surgical greens popped out, pushing a wheel chair. She flashed a smile at them, and the braces on her teeth gleamed silver. "Which one of you needs this?"

Jason sighed in relief. "That'd be me, miss." He read her nametag. "Miriam. You're a lifesaver."

She giggled. "Thanks. You won't die from a sprained ankle, but we can make it feel better. Doctor said to elevate your leg. Which one is it?"

Jason pointed, and she adjusted the chair. "All righty! Shall we go?" Without waiting for an answer, she pushed him into the elevator, with Rachel trailing behind.

When they got to the infirmary, Miriam helped Jason onto an examining table and untied his sneaker. "My, that poor thing is swollen, isn't it. Can you move it for me, hon?"

Jason screwed his eyes closed and rotated his foot. "Yeah. It kind of throbs, but mostly it hurts when I put weight on it."

"You poor dear." She felt the bones in his foot and examined his Achilles tendon. "Well, it doesn't look like anything's broken. Are you allergic to any medications?"

"Not that I know of."

"Taking anything? No? Well, Doctor said you could have a Lortab for the swelling and pain." She bustled off to the other side of the room and returned with a pill in a bubble pack and a glass of water. "You take that, hon, and I'll get an ice pack and Ace bandage. We'll get you all fixed up in nothing flat." She flashed a metallic smile at him, patted his knee, and left the room.

Jason downed the pill and then took the moment of privacy to speak to Rachel. "I'll show you my notes when we're alone. I've got a lot of information that connects the Gerion Group and crimes at this lab. Even if they can't be prosecuted, it would damage their reputation. They'd want to cover it up."

She looked disappointed. "Everyone knows this lab is connected to the Gerion Group. It's a matter of public record that they fund research here."

"No, I'm not talking about the grants everyone knows about. I'm talking about funding that's funneled through a rat's nest of shell companies. Money laundering, like the Mob does, except this involved one of the biggest companies in the country. Besides, those research reports I told you about are pretty damning evidence of abuses, crimes against humanity even. You need to look at them to really get the whole import. The people at this place have done some really bad shit, and it all ties back to the Gerion Group."

Her face returned to a stolid, professional calm. "I'll be interested in examining your evidence."

"Ha. I recognize that look, Agent. You know something. You've put what I just told you together with something you've got, and now you're not talking. Fair is fair. If I show you mine, you've got to show me yours."

The nurse stepped back into the room, and her face turned pink. "Well, I guess *we're* feeling better, aren't we? No hanky-panky in my infirmary, you hear?" She took a moment to throw a cold glare Rachel's way and then sat on an examining stool and tugged on Jason's leg. "Hold still while I wrap your ankle, hon. A compression bandage and that Lortab will make it feel *allll* better."

Jason lay back on the examining table and closed his eyes. He'd made his point. Rachel had to come clean with him, or he'd not tell her anything, by all that's holy and the First Amendment.

The door to the infirmary swished open, and Gary's voice grated against Jason's ears. "I got bored. The doctor sent me down here to get something for my poison ivy."

Miriam glanced up, and her mouth formed a little "oh" shape. Jason avoided rolling his eyes at her reaction to Gary's appearance. Her voice bubbled like Paris Hilton cooing over a new outfit. "Well, aren't you the handsome one! I'll be done here in just a jiffy, and then I'll help you out. Have a seat, hon."

Rachel nudged a chair toward Gary with her toe. "Yes, do have a seat. While you wait, I wonder if you'd mind answering a question or two."

He shrugged and flopped into the chair. "Sure. Why not? But you should know your boss already debriefed me."

A slow smile spread across her lips. "I'm sure he did. I'm curious, though, Mr. Dixon. Tell me, where did you pick up that poison ivy on your arm? Maybe you were someplace near the Hyde farm? Say, a couple of days ago?"

In the fluorescent lighting of the little clinic Jason couldn't be sure, but it seemed as though Gary's face turned ashen. He found himself liking Rachel even more, and waited for Gary's answer.

Chapter THIRTY

RACHEL'S heart raced, but she controlled her features and kept her breathing steady. Bits and pieces of evidence clicked into place, as though a jigsaw puzzle arranged itself into sudden, startling coherence. She loved this part of her job, where the threads began to weave together. She stepped closer to Gary, invading his personal space. "Where were you the afternoon the Hydes disappeared, Mr. Dixon?"

He slid his chair away from her and snarled, "I was at work. You can check with anyone there." She tensed as he reached into a pocket, but he just pulled out a business card case. "Here. Call them."

She accepted the card, glanced at it, and a thrill of recognition coursed through her. "You work for Grace Development, Mr. Dixon?"

"That's what the card says." He seemed to sense an advantage, and his tone became more belligerent. "They'll vouch for me and where I was. Brent knows I was working that afternoon. He called me. I told him I'd be late getting to the farm."

Jason looked up from where the nurse still fussed over his ankle. "I seem to recall Brent saying something about that."

She nodded and put on her best dumb and simple look. "I remember too. It's somewhere in my notes, from when I interviewed him. Anyway, I'm sure your colleagues at Grace Development will confirm your alibi." She scanned him from head to toe, and her gaze stopped at his shoes. "Say, those are pretty cool running shoes. Are they Reeboks, by any chance?"

He rolled his eyes. "I suppose. But they're walking shoes, not running shoes."

She knelt to examine them. "I was thinking of getting a pair for my cousin. What kind are these? Sporterra Extremes, by any chance? That's what he said he wanted."

"I dunno. What difference does it make?"

"I see they are." She kept her simpleton expression glued to her face while longing for a search warrant. "They comfortable? He does a lot of hiking in the woods."

"Yeah, they're fine." Impatience crackled in his voice. "Shoes are shoes."

She lounged in one of the chairs and glanced at Jason. He stared at her with narrowed eyes and seemed about to speak. She could see his synapses synaping, and gave him the slightest shake of her head, praying that he'd not reveal her suspicions by asking questions. She was certain the CSI team would tie Gary's footprints to the Zimmerman murder scene, but it wouldn't do any good unless she had a warrant to obtain the shoes. For that, she'd need to be sure he didn't know her suspicions and destroy the evidence.

Jason's eyes sparked, and his mouth quirked, but he didn't speak. She sighed. *I knew he was a smart one.*

For a diversion, she pulled out her notebook. "I'd like to go over one more time what happened that night, when the three of you were shot at. Jason, could you tell me what you remember?"

He blinked and seemed to pull himself away from his reporter's instinct to ask questions. He leaned back and closed his eyes.

The nurse *tsked* at him and tugged on his leg. "Now, now. Hold still. That's a good boy. I'll be just a second longer."

He blinked at her and returned his gaze to Rachel. "Sorry. Well, I'd gotten a tip from my source that Brent was in danger."

She nodded and made a note. "Any chance you'll tell me the identity of that source?"

"Even if I wanted to, I couldn't. He always called me. I tried reverse look-up on the number, but it was a prepaid cell." He paused and shrugged. "He used electronics to disguise his voice too. For all I know, he was really a woman."

She caught something in his tone. "A woman? Do you think that's likely? Tell me what you know."

His voice turned petulant. "I don't *know* anything, except that I got this call. Whoever it was said it was urgent that I warn Brent right away. So I drove to the farm and, well, warned him."

She jotted another note, killing time. "And then what happened?"

The nurse interrupted. "All done! We'll be feeling better soon." She batted her eyelashes at Gary before glancing at Rachel. "Would you mind if I treated his poison ivy?"

Rachel shrugged. "Go ahead. We can do this while you work."

The nurse shuffled through the contents of a drawer and then went to Gary. "How far up your arm does it go?"

He leered at her. "It itches all the way to my bicep. It was hell working out earlier today."

She gave him a sunny smile, and her braces gleamed in the fluorescent lights. "Well, maybe you should slip off your shirt so I can check you out." She turned pink. "I mean, so I can check out your poison ivy."

"Sure." Gary unbuttoned his shirt and pulled it off. Rachel avoided rolling her eyes while he flexed his muscles for the nurse. He pointed to where red welts ran up his arm.

The nurse pulled on latex gloves. "You poor thing. You must be miserable. Let me put some salve on that. I could give you a Benadryl too. It would help with the itching."

Gary flinched. "No drugs. I'll just tough it out."

She *tsked* again and applied a white cream to his arm. "Well, this will help, hon."

Gary flexed his pecs and leaned back, seeming to enjoy her attentions. If Rachel didn't know he was gay, she could have sworn he was flirting with the little nurse. She turned back to Jason, who glanced at Gary, then at her, and smirked. She chose to ignore his expression and asked, "So, this warning you got from your source. What exactly did they say?"

"Just that he was in danger, right then, and it was urgent I warn him."

"So you went to the farm. What happened then?"

"Gary answered the door holding a kitchen cleaver. Like he was expecting trouble."

She turned to Gary, who was murmuring something unintelligible to the nurse. "Is that right, Mr. Dixon? Did you have reason to expect trouble that night?"

He jerked his attention away from the nurse and to Rachel. "Not really. But Brent's parents were missing under suspicious circumstances. I was just being careful."

"With a cleaver?"

He shrugged. "It was what I had."

"Uh-huh." She pretended to make another note, and wished that Montel would return with Brent. "What happened next?"

Jason seemed to decide it was his turn to answer. "Well, I delivered the warning. They didn't believe me, which I guess isn't surprising under the circumstances. But then someone fired shots at us, and things happened pretty fast after that."

"Tell me what you remember, in order."

"Well, I'd tripped on the stairs and fallen down right before the shooting started. Brent hit the dirt next to me before the second shot, and Gary ran into the house."

Gary interjected, "I remembered seeing Brent's .22 in his bedroom. I went inside to arm myself."

Rachel turned to him. "Exactly when did you get shot?"

The nurse gave a little gasp and whispered, "You were *shot?* And you still went inside to get a gun? You brave thing, you!"

Gary shrugged. "The second bullet grazed my left arm. It's all healed."

Rachel tapped on her notepad. "Who called the sheriff?"

Gary puffed his chest, and the nurse wiggled closer to him. "I did, on my phone, while I was running upstairs for the rifle."

Rachel frowned. Something didn't fit. She flipped back through her notes. "Are you sure? For some reason I thought Brent called 911."

Jason piped up, his eyes alight. "No, it was Gary. I remember. I bet he called using Brent's mobile phone. I remember when we were hiding behind the stairs, Brent was going to call, but then he said Gary had his phone."

Rachel leaned back and stared at Gary. "You had Brent's cell phone?"

He shrugged. "Yeah, that's right. I guess I might have reached for his instead of mine in the heat of the moment. He'd given it to me earlier, in case the sheriff called while he was in the shower."

Keep your face passive, Rachel. Don't give anything away. "So you must have had his cell phone in your possession all evening?" That should be a safe question.

"I suppose. What of it?"

Jason's eyebrows crawled up his forehead, and his voice quivered with excitement. "But that means *he's* the one who did the money transfers, not Brent!" He turned to face Rachel. "Don't you see? This proves Brent's innocent." He paused while she again signaled him with a slight head shake. "Oh. I bet you already figured that out, huh?"

Gary's face turned ashen, and he brushed the nurse aside. "I don't know what the two of you are talking about. What money transfers?"

Rachel closed her notebook. "I think you have a lot to answer for, Mr. Dixon." She took a deep breath. "You have the right to remain silent. Anything you say can and will—"

The door to the infirmary swished open, and Montel stepped into the room. He listened for less than two syllables before he interrupted. "Just what do you think you're doing, Agent Morrison?"

She paused but kept her eyes on Gary. "I'm reading Dixon here his rights, sir. I think he's the shooter in the Zimmerman murder, and he just admitted that he had possession of Hyde's cell phone when the money transfers took place."

The nurse's face turned pink, and she looked at Gary like he'd crawled from under a rock. Brent stumbled into the room behind Strorm, with Dr. Jelnick at his elbow. When he spoke, he slurred his words. "Zimmerman murder? You mean our neighbor's been *murdered?*"

Strorm turned to face him. "That's right, with a 9mm shot to the head. Do you have a 9mm pistol, young man?"

Brent leaned into Jelnick and blinked. "What? No. All I've got is my .22." His fingers trembled through his hair, like bony little spiders.

Strorm's voice carried triumph. "Then why did you have a box of 9mm ammo hidden in your underwear drawer?"

Rachel interrupted. "Anyone could have put that there, sir." She nodded in Gary's direction. "This one had ample opportunity, for example. And he works for our friends at *Grace Development.*"

Montel nodded. "Yes, of course. I know. I've spoken to them, and they vouch for him." He scowled at her. "Don't get ahead of yourself in this investigation, Agent Morrison."

Gary leaned back with a smug look on his face. "See. I told you they'd vouch for me."

Despite herself, her face heated. She confronted Montel and didn't try to hide her words from the others. "Sir, we need to talk. Privately."

"All in due time, Agent Morrison. You're doing fine. Just don't get ahead of me." He looked around the room. "I've spoken with Dr. Holmes, and I think we can clear this all up with a visit to his lab back in town."

Rachel considered this for a moment. After what Jason had told her, she didn't trust the corporate security here at Grange Station. As a matter of fact, she didn't trust Montel. She remembered that the lab on campus just had passive security, with no hired thugs. Maybe that was better, after all. The thought of thugs reminded her of Montel's private contractor, and she asked, "Where did your agent go? Verloc? Was that his name?"

Montel's eyes narrowed. "You'd do well to forget you ever heard that name. I've sent him on an errand." His gaze swept over the room, as if dismissing her. "I think it's time to leave. Shall we go?" He held the door open.

She waited a beat, but couldn't think of anything else to do. "All right, boys, back outside." She caught an urgent expression on Jason's face and asked, "Do you need help?"

Relief flooded his face for an instant, and then his features turned impassive. "Perhaps you could lend me your arm, Agent Morrison. My ankle's still pretty sensitive."

Gary rolled his eyes. "Pansy." He hastened to Brent's side, snatched his hand. "How you doing?"

Jelnick spoke up. "He doesn't have a concussion, but he's suffering from fatigue and worry. He has every reason to be stressed, what with his parents missing. I gave him some Ativan for anxiety. It might make him sleepy."

Gary grunted and led Brent into the corridor, followed by Montel, Jelnick, and the nurse. The door swished closed, leaving Rachel alone with Jason.

Jason leaned into her and whispered, "What the fuck did they do to him? I don't like that they drugged him."

She frowned. "You mean Brent? He did seem a little spacey, but I'm sure he'll be all right. Montel won't let anything happen to him. He was really clear with me on the way to the Grange earlier tonight that we were to protect him, not let anyone hurt him."

Jason stood and leaned on her shoulder. "Who's gonna protect him from Montel?" He winced as they hobbled to the door. "Look, all our evidence is in folders under the backseat in the van. We've got to get those out of there, to protect them. We can't just leave them here."

Rachel nodded. "Agreed. It's certainly something the people running this place would want to get their hands on." She paused as they approached the elevator. The lights showed it was on the first floor. "Nice of them to wait for us."

"Gives you and me a chance to talk. Good move to offer to help me." He paused and chewed on his lip. "You know, I've been wondering why they just left those files laying around. They're clearly important, but they were just in an abandoned file room, with slap-dash security. That homeless guy hinted that he was watching them for Brent's mother, but I don't see how that can make any sense."

She sighed. "Nothing makes sense right now." The elevator dinged, and she helped him inside. "Those files. Will they fit in my handbag?"

"It's big enough. You might have to dump some stuff out to make them fit."

She nodded and pushed the button for the first floor. "Not a problem. When we join the others, just keep your mouth shut and follow my lead, okay?"

"Okay." He squeezed her shoulder. "I'm glad we're on the same side."

She muttered, "Me too." She hoped she wouldn't have to betray him.

Chapter
THIRTY-ONE

JASON'S ankle throbbed inside the Ace bandage as he leaned against the side of the elevator cab. Soft orchestral strings sighed from the overhead speakers, playing the Beatles tune "Nowhere Man." He screwed his eyes closed and tried to make sense of things.

The doors swooshed open, revealing the bright lights and polished terrazzo of the entry. Rachel tugged at his arm. "You need help?"

He tested his ankle with a hesitant step. "It still aches, but the wrapping and painkillers seem to have helped. Where is everybody?"

"Outside, waiting for us, I bet. Maybe you should still lean on me a bit, for appearances."

"Okay." His fingers wrapped about her arm, and found solid muscle coiled under her baggy sweatshirt. "Work out much?" he muttered.

"Shut up."

She pushed him through the glass doors, and he blinked against the flashing red and blue lights of a patrol car. "Looks like the cavalry's arrived," he whispered.

She shook her head, and her mouth formed a grim line. "I said, keep quiet." She tugged him forward toward the car.

Montel appeared from the shadows and hailed her. "Agent Morrison. I've commandeered a spare patrol car from the local security team for our prisoners. Secure them in the back, please."

They stopped by the car, and Rachel opened the rear door. Jason peered inside. A wire cage separated the backseat from the front, and the interior of the door had no handle. Brent huddled on the opposite side, his head resting on the door and his eyes closed. Jason cast his gaze around for Gary, but didn't see him in the flickering light.

Rachel reached for her handcuffs, but Montel called out, "Don't waste time with those. That's one reason I got this vehicle. Those two will be secure in the back. You can drive them to the lab."

She nodded and answered, "Yes, sir. Where's the other prisoner? Dixon?" She pushed Jason into the car.

"He'll ride with me, in my SUV. Everything secure?"

"Yes, sir. But I'd like to search the van, if you don't mind. Just to double check, make sure we haven't missed anything."

"It'll be safe here. The guards will see that no one disturbs it."

Jason clambered into the back of the patrol car, and Rachel slammed the door after him. He slid across the seat toward Brent. "You okay, man?"

His eyes fluttered open. "Yeah. I'm just kind of woozy. Let me rest, okay?"

Jason gripped his hand and squeezed. "Sure."

Rachel opened the front door but didn't get inside. "Sir, I still think I should check out the van. It'll only take a few seconds. If there's anything there, looking now will keep the chain of evidence with the FBI."

Montel's voice snapped with impatience. "Whatever. Just don't dally." He climbed into his SUV and called out through the open door. "You know where Dr. Holmes's lab is at on campus?"

"I visited it yesterday, sir. I can find it. Will you wait for us in the lobby?"

"We'll be in his office. I'll text you with the room number once I'm there." He slammed the door to his vehicle. In moments, he sped away.

Rachel stuck her head in through the open door. "I'll be right back. It's under the backseat, right?"

Jason nodded. "Right. A stack of file folders. There might be two stacks. My notes are there too. The bigger stack would be the stuff we found tonight."

She trotted away to his van, and Jason turned back to Brent. Jason rested his head against Brent's chest and listened to the steady *lub-dub* of his heartbeat. He pulled back and brushed his fingers through Brent's spiky blond hair, but the other didn't stir. He frowned, and wondered if he should wake him up. He didn't trust that doctor at all.

He pulled out his cell phone to check on the treatment of concussion, but the front door slammed open and Rachel slid into the drivers' seat.

She tapped her purse, which now bulged with documents. "Got them." She started the engine, shut off the flashing lights, and pulled into the roadway. "I'll be glad to get out of this place. I don't trust the corporate security here at all." Headlights flashed against the chain-link fence and cast ghostly shadows through the thick forest surrounding the facility.

Jason leaned forward. "You got all the files? Both stacks?"

"Yeah. I checked. Your notes are kind of messy."

"That's what my editor says." He looked back at Brent. "Hey, should I wake him up or something? I thought concussion patients shouldn't sleep."

"The doctor said he didn't have a concussion. I'd let him rest. Besides, it's fine to sleep after a concussion. That's an old wives' tale."

Whiskers bristled against his fingers when he stroked Brent's cheek. "You sure?"

"Yeah, I'm sure. I did the first aid refresher just last quarter." The car slowed as they approached the entrance to the Grange, and she dimmed the lights. "Good, that asshole guard's waving us through this time. Montel must have spoken to him."

Jason decided he'd already trusted her with everything else; he may as well trust her advice on Brent too. Besides, she knew things. "So, we're going to Dr. Holmes's office? What's *that* about?"

"I'm not sure." She slowed as she approached the crest of a steep hill. "You know, I wonder why he didn't arrange to take all three of you guys with him. I don't think he really trusts me. Maybe he wanted to be alone with Dixon for some reason."

Jason waited, but she didn't say anything else. He decided to press her. "I think you know something more, Rachel. How about we trade information?"

She glanced over her shoulder, and an impish grin flashed across her face. "I don't need to trade. I've already got your files in my purse."

His face heated. "That's not fair. Besides, we need to put things together before we get to Dr. Holmes's lab, and you can't do that in the time we've got. You said my files were messy, after all."

"Yeah, yeah. I was just foolin' with you. Tell me what you've got. You said you traced the funding for that lab back there?"

Jason leaned forward and gripped the wire cage. "Yeah. There's a big DARPA grant, but that's classified and no one would tell me anything about it. But the biggest part of the funding is from this consortium of a dozen or so private companies. At least, on paper, it looks like there's a dozen of them."

"But you found otherwise?"

"Yeah. All but three of them are shells. Tracking the ownership led me to a couple dozen more corporations, mostly shells that seemed to own each other. They all seemed to track back to just three companies."

"Let me guess. Granville Pulp and Paper, Brownfield Biologics, and Grace Development."

"How did you know?"

"You remember the brokerage firm, the one where Brent supposedly stole that money?"

"Yeah?"

"When I started following the source of the funds, it passed through sixty-some shells. Those three were the only companies with real names behind them."

His ears perked up. "You got names? I couldn't get at the incorporation papers."

"A National Security Letter does wonders to open up financial records. Yeah, I got names."

The wire mesh bit into his fingers as his grip tightened. Despite himself, his voice quivered. "So give."

"Aaron Holmes, for one. Charles Hyde, Brent's father, for another, owns twenty percent of Brownfield Biologics. That's worth several billion dollars."

Jason glanced toward the sleeping young man beside him. "Really? Sweet Jesus. Who else?"

"Hard to say. Someone named Minock, and some German woman I couldn't track. Zeigler. She had a funny first name. She owned twenty percent too."

A little thrill pulsed in his chest as the pieces clicked together. "Meike Zeigler."

"That's her. How'd you know?"

"That's Brent's mother's maiden name. Did you know she once worked for Holmes, before Brent was born? As a researcher?"

Her head jerked around to face him before she turned back to driving. "His *mother* worked there? This is even more fucked up than I thought."

"You're telling me. And that Minock guy? He's the homeless dude that Purcell killed, down in the file room. Before he died, he implied that Brent's mother set him up to guard the files."

She tapped on the steering wheel. "You know, Montel told me this was a big internal fight for control of the Gerion Group. I thought he was lying, or maybe crazy, but now I wonder."

"Yeah." He released the cage and flexed his fingers. He knew he was missing something. "Wait a minute. Where did you say that asshole Gary worked?"

"Grace Development."

"That's right. That's one of the companies. Shit! He's been up to his ass in this from the start!"

"That's what I think. Grace Development is almost certainly a CIA front company."

"You mean he's a fucking *spy*?"

"I'd say covert ops, more likely, except that he's way too young. It takes years of rigorous training to be an effective agent. They would have had to have started when he was just a child."

Years of training. Rachel's words jogged a memory of something from the last two days, but he couldn't quite make the connection. He frowned. Someone had said something about a school for training children to be soldiers. Who was it?

Streetlights flashed into the interior of the patrol car as they entered town. Brent stirred, and his eyes fluttered open. "Where are we?"

Jason reached out and squeezed his hand. "We're back in town. Rachel, the FBI agent, is taking us to Dr. Holmes's office, at the Stillwell Research Center."

Brent frowned, and confusion showed in his eyes. "Dr. Holmes's office? Why there?" He looked around. "Where are we? And where's Gary?"

"We're in the back of a police car. Gary went with that other FBI agent, Strorm."

Brent closed his eyes again. He slurred his words as he spoke in petulant tones. "Strorm. He was mean to me. I didn't like him."

"It's all right. I won't let anyone hurt you."

The car pulled into the parking lot of the Center and stopped. Rachel killed the engine and turned to face Jason. "We're here, and I'm not sure we know any more now than we did before."

That phantom memory still itched at his subconscious as he answered, "We know a lot more. It just doesn't make any sense."

Brent peered out the window and pawed at the door. "I know where we're at. It's Dr. Athair's lab. I work here. Why won't the door open?"

Rachel jumped out of the front and ran to Brent's side of the car. When she opened the door, he stumbled out of the car and weaved a bit before steadying himself on the door. Jason followed him out. "You okay, man?"

"Yeah. I was just dizzy for a second. Why are we here?" He surveyed the lot. "There's Dr. Athair's car. Are we here to see her?"

Rachel leaned into Jason and murmured, "She's another part owner of Brownfield Biologics. Did I mention that?"

Jason avoided her gaze as more bits fell into place.

Rachel gripped his arm. "You just figured something else out. Tell me."

He narrowed his eyes. "She's got to be Deep Throat—my source. I suspected before, but now I'm sure. It's got to be all about the money."

Brent's eyes gleamed in the moonlight as he looked from one to the other. "What are you two talking about? What money?" A light breeze rustled through the trees, and he seemed to sway in the gentle wind.

Jason's heart ached for him. "It's all right. Don't worry. I'll protect you." It might be all about the money for everyone else, but Jason knew better. For him, it was all about Brent.

The dark windows and brutalist façade of the Stillwell Research center loomed over them. A lone window on the third floor glowed, and ghostly figures moved about inside.

Jason pulled out his cell phone. Rachel's eyes flashed. "What are you doing?"

"I'm going to leave a message for my editor. Just the time, my location, and where we're going. Nothing more. I'll feel better if someone else knows where we're at."

She blinked at him and seemed to think about it. "Montel said this was secret, that national security was involved. Just in case he's not fucking with us, don't reveal any more than that, okay?"

"You can listen in." Jason flipped his phone open and spoke into the speaker. It transcribed his words and sent a text to his editor. "There. Shall we go?" He took Brent's hand, and together they followed Rachel inside the dark front entrance.

Chapter THIRTY-TWO

JASON'S skin prickled as they entered the air-conditioned interior of the Stillwell-Holmes Labs. Only the swish of a janitor polishing the terrazzo broke the deathly silence inside. Muted lighting cast golden shadows in the cavernous entryway, while dark corridors vanished into the bowels of the building.

Brent leaned into Jason and goggled at their surroundings. Jason murmured, "It'll be all right," while he squeezed Brent's hand and Rachel checked her cell phone.

Her eyes shimmered in the glow from the screen. "No text. Dammit. Montel *said* he'd text me where Holmes's office was at."

Brent spoke, his voice slurred and dreamy. "I know where his office is."

Her gaze jerked to him, and Jason instinctively edged closer, to protect him. When she spoke, her voice hissed over the whine of the floor polisher and bounced off the glass walls. "That's right. You worked here. Where do we go?" Her phone buzzed, and her hand gave a little start. "Just a second." She scowled while reading something on the screen. Jason peered over her shoulder while she announced, "Montel says suite 3B12. Now all we need is an elevator."

Brent tugged at his hand and murmured, "I know the way."

Jason took a step, and his leg throbbed. He faltered and winced. "Take it easy, okay?"

Brent turned to face him in a pool of moonglow passing through the exterior windows. His eyes glinted, and his pallid features seemed frozen, preternaturally placid. "I'm sorry." He paused and appeared to concentrate. "I forgot. You hurt your ankle doing… something. I don't quite remember what. How is it?"

"I'm fine. Just don't walk so fast, okay?" Jason leaned closer and whispered, "Are you all right? You seem pretty out of it."

"I'm not sure. Everything is so… distant, somehow. Like I'm floating in a dream within a dream."

Jason frowned. "That damned doctor gave you something. Ativan."

Brent turned a puzzled glance his way. "Doctor? What doctor?" He stopped at a bank of elevators. "Dr. Holmes's office is on the third floor."

Rachel pushed the button while Jason fretted. He turned and stroked Brent's brow. "I've got a bad feeling about this. I wish we'd taken him to a real doctor, not that corporate shill."

She shrugged. "He struck me as competent enough. Dr. Jelnick said he gave him an anti-anxiety drug. Sometimes those cause temporary cognitive impairment. I know." She shuddered. "I'm sure he'll be all right."

Jason chewed at his lower lip and peered into Brent's eyes: perfect amethyst eyes that reminded him of the color of the sky just before twilight. He wondered how he could have missed noticing how beautiful they were.

When they entered the elevator, Brent heaved a sigh and leaned against the wall. "I'm so *sleepy*. Maybe I could just lie down someplace?" The Muzak from the overhead speakers sighed into a string quartet playing "Scarborough Fair/Canticle." "Oh, that's nice. My mother loves that song." He started to hum along, out of tune and out of cadence.

The elevator stopped, and the doors slid open into another corridor of dark shadows. Rachel stepped out first and looked left and right. "The lights are on in the office down there. I bet that's it."

Jason pulled at Brent's hand. "Come on. We're here."

Brent gave a little start and stepped into the corridor. "His office is on the left. How nice of him to leave the lights on." He meandered off in that direction without waiting for them.

Rachel pushed past him, went into the office first, and then held the door open for them. She pointed toward an open door, beyond which bright lights glowed and muffled voices spoke. "Looks like they're waiting for us in there. Let me check it out first."

She slipped her hand inside her purse before she called out, "Special Agent Strorm? Agent Morrison here." Craggy shadows marched across her grim features. The back of Jason's neck cramped with tension, and he held his breath. What was she expecting?

Montel's hearty voice sang out. "Rachel. I see you found us. Do come in and have a seat."

She heaved a sigh, and Jason remembered to breathe. She stepped into the room and blocked the door for an instant before turning back. "Okay, boys, come on in and have a seat. It looks like we're all here."

Jason followed her inside and blinked against the bright lights. He stubbed his toe on a conference room chair.

Rachel steadied his elbow and pulled the chair out for him. "Have a seat. Your ankle will feel better if you don't put weight on it."

"Thanks." He peered into the room. He recognized Holmes from his news photographs. Strorm and Gary stood next to him in one corner, chatting about something. Athair sat placidly on the other side of the table from him, twiddling her thumbs, her eyes sparkling. Next to her a prim, middle-aged woman with a trim figure and striking amethyst eyes sat staring at the door. She looked familiar, and then Jason placed her from twenty-year-old photographs: Mary Hyde.

Brent stumbled into the room and gave a little gasp. "Mom," he sobbed. Mary stood with her arms outstretched while he staggered around the table to her. "Mom." His voice quivered and his hands trembled. "I was so worried about you. Are you all right?"

"Brent, baby, I'm fine." She cradled his head on her shoulder and stroked his hair. Tears shimmered in her eyes, eyes that were the same incredible color as Brent's. "Everything's going to be all right, baby." She pulled him away and caressed his cheek. "How are you, darling? You look so tired."

He blinked, and his head wobbled. "I'm fine, Mom. Where have you *been*?"

"I've been busy, dear. But now we're together. Here, sit with me." She pulled out a chair and helped him into it. "That's good. Just close your eyes and rest your head on my shoulder. Everything's going to be all right."

Brent complied, but then he tensed and jerked upright. "Mom, where's Dad? I lost him too."

Her eyes glinted, steel-like, for an instant before melting into pools of warmth. "He got called away, dear. He sends his best."

Jason's eyes narrowed as Athair gave a little snort, but no one else appeared to notice.

Brent's features relaxed once more, and he settled back into his seat, his head resting against his mother's shoulder. She stroked his features. "That's my good boy." When he didn't stir, she glared at Strorm. "What have you done to him?"

Jason piped up, "He hit his head. The doctor gave him Ativan."

"Ativan. But that will…." Her voice trailed off.

Jason turned as Holmes rapped his knuckles on the conference table from the other end of the room. "Ahem. Could I have your attention, please?" He waited until everyone was staring at him. "So, I believe we have some outstanding business to close tonight." He glared at Jason. "First, though, I think we need to attend to security matters."

Montel smiled, and Jason thought of snakes and the devil. "No need. I've already signed a directive classifying this meeting as a matter of national security. The directive forbids revealing the existence of the classification, let alone the content of what we discuss." His face hardened as he turned to Jason. "That means you, Mr. First Amendment. I'm sure you've heard of extraordinary rendition. You'll disappear overseas if you so much as breathe a word of this."

Jason gave him a curt nod but didn't say anything.

Holmes steepled his fingers and looked like he'd bitten into a lemon. "Really, you bureaucrats have such faith in regulations. I prefer more direct methods."

Montel's smiled broadened. "Those are available too, as needed."

Rachel's face remained impassive, but she tapped Jason's foot, and her head gave the slightest of shakes.

Gary leaned forward, a predatory expression on his face. "Just give me the word, sir. Just give me the word. That's one job I'd love to handle."

Jason decided now was not the time to argue the niceties of constitutional law, and held his peace. Besides, he'd given all his evidence to Rachel. Now all he could do was trust her, wait, and watch.

Silence stretched for a moment. Holmes glanced first at Rachel, sniffed, and then turned to Athair and Mary Hyde. "Do the two of you agree? Everything we discuss stays in this room."

Athair rolled her eyes. "Really, Aaron, isn't it time to stop this charade? You know it doesn't matter what these... *people* know. Why don't you just come out with it?" She pointed at Gary. "Tell them about him."

Holmes shrugged. "Strorm already knows, and his security directive will silence this other agent." He tossed an indifferent glance in Rachel's direction. "I'm sorry. I forget your name." It was obvious to Jason he wasn't sorry. Holmes glanced around the table. "I see no advantage in revealing anything further."

A languid expression flowed over Gary's features, and he lounged back in his chair. "Why not, *Dad*? Are you ashamed of me?"

Holmes's expression softened, and he patted Gary on the shoulder. "Of course not, son. You've exceeded every dream I ever had for you. You know that."

Pleasure oozed across Gary's features, like a cat having its chin scratched. "Yes, Father. You've always been the one who cared for me." But then he turned to face Athair, and his expression turned feral. "As for you, you evil witch, you never appreciated me. You never acted like my mother. All those years in the school, and all you ever did was bitch at me. I'll show you. I'll show all of you." He pulled out his 9mm and slammed it on the table. The barrel pointed at Jason, like an enormous black gate to hell.

Athair's face turned ashen, and she glared at Gary. "What we did was all for you, Gary. We *made* you what you are. My conditioning and Aaron's biology, working together. Everything we did, we did together, for you."

Jason stared down the chasm of the gun, and his head spun. *Years of training. Covert ops. The story that Mandy told her friend about the special school at the Grange. Gary's weird ability to heal and his supernatural woodcraft skills.* It all fit. "I've got it. You've spent the last twenty years doing some kind of genetics experiments to produce super-soldiers, and he's one of them." He pointed at Gary, and the triumph of certainty filled his voice. Then he caught sight of the color draining from Rachel's face, and his elation froze into a cold ball of fear.

Holmes sneered at him. "Not genetics, you idiot. Epigenetics. The products are human, but with enhanced naturally occurring genetic traits and abilities. This one *already* had superior genes. Mine." He looked smug and patted Gary on the shoulder. "He just needed the right chemical triggers and conditioning to optimize his natural superiority."

Despite his fear, Jason couldn't stop himself. "My God, you experimented on your own son?"

Athair's voice still trembled, and anger flushed her face. "*Our* son." Her index finger stabbed at the tabletop. "Those sexist ingrates won't even acknowledge my part in this. He's *our project*, Aaron's and mine, and our genetic offspring." She paused and caught her breath. "As to what we did, why not? What parent doesn't want the best for their children? We gave our child the best." Tears pooled in her eyes as she stared at Gary. "So many attempts, so many failures, just one success. But it was worth it. It was all worth it."

Holmes steepled his fingers again and purred, "Enough of this. Yes, we gave our son his birthright. He's smarter, and stronger, and *better* than the human cattle. He's the *future*. Now that we have proof-of-concept, we can move to the next phase: a whole army of perfect soldiers."

Brent whimpered in his sleep and stirred against his mother's shoulder. She stroked his hair and whispered something in his ear. When she looked up, her eyes blazed. "Aaron, I've heard enough. I'll do what you want. You can have the company, the patents, the money, all of it. I'll tell you where my files are, and I'll sign anything you want. So will my husband. Just let Brent go."

Montel leaned forward and whispered, "Let *Brent* go? I think not."

Chapter
THIRTY-THREE

JASON looked into Montel's reptilian eyes, and a cold ball of fear clenched his gut. The back of his neck prickled as he followed the FBI agent's gaze toward where Brent cuddled, asleep, against his mother's shoulder. Across the room, Gary had retrieved his gun and leveled it at Jason, or maybe at Rachel. She sat next to Jason, stiff and unmoving.

Holmes frowned and cast a puzzled look at Montel. "Don't get above yourself, Strorm. We've proven the concept, about our son's—our agent's—breeding and conditioning. He even simulated homosexuality for the surveillance assignment we gave him, to watch the Hydes."

Jason wanted to spit at that fuckwad Gary. What a heartless tool!

Holmes continued, too self-absorbed to notice Jason's expression. "But now we need to clarify the ownership of this project, and do it in a way that doesn't ruin the senior financing for the next phase." He glanced at Mary and looked away. "We took care of her oafish husband with threats and cash, and then helped him to disappear. Let's buy her off too, now that we've got her price."

Jason was sure the glint in Montel's eyes didn't have anything to do with buying people off. His gaze wandered to Rachel, but her blank features revealed nothing. She kept her hand close to her purse, though. Jason remembered that's where she kept her weapon, and that heightened his sense of danger. Gary had the drop on her. What could she be thinking?

Montel gave Holmes a disgusted look before he nodded toward Mary Hyde. "I don't think we can trust her, or her husband. I'm sure corporate agrees. The money men don't like bad press, and like being threatened even less. I've known all night the time for negotiations was over."

Rachel's hand gave the tiniest of flinches, so small that Jason was sure he was the only one who noticed. *She can't deny it now. He's part of a criminal conspiracy. What's she going to do?* He reflected that dead men tell no tales, and that applied to her as much as it did to him. The thought didn't comfort him. Gary's hard expression and his unflinching aim with his gun didn't help either.

Jason flinched when Rachel straightened in her chair, glared across the room, and snapped, "Montel!"

The man's eyebrows crawled up his skull. "Not now, Agent Morrison. I'm not done discussing strategies with Dr. Holmes."

"We're federal agents, Montel. We took an oath to bear true faith and allegiance to the constitution of the United States. A sacred oath."

His eyes narrowed. "I said, *not now.* Perhaps you'd like me to have Mr. Dixon here silence you?"

A grin stretched across Gary's features. "I'd like that order. Just give me the word."

Jason reached out and touched Rachel's arm. She snatched it away. "You don't need to set your dog on me, Montel. I just wanted to be sure where you stood. I can't wait to put the cuffs on you and read you your rights."

A languid smile spread across Montel's features, and his eyes sparkled. "Why, Agent Morrison, I didn't know you cared. But handcuffs are so *déclassé*, don't you think? I do prefer my sex partners use whips and chains." He turned back to Gary and snarled, "If she moves, kill her."

"It'll be a pleasure."

Holmes scowled and drummed his fingers on the polished table. "This is getting out of hand. This isn't the same as that ridiculous Geary woman and her pathetic blackmail attempt." He nodded toward Mary and Brent. "She knows things, and can back it up with documents. If you're really worried about bad press, we need the originals."

Montel's words oozed from his lips, full of menace. "There's more at stake here than some old documents, *Dr.* Holmes."

An exasperated expression flashed on Holmes's face, and he snapped, "Whatever are you talking about? Of *course* it's about the documents."

Athair jumped to her feet. "Oh, Aaron, you are so fucking *stupid* sometimes. It's as plain as the nose on your face. Literally." Staying out of Gary's line of fire, she stepped to Brent and twisted his head around to face into the room. "Just *look* at him."

Brent's face gleamed ghostly pale in the brilliant fluorescent lighting. He squinted his eyes open, and his mouth formed a little "o." He mumbled, "What? Lemme alone. I need to sleep." He pushed Athair's hand away, rested his head on his mother's shoulder, and seemed to fall back asleep.

Athair repeated, "*Look* at him, Aaron. I saw it the day he showed up a year ago, applying for a job in my lab. *Look* at him."

Holmes seemed about to explode, but then controlled himself. "Don't get above yourself, *Dr.* Athair. Remember who's in charge here." His gaze raked over Brent, and he shrugged. "What am I supposed to see? He looks a bit like his mother."

Athair's red rage exploded in her features. She stalked across the room and shoved at him. "He's *your son*, Aaron. Your *other* son, by Mary Hyde. You never could keep it in your pants, you asshole."

Holmes gaped at Brent, then at Mary. "My son? You never told me?"

Mary's mouth formed a tight line, and her eyes sparked as she glared at Holmes for a brief instant. She seemed about to speak, but then Brent stirred and muttered something unintelligible and her attention returned to her son.

Prickles of shock tingled out Jason's fingers. He examined Holmes's face, and it became obvious, in retrospect. The cant of the eyes, the thrust of the jaw, these were unmistakable now that Athair pointed them out. Brent looked like his mother, Mary, for sure. But he looked like Holmes too. The man had to be Brent's biological father. Except there was a difference. Features that ennobled Brent, like a Greek statue, on Holmes softened to self-indulgent indolence.

Athair's voice dripped with scorn. "Yes, your other son. Not your fake adopted family. Not our perfect creation." She stopped for an instant to simper at Gary and stroke his hair. He scowled and pushed her hand away. Her icy smile turned sour as she turned back to Holmes. "Don't let *her* and her little bastard that you sired destroy all that we've built."

Jason frowned at her, confused by her sudden hostility toward Brent. "I don't understand. If you hate him, then why did you contact—" Rachel stomped on his foot, and he shut up.

Athair laughed at him. "Why did I *what*, you obnoxious little snoop? Why did I feed you information? I knew you'd root around and make waves, and that corporate would notice and send in *that* one," her finger jabbed at Montel. "I knew *they'd* fix her clock, while Aaron dithered and tried to fucking negotiate."

"But then why send me to warn Brent that night? Oh, you knew your *magnum opus* Gary was there. You wanted me to warn *him*."

He winced as Rachel jabbed him and snapped, "Will you just shut the fuck *up*, for God's sake?"

Montel chuckled. "Too late for that, I'm afraid, Agent Morrison. Far too late for that."

Athair sneered. "Don't forget what was going on at that farm." She turned back to Mary with a look of triumph. "When corporate finds out about the strain of *M. vaccae* we found in those cows, you're toast."

Montel glanced at Mary Hyde and then smirked at Holmes. "It turns out young Mr. Hyde is your progeny in more ways than one, Professor." He turned back to Brent's mother, and a tight little smile slithered across his features. "I can't wait, Mrs. Hyde, to inform New York about your personal little science project. By the way, how's that working out for you?"

Her eyes widened, and then enormous pride flooded her countenance. "Just fine. Better than I ever hoped." She squeezed Brent's hand, and a feeble smile fluttered on his lips.

Jason peered across the table into her face, and then at Brent. His heart sank as he figured out the rest of the secret. He wished he was wrong, but he knew he wasn't.

Chapter THIRTY-FOUR

JASON jerked his attention away from Brent's peaceful, sleeping face when Montel's voice rapped into the room.

"Mr. Dixon. Listen to me."

Gary turned to face him, his features rigid as granite. His body quivered on tiptoe, as if queued for action.

Montel continued in more forceful tones. "Agent Morrison is armed. *Loose the wineskin's jutting neck.*"

Jason frowned. This was a hell of a time to start misquoting Euripides.

But then Gary's body lurched. Things moved faster than Jason could have imagined possible.

Gary dropped his weapon, jumped onto the tabletop, and bounded across it in two giant steps. His foot slashed out and caught Rachel in the jaw. Her head snapped backward, and she slid toward the floor. In an instant, Gary was beside her, snatching her purse from her shoulder and snagging her weapon from inside. She was still half in her chair, but he flipped her over, jerked up her sweatshirt, and pulled a second gun from a hidden holster in the middle of her back. With a gun in each hand, he whirled and kicked Jason's chair away. Jason tumbled to the carpet, where the stale stench of an old coffee stain fouled his nostrils.

Rachel slid the rest of the way to floor, like a deflated air bag, her eyes closed and her face expressionless.

Jason levered himself back to his feet and balanced against the wainscoting. His gaze never left Gary, who glanced at him though eyes that had narrowed to pinpoints. His cheeks had flushed, and the muscles in his arms writhed and the veins bulged. When he whirled to survey the room, his body pulsated with energy.

Montel snapped, "Mr. Dixon. Listen to me. *Troezen's daughter sleeps.*"

Gary heaved a sigh. His pupils dilated to normal size. The veins in his arms no longer threatened to explode from internal pressure. His mouth twitched.

Holmes lounged back in his chair and started to clap his hands. "Marvelous! Simply marvelous." *Clap, Clap.* "Another demonstration of his prowess."

Jason gulped in air that suddenly swirled with Gary's pheromones. "What the fuck?"

Athair beamed with pride. *"Good* job, Gary." But then she frowned, stood, and ambled around the table. "Still, I hope your kick wasn't lethal. That could be inconvenient." She knelt by Rachel and probed the agent's neck for a pulse. "Still beating." She peeled back an eyelid. "Looks like she's just knocked out, no thanks to you." She wiped her hands on Rachel's sweatshirt before she stood. "Really, Gary, you should be more careful when you're in accelerated mode." She wandered back to the front of the room, near Montel and Holmes.

Gary's hands trembled, and his breath came in short spurts. He glared at her and panted, "Bitch. Nothing's ever good enough for you, is it?"

Montel snapped. "Check the reporter. Make sure he's not carrying."

Gary stopped to slide the two weapons he'd taken from Rachel across the table toward Montel before he grabbed Jason and jerked him upright. "Hold still, creep." Pain shot through Jason's arm from Gary's vicelike grip.

Jason shuddered as Gary's searching hands dug into his torso. Then Gary grabbed him by the shoulders, twisted him around, and kicked his legs apart, so that he had to lean against the conference room whiteboard to stay upright. He winced when Gary's fingers probed between his legs and then groped his thighs.

As if this humiliation weren't enough, Gary stepped back and ordered, "Strip."

"What?"

"Can't do a cavity search with you dressed. Strip." He snatched at Jason's sweatshirt and wrenched it over Jason's head. Pain screamed from Jason's shoulder and down his right arm.

Montel laughed. "I don't think that's necessary, Mr. Dixon. He's too tight-assed to have a weapon up his butt."

Gary finished pulling off Jason's sweatshirt and flung it across the room. "Yeah? There's no telling what *else* he's had up there. I think I should cavity search him."

Montel shook his head. "Enough, I said. Come back here and pick up your weapon. We need you to watch all our captives while we consider our next steps."

Chill air from the wall units wafted across his naked torso, and Jason shivered. He folded his arms about his chest and squatted next to Rachel. Her chest rose and fell, and when he leaned close he caught a whiff of jasmine and sandalwood. He stroked her hair and whispered, "Come on, Rachel. Wake up. Please be all right."

She stirred, and her eyelids fluttered.

"That's it, Rachel." Her cheek was soft as lambskin under his fingers. "Wake up."

Someone knelt on her other side, and Mary Hyde murmured, "How is she doing?"

Rachel opened her eyes and pushed Jason's hand away. "Jesus. What happened?" She reached for her chin and wobbled it back and forth. "My jaw feels like someone stomped on it."

"Gary kicked you and took your gun." Jason glanced at where her purse lay, discarded nearby on the floor. At least the documents were still there.

Her eyes darted back and forth as she gazed around the room. She whispered, "Not to worry. I've got a spare weapon."

Gary laughed from the other side of the room. "I heard that. I took your spare too, moron."

Rachel sat up, twisted an arm behind her back, and then slumped, her face ashen. "Shit."

Brent's mother muttered, "Hold still for a second." She held up an index finger. "Follow my finger.... Good. Quick, what's seven times nine?"

"Sixty-three."

"And what day is today?"

"Tuesday, the twelfth."

Mary nodded. "Well, it's not conclusive, but I think you'll be all right. Do you need help standing up?"

Rachel struggled and grabbed Jason's arm. She levered herself to her feet and stared at him. "Where's your shirt? I knew you were skinny, but you look like a broomstick with a mop on top of it."

His mouth turned downward. "Gary took it when he searched me." He glared across the room, where Gary aimed a gun at them. Athair, Holmes, and Strorm huddled behind him, in a muttered conference. Brent sat across the table from them, his head on his hands and his eyes closed. A little sliver of drool ran from the edge of his mouth and pooled next to him on the table. Jason tried to keep his body from shaking. "I think we're in deep shit."

Mary's eyes glinted. "Don't do anything rash, either one of you. Just wait."

Jason gave a little laugh that threatened to spiral into hysteria. "Wait for what? One of those maniacs to put a bullet in our brains? You know that's what they intend." He cast a worried glance at Brent.

Mary followed his gaze and touched his hand. "He's going to be all right. Trust me. I know what I'm doing."

Jason heaved a shuddering breath. "God, how did we ever get into this mess?"

Rachel reached down and retrieved her handbag, her voice flat with despair. "I don't think what we do now matters."

Athair chose that moment to stomp her foot and push at Holmes. "Shut up, you fool. I will *not* have you risk this project just to show off."

Montel held up his hands. "Enough of this. We need to bring this to closure, and we have a tool to achieve that end. Mr. Dixon. Listen to me."

Gary's gaze never left Rachel and Jason, but his body tensed once again.

A new voice spoke from the doorway, loud and commanding. "That's enough, Montel. Another word and I'll splatter your brains all over the wall behind you."

Jason staggered against the table as he swiveled to the door. The commando guy stood there, a machine pistol gripped in both hands, pointed at the far side of the room.

Chapter
THIRTY-FIVE

JASON wondered if he'd lost the ability to be surprised. The arrival of the commando and his automatic pistol seemed to have frozen time. Gary's body still vibrated, like a piano wire about to snap. Montel's eyes threatened to pop out of his skull. A furious expression plastered itself across Holmes's face. Brent's mother had somehow returned to the side of her sleeping son. Rachel, incredibly, appeared calm and alert, almost as if she were assessing a new tactical situation. But Athair... why did she look so smug?

Jason tried to remember the thug's name. *Verloc? No, that can't be right. That's from Conrad.*

Montel turned to the newcomer and tried to speak, but only a croaking sound came out. His jaws clenched, he heaved a breath and spoke again. This time his voice was as cold as a witch's kiss. "Verloc. What are *you* doing here? I sent you back under your rock."

Jason narrowed his eyes. The name had to be fake. The guy was a *secret agent*, after all.

Holmes snapped, "Yes, and I told him to stick around and monitor the situation in case it got out of hand. He takes orders from corporate, as you well know, Montel. And *I'm* corporate, at least around here."

Beads of sweat gleamed on Gary's brow. His gun still pointed at the prisoners.

A sly smile etched across Athair's features. She edged toward a corner of the room, away from Montel, Holmes, and Gary.

Silence stretched for moments that seemed like hours. Outside, a siren wailed, and then faded into the distance. A soft, mechanical sound repeated over and over again from the hallway. *Thunk, pause, thunk, pause, thunk.* Jason's heartbeat drummed in his ears in cadence. Details etched in his brain: the mysterious sound, the sweat on Gary's brow, the glow of the lights on Brent's hair.

Montel chewed on the side of his mouth and contemplated Holmes. "You may be corporate, but they put me in charge of security." He turned to Verloc and pulled a set of handcuffs from his belt. "As long as you're here, make yourself of use. Secure Agent Morrison. She's the only one that's any threat."

Verloc didn't move, and his aim never wavered from Montel, Gary, and Holmes. Jason frowned. The dynamics were all screwed up here. What was Verloc up to? He didn't act like he was Holmes's subordinate at all, to say nothing of Montel's. From the puzzled expression on Rachel's face, she was confused too.

Only Mary Hyde seemed calm. She sat, a sorrowful expression in her eyes, caressing her sleeping son.

Verloc spoke. "If you still believe I'm taking my orders from you, Montel, you're even stupider than I thought."

Montel blinked. His face stayed impassive, calculating.

Holmes's triumphant voice filled the room. "See, Montel? I told you. He's working for me."

The beads of sweat on Gary's brow congealed into rivulets that streamed down his handsome features. His eyes gleamed, and his muscles flexed, but he stayed rigid. Jason couldn't be sure, but it looked like his aim now included Verloc as well as the others.

Athair's sudden peal of laughter broke into the room like fine crystal shattering into a thousand shards. "Men! You're all such self-absorbed fools. He works for the highest bidder. He works for me!" She turned and spat out her words. "Take him out, Verloc." Her laughter turned hysterical. "Take both of them out. How I loathe them!"

Montel's voice rapped out, "Gary. Listen to me."

Gary quivered, ready for command.

Verloc licked his lips. His eyes gleamed, and sweat stained his shirt.

Jason dropped his gaze, where it passed over the commando's crotch. Nausea burned the back of his throat when he realized the man was sexually aroused.

The machine pistol rasped, like a chain saw tearing through corrugated steel.

Montel slammed backward, his chest a bloody ruin. He still had a superior little smile frozen onto his face.

Another salvo ripped from Verloc's machine pistol.

Athair screamed.

Gary's body danced as bullets riddled his torso. Blood spurted from his wounds in little fountains and splattered onto the table. Even with his injuries, he stood his ground. He turned to Athair, gripped his pistol, and aimed. A single shot rang out.

Athair's screams stopped forever.

Verloc's pistol barked one more time, and Gary's head exploded in a spray of blood, brains, and bone. His body stood frozen for a second longer before it collapsed over the table and slithered to the floor, leaving a crimson trail of slime behind.

Jason gagged, and sour vomit hurled from his mouth.

Verloc smiled, and a little sigh of pleasure oozed from his lips. His body twitched once, then two more times. A wet stain jetted across his crotch.

Holmes sputtered from across the room. "What have you *done*, you fool?"

Rachel had eased around the table, away from Verloc. He pointed his weapon at her and spoke with the calm cadence of a priest consecrating the Eucharist. "I wouldn't do that if I were you. The clip for this thing holds over a hundred rounds."

She stopped. "Who *do* you work for?"

He shrugged and sneered. "Why should I tell you?"

"Call it a last request, before you kill me." She nodded at Holmes. "And you can show that asshole how you outsmarted him."

Verloc's suave smile sent chills down Jason's spine. When the man spoke, his words flowed with precise diction. It was as though Lawrence Olivier had taught him elocution. "Ah yes. They all thought they controlled me, but I showed them." He beamed at her. "I work for myself, of course. Always. No one controls me. Today, though, today I'm being paid by some nice men in London." He motioned toward where Brent huddled, awake at last, his eyes blinking and his face blank. "Now I'd like for all of you to gather over by this young fellow, please."

Holmes stood at the far end of the room, wiping Gary's blood and brains from his face with a handkerchief. "London? Those assholes are trying to take over the Gerion Group. What are you doing with them? You're working for *me*. I paid you enough."

Verloc rolled his eyes. "You really are an idiot, aren't you?" He grinned. "You know what? I love my job. I really do." He nodded at Holmes. "Yes, you paid me, and thank you very much. I'll make a donation to my homeless shelter in your name." He tipped his head toward Athair, who lay on the floor in a pool of dark blood, unconscious and twitching. "*She* paid me. That asshole *Montel* paid me. You *all* paid me. But then I got this polite call from London. They paid best of all." His grin transformed in an instant, no longer childish with joy, but sinister and crocodilian. "Now," he snapped, "I want *all* of you over here. Move!" He waved the barrel of his weapon in Brent's direction.

Jason's stomach clenched with fear. He stumbled across the room and gripped Brent's hand. At least he had time to stoop and kiss his cheek. "I love you." He hadn't meant to say that. The words sent a thrill of surprise tingling down his back. "I just realized…."

Brent squeezed his fingers. "I know. I love you too." His gaze roamed over the blood-soaked chaos and paused on Gary's crumpled body. All the remaining color drained from his face, but then his mouth firmed and his eyes pierced Jason's soul. "I'm not sure what's happened here, but I'm sure of this. You're my hero."

Verloc snapped, "Shut up, you two."

Mary Hyde leaned forward. "Brent, darling."

"Yes, Mother?" His voice wavered, and Jason's heart broke at its weakness.

"Brent. Listen to me." Her tone turned sharp, commanding.

His head jerked up, and his gaze locked onto his mother.

She kept her voice low. Her taut words now carried the faintest German accent. "Three cows are in the pasture. One of them is purple."

Brent's eyes narrowed to pinpoints. He leaped to his feet and grabbed Jason by the hair.

Jason had just enough time to wonder what Brent was up to before his head slammed into the table and blackness closed in.

Chapter THIRTY-SIX

RACHEL ignored the nonsense sentences that Mary Hyde whispered to her son. Instead, she kept her gaze locked on Verloc. Her muscles quivered and screamed for action. Her breath raced in shallow puffs, in and out, in and out. Her weapon called to her from where it had fallen, in a puddle of blood next to Gary's body. So close, so near, so tempting. In just an instant she could have it in her grasp. A movie ran in her mind: drop, roll behind the table, grasp her weapon, fire. It would only take a few moments, or maybe the rest of her life. All he had to do was look away. *Please look away. Just give me three seconds. Two.*

A flicker of motion erupted on her left. Brent leaped to his feet, grabbed Jason's shaggy hair, and slammed his face onto the conference table. Time stretched, each instant an eternity. Verloc's eyes twitched, and his pistol pivoted.

Now! Rachel threw herself to the floor and rolled. The automatic pistol barked. Splinters rained down around her. Her fingers stretched, and she gripped her weapon. Something—footsteps?—thumped on the table above her. Verloc's machine pistol spoke again: a rapid *rat-tat-tat*. Three rounds only.

Rachel thrust her weapon forward in a two handed grip and crouched. She peeked over the edge of the table. Brent stood behind Verloc, with his hands cupped over the hit man's ears. He twisted, and a sickening *crack* filled the room. Verloc's body convulsed, and then it sagged, as if his bones had melted. Brent released him and staggered against the table. Blood soaked the right side of his T-shirt.

Verloc collapsed in a silent heap on the floor. The stench of urine and feces filled Rachel's nostrils. She stood and tried to control her trembling arms. "Sweet Jesus, what just happened?"

Mary Hyde rushed around the table to her son. "Brent, sweetie, you've been shot."

He looked at her with glazed eyes, gasping.

She caressed one of his cheeks. "Brent. Listen to me."

His head gave a little jerk, and a spasm seized his body.

She spoke once more, in precise syllables. "Three cows are in the pasture. One of them is brown."

His eyelids fluttered, and his chest heaved. "Oh my God." His gaze roved over the room, stopping for an instant on Verloc and then passing to Jason. "What have I done?"

His mother's fingers danced over his features, and tears pooled in her eyes. "Brent, honey, you've saved our lives. But you've been shot. Lie down, now, and let me take a look at you."

Brent shook his head. "Jason. Check on Jason." His voice quivered. "He was right next to me. I needed him out of the line of fire before I attacked Verloc. I didn't know what else to do, so I knocked him out. Is he all right?"

Rachel kept her weapon at the ready and stalked Verloc's body. "Is he dead?" She pushed his gun away from his hand with the toe of her shoe.

Brent slipped to his knees. His head wobbled. "I broke his neck. He's dead. Please. Check on Jason."

Rachel whirled as a choking sound came from behind her. Jason leaned against the wall, his hands swiping blood from his nose. "What the fuck happened?" Panic lit his eyes, and they hunted the room. "What happened to Brent?"

Rachel relaxed. "He killed the guy with the gun. But he got shot."

Jason turned pale as skim milk and hobbled around the room to Brent's side. Blood streamed from his nose, down his chin, and over his bare torso.

Mary knelt next to her son, murmuring, "Lie flat, darling. Just relax, and I'll take care of you." She turned pleading eyes on Rachel. "I saw a level one biohazard sign next to a lab down the hall by the elevator. There should be a first aid kit just inside the door. Get it!"

Rachel hesitated and scanned the room. Where was Holmes? A whimpering sound caused her to stoop down and look under the table, where she found him cowering. "You!" she snapped. "We need that first aid kit now! Come on." She kicked at him.

He crept out of his hiding place. "This can't be happening to me," he whined.

Rachel gestured at him with the barrel of her weapon. "Move. Take me to that lab now."

"All *right*. No need to get nasty about it." Holmes trotted outside the conference room, and Rachel followed.

The sound of elevator doors thudding repeatedly against an obstruction filled the hallway. Rachel kept her gun at the ready and ran to investigate. The maintenance man who had been polishing the floors downstairs lay half in and half out of the cab, a pistol clutched in one hand and a bullet hole in his skull. She toed his body and read his nametag: Milo, and then she saw the name of the company stitched underneath. "Shit. Grace Development provides your maintenance?"

Holmes's mouth turned down as he approached the corpse. "He's really building security. The university didn't want me to post armed guards, so I had to pay extra for undercover support." He shook his head and turned petulant. "I paid them good money to protect me. I'm really going to have to speak to the company about this."

"Right. Well, he's sure not going to protect anyone now. Come on. Where's that lab?"

He led her another dozen steps down the corridor, where he swiped at a door with his ID card. "You know, this isn't over." He seemed more confident now as he spoke to Rachel. "If you cooperate with me, things could still work out really well for you. Really well indeed."

Rachel thought her head might explode. Or his, if she shot him. God knows the fuckwad had it coming. "Just get that damned kit."

He nodded. "Consider your options, Agent. If you think you're on some kind of crusade, think again." He opened a cabinet marked with a red cross and pulled out a small knapsack. "The amount of money at stake here is enormous. You can't fight that kind of money. It always wins. You may as well benefit."

She wanted to slap him, but she just shoved him toward the door. "Hurry up."

He gave her a smug little smile and trotted back to the conference room.

Jason sat next to Brent, tears streaming down his cheeks and a bloody handkerchief at his nose. Brent's mother knelt next to him, daubing at her son's wounds with Jason's discarded sweatshirt. Her eyes threw daggers at Holmes when they entered the room. "Took you long enough. Give me that." She snatched the first aid kit from his hands.

Brent reached up and touched Jason's cheek. "Are you all right? Your poor nose. I'm so *sorry*...."

"Sorry, hell." Emotion choked Jason's voice. "You saved us all. Just don't die on me, not now that I've got you."

Brent's mother wiped blood away from the wounds. "Looks like a through-and-through. He's already clotting. He should be healed up in a couple of days. All he needs is a couple stitches, a sterile bandage, and some antibiotics."

Rachel leaned closer. "A couple of days? Nonsense. Any abdominal wound is dangerous. We need to get him to a hospital."

Mary Hyde shook her head as she tore open a surgical packet. "No hospitals. It's not safe. Don't worry. He's designed to survive more severe wounds than this."

Holmes pushed Rachel aside. She resisted the urge to kill him.

His voice held awe. "Amazing. I can see the wound closing as you speak. His healing powers are superior even to Gary's. Or what Gary's were." He turned his attention to Mary. "Did you alter the protocols, or is he just more susceptible to the treatments? Or maybe you had a mutated strain of *M. vaccae*?"

Rachel scowled. "What the *fuck* are you talking about?"

Jason raised his eyes to look at her. "*I* know. He's like Gary. Or like Gary was."

Brent's head jerked at that. "What do you mean, 'like Gary'? I'm not like him."

Rachel frowned, and then everything fell into place. Bioengineering. Experiments on children twenty years ago, exactly when Brent and Gary were born. Gary's impossible speed when he attacked her, and now the way Brent was reacting to what should be a debilitating injury. They were both genetically engineered, maybe to be spies or soldiers. No wonder that fuck Holmes thought he had all the cards. Governments would do anything for this technology.

Jason squeezed Brent's hand. "Sweetheart, you're *nothing* like Gary. You're sweet and brave and good. But you've got the same abilities he had. Thanks to your mother."

Mary tore off a strip of white adhesive tape. "And my husband. We taught him together."

Holmes shook his head. "But the indoctrination requires total control of the subject's environment. How did you manage that, outside of a lab?"

"Our farm was our lab. The family cows incubated my strain of *M. vaccae* for us, as needed. So far as anyone knew, we homeschooled him. The program worked beyond our wildest dreams. He doesn't even remember the training."

Holmes smiled. "Excellent work—he's a weapon, cocked and ready for you to pull the trigger. Brilliant. I do hope you kept proper documentation. We'll want to duplicate your processes as we move to phase two. We suspected you might be up to something, of course. That's why I sent my agents to secure your bacterium from the animals' mucus membranes." He pursed his lips and gave Brent a calculating look. "It's a good thing we've got another specimen to show the bean counters in New York, now that we've lost our first prototype."

Rachel had enough of this asshole. She exploded. "What kind of a sick fuck are you? One of your sons is dead, your other one is wounded, and you call them *specimens*?"

Holmes shrugged. "Really, Agent. It's just business. Montel understood that. So do his superiors at Justice. And if there's a problem with any of them, well, our division at Langley is quite capable of handling things for us. I told you. You can't fight the kind of big money that's behind this. Our discoveries are going to make a lot of people very rich."

She stared at him, thinking. She couldn't let him get away with this. She glanced at her purse. All the evidence she needed was there, in Jason's files. She just needed to get out of here.

Holmes must have mistaken her hesitation as a bargaining ploy. He nodded, and asserted in a confident tone, "There's enough money to go around, if you play along, Agent."

Her eyes narrowed. *Let him offer me a bribe. Please. But I need witnesses.* Jason seemed about to speak. She couldn't let him screw things up. The guy just didn't know when to shut the fuck up. She spoke before he had a chance. "Tell me more, Dr. Holmes."

Holmes's face relaxed into an expansive smile. "I knew you'd be reasonable, Agent Frederickson. People almost always are."

Rachel's throat constricted, but she didn't correct him. *The asswipe is too arrogant to admit he doesn't remember my name.*

Jason snorted. "And if people aren't reasonable?"

A smarmy smile oozed across Holmes's features. "Why, then we have other means to solve our problems. I think you visited the location of one of those alternative solutions recently. A little place called Lost Springs?"

Rachel frowned. She recognized that name from someplace but didn't have time to sort it out now. She considered her options for another beat and then holstered her weapon. "So what's your offer?" She stooped to pick up her purse and slung it over her shoulder.

Jason glared at her. "What are you doing? I *trusted* you." He scrambled to stand up, but Brent's mother reached for him and held him back.

Mary muttered, "Wait. We're not out of this yet. He's right. They've got unlimited resources." She stood and faced Holmes. "I'm willing to make the same deal as before."

Holmes turned and beamed at her. That was the opportunity that Rachel needed. Her fingers found her cell phone in her bag and turned on the voice recorder.

Holmes simpered, "You always were the smart one, Mary. I'm sure we can work out a satisfactory arrangement."

Rachel tilted an eyebrow toward the bodies. "It's more complicated now. If you think I'm going to go along with covering up four deaths, you're crazy."

Holmes ran bloodstained fingers through his hair, mussing it and leaving a rusty trail in the gray. "Who said we would cover it up? You and Agent Strorm were interviewing me when *this* creature broke in," he pointed at Verloc. "By good fortune, young Brent overpowered him. What's to cover up?"

Mary shook her head. "No. Leave Brent out of it. It was a shootout, and Gary did it all."

Holmes shrugged. "That's satisfactory. We'll have a nice story for the investors about how his enhanced abilities saved the day. He'll be a hero, and we'll get our next round of financing." He frowned. "Of course, I'll need guarantees from you. Like the location of those files you hid away, Mrs. Hyde."

Mary snorted. "Those files are my only leverage." She frowned. "Tell you what. Let Brent go, with enough money that he can disappear. I'll sign our share of the company over to you and stay here, under your lock and key. When I'm sure my son's safe, I'll tell you where the records are."

Rachel glanced at Jason, who had locked his gaze on her purse. She hitched it up on her shoulder and prayed he'd keep quiet. "How about the FBI? They're going to be all over this, with one of their senior agents dead."

Holmes sniffed. "I think I can handle the FBI. Money talks in Washington. I told you there will be plenty to go around." He stopped and seemed to consider the situation. "My colleagues in New York will love it if we tie this to their rivals in London. That will put a stop to all this hostile takeover nonsense."

He turned a beatific expression on Rachel. "Montel made millions, working for us. You can do the same, Agent Frederickson."

"Morrison. My name is Morrison. Exactly what are you offering?"

He blinked. "Shall we say, as a retainer, ten million, in a numbered bank account in the Caymans?" He glanced at Mary. "Young Brent can have the same amount." He chuckled. "I'd even extend that offer to that nasty little reporter over there, although I'd rather just turn him over to my security people."

Jason didn't even glance at Rachel's handbag. "I accept your offer."

Rachel breathed a sigh of relief. She knew he was smart. And now she had the bribe offer recorded on her phone.

Holmes nodded. "It's probably simpler that way. More expensive, but less of a mess to clean up. Just remember, we're buying your silence. If any of this comes out... well, it could be unpleasant for everyone." He surveyed the others. "So, do we have a deal? I'd like to get out of this dreadful room. I'm afraid I'll have to have the whole thing redecorated."

Mary nodded. "Yes. I already said I'd agree to this."

Brent struggled to a sitting position and looked at Jason. "You're okay with this?"

Jason nodded, his eyes wide. "I think it's the only thing we can do."

"You'll come with me? I don't want to lose you."

Jason's blushed. "I don't want to lose you either. Yes, of course I'll come with you."

Brent turned to face Holmes. "Then I agree too."

Holmes looked like two snakes just crawled into his conference room. "Aren't the two of you sweet? Agent Frederickson? You agree too?"

A slow smile bent Rachel's lips. "It's a done deal, Dr. Holmes. It is indeed." She pulled out her cell phone.

Holmes held up his hand. "Who are you calling?"

"The FBI office in Des Moines."

"No, no. They'll be all over this with scientific investigators. I've already alerted my security company. They'll arrange the scene to conform to whatever cover story we need. They'll bring in a local deputy who's on the payroll, for appearances." He gave her a pensive look. "The locals are loyal, but not too bright. Maybe it would be better if you weren't here when they arrive."

Rachel kept the relief that flooded through her from showing in her voice. "I agree. I've got a car in the parking lot. I'll get Jason, Brent, and his mother out of here. Is there anyone else in the building?"

He peered at her and then guffawed. "Really, Agent, do you think I'll let you take my specimen with you? We've got a deal, but I'm not stupid. Brent stays with me."

Mary interjected, "I'll be your hostage. I want Brent safely out of here and in bed, so he can heal." She touched her son's arm. "Honey, can you walk?"

He pulled himself to his feet, winced, and leaned on Jason. "I think so."

Holmes shrugged. "All right. Come to think of it, you're more valuable to me anyway. You know the process." He smirked, as if satisfied with his cleverness. "Keep it simple." He pulled out a business card, scribbled on it before handing it to Rachel. "This is your first assignment, Agent. Secure my specimen, and call this number with the location once you're done. Don't fail me."

It was Brent's turn to object. "I'm not going anywhere without Jason."

Holmes rolled his eyes. "Whatever. Just get them out of here."

Rachel edged toward the door. "Yes, sir. You didn't say if anyone else was in the building."

"No. There was just one guard, the one we found in the elevator."

"Students? Researchers?" She stood aside while Jason and Brent hobbled into the hall.

"No. We close down at six every night. Security makes sure everyone leaves."

Rachel let her features relax in a smile. "Good. You can trust me, Dr. Holmes. You're calling the shots now." She made sure her recorder was still running when he answered.

"I am indeed calling the shots. You're bought and paid for now. I own you, all of you."

Rachel rushed out the door. As soon as she was out of his sight, her smile turned sour, bending her lips downward. Just wait. She'd show this asshole who owned who.

Epilogue

Eighteen months later
Café Kaffee
Ponsonby Road, Auckland, New Zealand

BRENT recognized the scent of Rachel's perfume even before she walked through the door of the coffee shop. Although he expected her, a touch of tension still sizzled in his chest. He turned to the older man who stood behind the counter next to him and murmured, "She's here. Handle the customers while we talk, will you?"

A wry grin wrinkled the other man's leathery features as he surveyed the dining area. Jason huddled in one corner peering at his laptop screen, but otherwise the place was empty. "What customers?"

"Just look like you're busy. Clean the steamer, or something." Brent removed his forest green apron and walked out to greet the FBI agent. "Rachel, it's so good to see you." He opened his arms for a hug, but when she hesitated he changed to a handshake. "Come, have a seat. Would you like coffee or anything?"

Her face glowed in a genuine smile. "Thanks, I could use some caffeine." She put her hands on her hips and surveyed him, head to toe. "You're looking fit. Much better than last time I saw you."

Jason slipped past Brent and pumped Rachel's hand. "We're so glad to see you." He glanced at his partner. "Brent will get your coffee. You're married now, right? You've got to show me pictures." He grabbed her elbow and maneuvered her to the corner where he'd been sitting.

Brent returned to the counter, where the barista had already prepared the latte. "Just thinking ahead, kiddo." The older man winked.

Brent accepted the steaming cup. "Thanks. You're a lifesaver, as always." With a worried glance backward, he rushed to the table where the other two sat, staring at pictures in Rachel's phone.

He served the coffee and peered over Jason's shoulder at the photos of her husband. "He's a hunk. You done good, girl." He sat next to Jason and held his hand.

"I got lucky. We're here visiting his family, you know. They're nice, although the local accent drives me crazy sometimes."

Brent chuckled and tried to relax. "Enzers have their own way with English, I'll admit. How did you meet him?"

"He works for OCDESC—the Officials Committee for Domestic and External Security Coordination. That's kind of the local version of Homeland Security. Anyway, he was in Washington as their liaison officer to the FBI, and I got promoted to an antiterrorism unit. We met, and it was love at first sight." She blew on her coffee and took a sip. "This is great. Thanks!" She glanced around the empty shop, but didn't say anything.

Jason grinned. "Good thing you didn't come this morning. We're packed until about ten or so, but this is the midafternoon lull. It'll pick up again tonight. The business is doing fine." He paused, and a sad smile bent his lips. "Of course, it's mostly cover. It's not like we need to work."

"Yeah. Lucky you." She put her coffee down. "I doubt that you're in any real danger. Still, there are people who would like to get their hands on Brent. We think the French and the Chinese have been sniffing around Holmes."

Brent scowled. "That fucking asshole. He'd use his own mother as a lab rat."

Jason squeezed his hand, and Rachel nodded agreement before she gave a little start. "Hey, before I forget, I wanted to hand deliver this to you in person instead of using our usual courier." She dug in to her voluminous purse and handed Jason an envelope.

Brent's eyes narrowed for a moment as he caught a glimpse of her handgun. A quick inspection revealed the telltale bulge of an ankle holster under her slacks, and from how she was sitting he concluded she had yet another weapon hidden in the back of her waistband. He trusted her, but still… why had she come here armed? He avoided looking at the barista.

While Jason opened the envelope, Rachel gushed, "It's the letter from the Pulitzer Committee, informing you of your nomination for your article in *Vanity Fair*."

Jason frowned and leaned back in his chair. "It didn't win." His fingers lingered on the document for a moment before he folded it and returned it back in the envelope. "Thanks. But that part of my life is over. Of necessity."

A pang of guilt caused Brent to touch his lover's cheek. Jason gripped his fingers as though drowning and they were his lifeline.

Certainty flashed from Rachel's eyes, and her firm tone carried conviction. "Your article was what blew the lid off the whole scandal. That bastard Holmes and his slimy boss Stillwell were so well connected, they could have buried everything. They almost did." Her finger jabbed at the table. "You done good, Jason."

Jason's fingers twisted with Brent's, and his face soured with disgust. "Right. So who wound up going to jail again? Last I heard, Brent's *mother* is the only person who's going to prison over this. Holmes and Stillwell got off free and clear. Worse, they got to keep their billions."

Brent's throat tightened at the mention of his mother. He glanced again at the barista, who stood out of earshot behind the counter, polishing the stainless steel coffeemakers. He pulled his fingers free from Jason and whispered, "She told me she deserved to go jail for what she did. She wanted to do penance for her sins."

Jason's eyes softened. "I know. I didn't mean to criticize your parents. You know, what burns me is that she's in jail and the ringleaders of this basically got by with murder."

Rachel leaned back. "Look, maybe they didn't go to prison, but your exposé stopped their super-soldier project. Holmes got fired from his cushy professor job, and Stillwell's being sued by stockholders for the Gerion group. Besides, the actual killers, Strorm, Verloc, and Gary are all dead."

Gary's dead. That comment slashed at the scar on Brent's memory. He winced and reached for Jason. *I'm the one who needs a lifeline now.*

Rachel must have caught his expression, for her voice softened. "I'm sorry. I didn't mean to hurt you. You've already been through so much."

"It's all right." He ruffled Jason's unruly hair. "I lucked out and wound up marrying the prince."

Jason's face turned an adorable red. "That works both ways, you know." He turned to Rachel and smirked. "I heard that Holmes lost his job as a commentator on Fox. Is that right?"

She smiled. "Sure is. He took the wrong side on global warming, and they canned his ass. Serves the SOB right." She paused and then asked, "So, how are you guys doing?" She glanced at Brent. "Have there been any… uh… side effects?"

Jason scowled and started to speak, but Brent beat him to it. "You mean from my, er, training? I haven't turned into RoboCop, or anything. At least, not since that night in Holmes's conference room."

Rachel's eyes narrowed, and she nodded. "Yeah, that's what I meant."

Jason's voice turned defensive when he spoke. "We even tried that trigger phrase, just to see what would happen. The one about the purple cows. It didn't work. *Nothing* happened."

She seemed to relax. "Well, I suppose that's for the best." She sipped her coffee, and silence stretched for a few moments. She fiddled with her purse, and Brent tensed, but she just pulled out a notepad. "I thought you might want to know our progress on searching for your father."

Brent kept his gaze locked on her face. "I assume you mean Chuck Hyde, not Dr. Holmes. Sure." *Stay cool.*

"Well, in the first place, your mother's testimony cleared him of any involvement in research misconduct."

Brent nodded. "Yeah, she told me. As far as I'm concerned, he was a good father. He protected us and took care of us."

Rachel nodded. "I'm sure he was. But he had to be working for either the Gerion Group or the CIA, or maybe both."

Brent shrugged. "So what? He didn't hurt anyone, did he?"

"Not so far as we can tell." She hesitated and licked her lips. "You know, we originally thought that body we found at the DEA raid was him."

Brent gave her a quick nod, and Jason said, "But the dental records didn't match."

"Yeah. But Chuck Hyde's ID was on the body, so it has to be connected somehow. That got me to thinking. Just for kicks, I had them pull your dad's—I mean Chuck Hyde's—old military dental records." She flipped to a page in her notebook but didn't bother reading from it. "Care to guess what we found?"

Brent shrugged and let irritation creep into his voice. "Just tell me. Don't play games, like that asshole Strorm."

Contrition showed in her eyes. "Sorry. Force of habit. Chuck Hyde's old military records *did* match the body."

Brent frowned. "What are you saying? You think that was his body after all?"

Jason frowned and said, "Surely you're not saying you think the man who raised him is dead."

Rachel held her hands up, palms forward. "No, no. I don't think that at all. The old military records didn't match the ones at your dad's dentist. At least, not unless he grew two new wisdom teeth after he left the army. As nearly as we can tell, the dentist's records are the real thing. But the old X-rays *did* match the dead body." She glanced at her notebook. "I think the plan was to fake his death, that the body we found was a plant. We just found it too soon, less than a day after they dumped it and before they could finish swapping records around."

Brent asked, "They?" He kept his voice cool, even.

She sighed. "I wish I knew. The trail's cold. I was hoping you guys might have some ideas."

It was Jason's turn to shrug. "Look, you said he might have been CIA. The financial records point to their involvement too. Those spooks could do anything."

Rachel nodded her agreement. "Yes, they could. The question is, why *would* they?"

Jason's brow furrowed, and he drummed his fingers on the table.

Brent knew he could trust him to not spill anything to Rachel, even though they both trusted her.

When Jason spoke, his words came with slow deliberation. "Holmes said that they'd bought off Chuck Hyde, remember?"

Rachel nodded.

"And a CIA front company was involved in the financial swindle, milking assets from the Gerion Group." His words accelerated with conviction. "Why wouldn't the CIA help cut a deal with Hyde to help him disappear, in return for his silence?"

She nodded, and, for the first time, Brent caught her peeking at the barista behind the counter. "I thought of that," she agreed. "It makes sense, even. I'm thinking that the body probably belonged to that neighbor, Zimmerman. We never did find him, you know." She glanced at her notebook again. "Turns out, he was a plant, a long-term spy on Brent's mother for the London faction of the Gerion Group. I'm convinced it was Gary who killed him. Anyway, his body was available. They just didn't have time to take care of all the records, to make it a smooth switch."

Brent's muscles tensed. "Problem solved, then." He had to ask. "So why bring it up now?"

She leaned back and stared at him with hooded eyes. "Good question. The FBI has closed the case. The CIA's not talking. The Gerion group is a financial ruin. I told you foreign agents are sniffing around Holmes. I ran into a Chinese diplomat a few weeks ago. He was attached to the UN mission, but he knew all about this case. He asked me all kinds of questions, including ones about the elder Mr. Hyde. He was subtle, but it was clear he was digging."

Jason asked, "Why would they care?"

Rachel smiled. "Well, the CIA now has all the research data on how to create a mega-soldier. You think they're just going to leave it lying around and do nothing with it? Anyone involved in this needs to be careful. You, especially, Brent. They'll see you as a specimen, not a person." She glanced again at the counter, where the barista was whistling "Me and My Shadow." She gave Brent a tense little smile. "You guys watch out. And if, by any chance you run into your father, you might be sure he knows that his little disappearing act didn't work quite as flawlessly as he thought. Understand me?"

A tidal wave of relief flooded through Brent. *She knows, and she's warning us.* He nodded. "I understand."

"Good." She slurped at her coffee. "So, you guys said this place is just a cover for you? What do you plan to do with your lives?"

Brent smiled and relaxed. "I was thinking of medical school. I got accepted at Massey, right here in Auckland. And this one"—he squeezed Jason's hand—"is working on a novel."

She beamed at them. "That's great. What kind of novel? You've got the right experience and brains for a dynamite spy thriller."

Jason shook his head. "I'll stick with romance, thank you. After all, love is what makes the world go 'round."

She snorted. "Hah! I don't know what universe you live in, but money is what makes the real world go 'round."

Brent let his face relax into a slow smile. "I guess it depends on what kind of world you choose to live in. We choose love. Shouldn't everyone?"

After she left, Brent returned to the counter to help set up for the evening rush. The old barista gave him a warm smile. "Everything go okay, son?"

"Everything's fine, Dad. Just fine."

MAX GRIFFIN writes romance, thrillers and science fiction stories, often with a dark twist. Authors as diverse as John Gardner, Dean Koontz, and Lawrence Block inspire and inform his literary style.

Max Griffin is the penname of a mathematician and academic who grew up in Iowa and currently lives in the Southwest. He is the proud parent of a daughter who is a librarian and the grandparent to two beautiful little boys. He is blessed to be in a long-term relationship with his life partner, Mr. Gene, who is an expert knitter. When he is not writing fiction, his days are filled with teaching mathematics and statistics, research, and administrative work at a major comprehensive university.

The two humans in Max's household are the pets of an Abyssinian cat named Mr. Dinger, who graciously lets them live in his home in return for food and occasional petting. Mr. Dinger's full name is Erwin Schrodinger the Cat, named after the famous physics thought experiment.

Visit Max's website: http://maxgriffin.net, find him on his blog, http://maxgriffin.net/blog, or e-mail him at author@maxgriffin.net.

www.ingramcontent.com/pod-product-compliance
Lightning Source LLC
Chambersburg PA
CBHW051638260626
47170CB00004B/1229